MYSTERY
AT
WINDSWEPT
FARM

MYSTERY
AT
WINDSWEPT
FARM

A Rosalie Hart Mystery

Wendy Sand Eckel

LEVEL
BEST BOOKS

First published by Level Best Books 2022

Copyright © 2022 by Wendy Sand Eckel

This novel is entirely a work of fiction. The names, characters and incidents portrayed in it are the work of the author's imagination. Any resemblance to actual persons, living or dead, events or localities is entirely coincidental.

Wendy Sand Eckel asserts the moral right to be identified as the author of this work.

First edition

ISBN: 978-1-68512-160-0

Cover art by Level Best Designs

This book was professionally typeset on Reedsy.
Find out more at reedsy.com

This one's for Bob Roth

Chapter One

The kitchen glowed in the early morning light as I fired up my favorite coffee maker and watched as he hissed out a cup of Columbian roast. Although he was showing his age, Mr. Miele had been my first and only improvement when I moved into this drafty, old farm house. I liked to think those initial espressos helped restore my will to carry on, and, not long after, bring Barclay Meadow back to life.

I sat at the table and gazed out the window. A pale gray mist hovered over the Cardigan River as a flock of Canada Geese fluttered onto the water. Sweeney Todd, my adopted Maine Coon cat, hopped onto the table, his massive tail switching back and forth. I eyed him and gripped my mug with both hands. His arrival was anticipated. And sure enough, just as I was about to take my first sip, he chin-bumped my coffee cup. But I was on to him, thus the mug grip. I didn't spill a drop.

It was unusual for me to have idle time in the morning. But the Day Lily Café, my restaurant in the small Eastern Shore town of Cardigan, Maryland that offered authentic farm-to-table cuisine, was getting an upgrade .

Sweeney hopped off the table, his back legs scattering yesterday's mail. I noticed an envelope from the Maryland State Department of Agriculture. My farm's annual organic certification was due soon. Passing was as important to my restaurant, as it was to Tyler Wells, the man who leased my farmlands, and the man I had recently shared several kisses with. Quite lovely kisses I should add. Down right knee-weakening.

The front door creaked open and I looked up to see Tyler and his aging chocolate Labrador, Charles Dickens, come into the kitchen. The scent of the outdoors and a hint of sandalwood soap breezed in with him. I stood and smiled. "Ready for coffee?"

"Always." He kissed my forehead and reached for one of the mugs hooked under the cabinets, a faded Orioles cap stuffed into his back pocket. After spooning several scoops of sugar into his cup, he leaned against the counter and took a long sip. How it didn't scald his tongue, I would never know.

I stood next to him, mirroring his posture. My heart did a little flip at his proximity. I handed him the envelope. "Care to do the honors?"

He stared down at it, a stitch forming between his eyebrows.

"Is this about the re-certification?" I asked.

"This is probably the dates for the inspection." He set his coffee down and slid his finger under the seal. His vivid green eyes darted back and forth as he read. "Damn it." He started to crumple the letter.

"Tyler." I put my hand on his arm. "What are you doing?"

"The dates are too far out." Dickens exhaled a small groan and walked over to Tyler, harrumphing onto his boots. "You know our neighbor? Windswept Farm?"

"Ronnie Kline, right? I've never even met the man."

Tyler shook his head. "You don't want to. He's as mean as a badger."

"Yes, that's what I've heard. But what does he have to do with our renewal?"

"His winter wheat is in. He's getting ready to crop dust his fields." Tyler lifted his chin. "And there's a chance the pesticides could blow over here and compromise our test."

The front door slammed. Bini Katz's boots were hard on the pine floor as she walked into the kitchen. Bini was the farm's only employee and a long time family friend of Tyler's. She had a no-nonsense manner and no clue that Tyler and I were a thing, which is exactly how he wanted it.

She looked at the letter in Tyler's hands. "When?"

"Four weeks."

"I knew it." She crossed her arms tight against her chest. In her mid-thirties, and despite her small stature, Bini's powerful presence could change the barometric pressure in a room in a nanosecond. "Can we move it up?"

"Then what? They will want to know why."

2

"We have to stop him, Ty."

"I've been talking to some of the guys in the co-op. We're going to draft a letter."

"A letter?" Her face contorted. "He could be hiring that plane today for all we know."

"Why hasn't this been a problem in that past?" I said. "He's owned that farm for as long as I can remember."

"His nephew took over the farming last year. Kline is so busy drinking Maker's Mark all day he doesn't give a flip what Barty does to the crops."

"I'm going over there," Bini announced. Her fair skin had flushed a deep crimson.

"No, you're not." Tyler's eyes narrowed. "Let's think about this. The wind comes from the northwest. Right, Bin? Maybe we are worrying for no reason."

"You willing to take that chance?" Bini pushed her short-cropped brown hair back from her forehead.

"What about the sheriff?" I said. "Isn't it illegal to spray the chemicals Kline uses?"

"Not yet," Bini said. "But it should be. Chlorpyrifos is about as toxic as you can get. It's been linked to all kinds of diseases. And don't get me started about what it's doing to the Chesapeake Bay."

"You just made my case," Tyler said "No one, including you, is going to tell a Devon County farmer how to grow his crops."

Bini looked down at her tightly-laced boots. "We have to do something."

"I agree. But let me ruminate on this for a bit. I think the letter will help. Everyone knows how toxic this pesticide is. He isn't going to want to alienate the county's entire farm community."

After a brief silence, Bini spun around and stomped outside.

Once the door closed, I said, "She's going over there."

He gazed at the space she had just occupied. "I know."

My shoulders fell. "Is this Kline guy really that bad?"

"Oh, yeah." Tyler faced me. "And he loves to piss people off. Bini going over there will only make things worse." He shook his head. "If the organic

3

board got even a trace of that stuff in our test, we'd have to start all over again."

"This is awful," I said, exasperated.

Tyler took me in. "Come here." He reached out and pulled me into his arms.

I rested my cheek on his chest.

"How's the café coming along?"

"I got the all-clear last night. I'm headed over there after I shower."

"That's really great, Rosalie." He kissed the top of my head and stepped back. "Once Bini settles down, we need to get the goat barn finished. We've got five kids arriving early next week."

"Five? That's wonderful." I looked up at him, those green eyes, the tanned skin, sandy blond tousled hair. "We could lose everything, Tyler."

"Yeah." He pulled his cap onto his head. "I've got to figure out a way to stop that plane."

Chapter Two

After a long, scalding shower, I pulled a lightweight black sweater over my head, and slipped into my favorite jeans, a hand-me-up from my Annie who was in her third year at Duke. I fluffed my hair and glossed my lips. And, as I did every morning, clasped my mother's pearls around my neck and said, "Miss you, Mom."

Worry for the farm clouded my thoughts as I trotted down the narrow stairway of my two-hundred-year old home. This house and vast farm were bequeathed to me by my dear Aunt Charlotte and, for a few years before I moved here, I pretended it wasn't mine. But when I learned, quite by accident, that my husband of twenty years was in love with a much younger woman, I decided it was time to leave my shattered life in the DC suburbs, and make the Eastern Shore of Maryland my home.

Hitching my purse on my shoulder, I stepped out into the crisp innocent October day. Built in the early 1800's, my house had floor-to-ceiling windows, a fresh white coat of paint, and forest green shutters. I rounded the corner and tossed some breakfast scraps to our free range chickens. A hammer pounded in the distance as I made my way to my car.

I was relieved to see Bini's F150 in the drive. Tyler must have persuaded her not to go to Ronnie Kline's. I climbed into my undersized red Mercedes convertible and dropped my purse on the passenger seat. I had never felt comfortable in this car. My ex-husband gave it to me for my fortieth birthday five years ago. My previous car was a beige Prius. When Ed wrapped my fingers around the keys, he said, "To keep you young." I should have realized then he was in the market for a newer model.

The scent of sawdust met my nose as I stepped into the Day Lily Café. A clear plastic tarp separated the original café from what was once The Little Lamb, a children's clothing store that had gone out of business.

My breath caught in my throat when I stepped into the addition. The new walls had been painted the same warm shade of ochre as the rest of the café, just like a Tuscan villa at sunset. New windows sported stickers in the bottom left panes. The area that was to be the bar extension was finished and the marble top installed.

As I walked back into the original space, I noticed yellow caution tape tied outside the front door. The concrete that was once my front steps had been jackhammered into chunks and now lay in a puddle. A flimsy sign read: *The Next Big Thing*. Cardigan was finally getting fiber optic cable, but there wasn't a worker in sight.

I looked up to see Alessa, a good friend and local winery owner, standing outside the door. Born in Italy, she held a bottle of wine in one hand, and lifted the other as if to say, what's going on?

I motioned her around to the back door that opened into the kitchen.

We shared a quick hug. Her thick dark hair was back from her face, her lips a bright red. Dressed in spiky pumps and a flowery skirt, she handed me the wine and said, "This is our latest *vino rosso*. Sixty per cent of the grapes are from Sonoma County. My cousin is flying over from Florence next week to see if he wants to serve it in his restaurants."

"It sounds amazing. And if I like it?"

"Put it on your wine list." She set it on the counter and looked around the room. "Darling, this place looks fantastic. Look at that range. It's beautiful. I want to move into this room."

"I'm beyond excited. Come and see the rest."

After a quick walk through, she turned to face me. "Rosalie, do you mind my asking how you could possibly afford all this? You've been closed for two months."

"Of course I don't mind." I smiled. "Have a seat. I'll make us an espresso."

She sat on one of the tall chairs at the bar and crossed her legs. I watched as she picked up the well-handled brochure I had left on the counter. "Tuscan

Culinary Adventures. A cooking school? In Italy?"

"Located in the hills of Tuscany."

"First the addition and now cooking school? Have you been going to Vegas?"

"Hah," I said as I set the small cup in front of her, a lemon zest on the saucer. "It's just a dream. Reading that brochure calms me down. Growing up I had a best friend, Carly, who lived on a farm about a mile down the road. I used to ride my bike over to her house every chance I got. Her Italian 'nonna' lived with them and the house always smelled of oregano, red sauce, and freshly baked bread. Sometimes I would linger hoping they would invite me to dinner, but my mother was on to me. She would call at 4:00 every day and tell them to send me home." I closed the brochure. "So no cooking school. And the café expansion is all due to my brother, Oliver."

"I've never heard you mention a brother." She stirred the zest into her espresso.

"I adore my brother, but I haven't seen him since our mother's funeral. We try and talk at least once a month, but that's about it."

"Why didn't your brother get Barclay Meadow?"

"It's a thing in my family." I rolled my eyes. "Don't burden Oliver, he's going places."

"And you weren't?"

"That was always my question, too. But we were raised in a very traditional family on a very traditional farm. So the someone who was expected to not move too far away from the parents, and maybe pop out a grandchild or two, was me."

"And did he? Go places?"

I nodded and took a small sip. "He makes a lot of money and he makes other people a lot of money. Don't get me wrong, he works very hard. But I learned long ago to not get in his way or add to his busy life. That's the rule in the Finnegan clan."

"Because he's going places."

"Exactly."

"It all sounds very Italian." She flashed me a wry smile. "And so he gave you the money to expand?"

"Technically he's co-owner of the café. But, yes, this is all because of Oliver. The good news is he's finally coming to visit to see his investment." I gazed down at the brochure. "Check out that view." I looked up. "Didn't you grow up in Tuscany?"

"Mm, yes I did. And it is as beautiful as the photograph." She put her chin in her hand and drummed her fingers along her cheek. "This has always been your dream?"

"I'm still in awe of what Carly's grandmother could do with a tomato."

Stomping boots sounded from the kitchen. A voice called out my name. Well, my last name. Sheriff Joe Wilgus only referred to me as 'Hart.'

He walked into the room in full uniform, hat low on his forehead. He shifted his holster and said, "You open?"

"Hello to you, too." I brushed my hands on my apron.

He looked around, taking in the changes in the café. When he noticed Alessa, he took off his hat, exposing his thick dark hair. "Miss Alessa. It's a pleasure to see you."

She flashed a playful smile. "Good morning, Sheriff. Are you well?"

"I am now." He looked over at me. "So, Hart?"

"Yes?" I put my hands on my hips.

"You open or not?"

"No. My steps have been demolished. Why are you so interested?"

He nodded toward the row of coffee makers.

"I should have known." I walked over to the machines and started up his favorite roast.

"I've got to go." Alessa stood. "This was fun, Rosalie. Do I get to meet your brother?"

"Can we tour the winery?"

"Sì, my dear. Oh, be sure to let the wine breathe for at least ten minutes." She blew me a kiss and winked at the sheriff. The scent of an expensive perfume trailed behind her.

Sheriff Wilgus stared after her. "How did such an exotic woman end up in Cardigan?"

8

"She loves her American husband." I set a mug of coffee and a small pitcher of cream in front of him

He sat down, setting his hat on the bar. "Place looks the same, just bigger."

"I'll take that as a compliment." I set a spoon on a napkin next to his coffee. "Anything new in town?"

"You don't happen to know who's driving around in that red Porsche." The sheriff looped his finger through the handle and pulled the mug closer. "Fancy friend of yours?"

"Not everyone driving a red sports car knows one another. And I don't particularly like mine. So, not a clue."

A scratchy voice emanated from the radio attached to his belt. *"Sheriff—"*

He stood and grabbed his hat.

I reached for a to-go cup. "What's happened?"

"That's for me to find out and you not to know."

I popped the lid on his cup and he headed back through the kitchen.

"You're welcome," I called after him, noting he hadn't paid. The door connecting the café to the kitchen swung back and forth until it fluttered to a stop. I tucked my unruly dark hair behind an ear and set the sheriff's mug in a dish bin. I wondered what classified as an incident in Cardigan. A dinged car door at the Acme? A tractor stalling traffic?

A faint noise sounded in the distance. As the siren grew louder, a police cruiser careened down Main Street, a dizzying array of blue and red lights flashing on the walls of the café. An ambulance followed close behind. They were headed out of town on my road. The road to Barclay Meadow. My stomach tightened. And the road to Windswept Farm.

I swallowed back an uncomfortable feeling. Did Bini? No, her truck was in the drive. But what if? It was a mother's worry. That faint idea that very quickly ballooned into the worst case scenario. I grabbed my phone and texted Tyler. *Did Bini go to Kline's?*

I set my phone on the bar, willing a speedy reply. I crossed my arms and bit my bottom lip. Tyler always answered my texts. He kept his phone on vibrate in his back pocket. He would have been notified by now. I gazed down at the black screen. Nothing. We should have pushed harder for her

9

to not go. The worry had reached full throttle. I shut down the café and ran to my car.

The tires skidded on the gravel as I rounded the circle in front of Barclay Meadow. I checked the drive. No pickups. I rushed up the steps and through the door.

I found Dickens under the table on his dog bed. His ears twitched but he remained asleep. Tyler's faithful dog never left his side. He was a fixture on his front seat. The few times I rode in Tyler's truck, Dickens sat between us, his hot breath fogging the windshield. I froze when I saw Tyler's phone next to the coffee pot. He must have been in a hurry.

At last my phone chimed. It was a text from Bini. She never texted me. My fingers trembled as I opened the message. *Ronnie Kline's dead.*

Chapter Three

I paced and fretted for over an hour imagining the worst. Had Tyler gone after Bini? Did he get in a struggle with Kline?

I considered going over there but thought better of it. Sheriff Wilgus was on the scene and he already found my curiosity to be beyond annoying, and at one point, worthy of throwing me in a jail cell.

When I at last heard a truck engine, I ran to the front door, stumbling over Dickens as we competed for first place to intercept Tyler.

"I left in a hurry." Tyler's face was lined with tension. "I forgot my phone." He bent down and gave his dog a quick scratch.

"The sheriff got a call while he was in the café. Then I got a text from Bini." I searched his face. "How did Kline die? Please tell me you didn't have anything to do with it."

"No, of course not." He rubbed his forehead roughly. "Why would you say that?"

"Because you said Kline was mean as a badger, that's why. When did Bini go over there? Did you follow her? Did Kline and Bini get into some kind of struggle?"

Tyler let out an exasperated laugh and shook his head. "So many questions." He continued into the kitchen and checked his phone. After stuffing it in his back pocket he turned to me. "Would you like to know what happened?"

"Does a chicken have feathers?" I crossed my arms. "Yes, please."

"Kline was already dead when Bini got there. He was just inside the door. She called me because she was afraid."

"Oh, my goodness. Poor Bini. What a horrible thing to discover."

"When the coroner got there he said it looked suspicious." Tyler frowned. "I'll spare you the details."

"You mean he may have been murdered? In *Cardigan*? That's terrifying."

"Yeah. I agree." He cocked his head. "This isn't your problem, you know." He gave me a small smile. "Okay, Nancy Drew?"

"Of course." I tried to sound incensed but the man had a point. "Sounds like the sheriff is actually going to look into this one."

"He already is. Asked Bini and me lots of questions. Like why did Bini call me before the cops."

"She should get a lawyer."

"I'm sorry?" Tyler fired up an espresso. "Kline was dead when she got there."

"Nobody knows that for certain but Bini."

"What are you saying?" He looked over his shoulder at me. "Are you suggesting she killed him?"

"No, Tyler, of course not. I would never, ever think that. But Joe Wilgus might. And he likes to wrap things up quickly." I combed my hand through my hair. "Poor, Bini. This is so awful." I walked over to Tyler while he stirred some sugar into his cup. "How is she?"

"Pretty shook up." He downed the entire espresso. "Up until today, Bini has lived in a bubble. Nothing even close to this has ever happened to her before."

I tucked my arm through his. "Doesn't she still live with her parents?"

"She's there now. I told her to take a few days off." He patted my arm. "We'll see if she does."

"Should I go over there?"

"No need. She's with her folks, and they will all deal with this in the Katz manner."

"The Katz manner?" I peered up at him.

"Say a few prayers for Ronnie Kline and reassure Bini this was God's will." Tyler paused. "And then her mother will say, 'It's a blessing Bini found him before the critters did.'"

Chapter Four

The next morning, Bini arrived for work and went about her business as if nothing had happened. She kept her back to me when she came into the kitchen for coffee.

"How are you, Bini?"

"Fine," she said into her mug. "Why wouldn't I be?"

I studied her, wondering if I was witnessing the 'Katz manner' in action. "That's great news about the goats. Five sounds perfect. Will they all be . . ."

She spun around. Clutching her mug she said, "I need to get to work." Just before she got to the door she said, "You're feeding the chickens too much bread."

I shook my head and realized I needed to give Bini some space. She must be feeling all kinds of mixed emotions, the worst being Tyler and I both warned her not to go to Ronnie Kline's.

Although I was dressed and ready for my trip into town, I had an idea. I was happy to let Bini handle this the Katz way. And I would handle it my way. I felt badly for her even though that's the last thing she wanted. So after making a decadent batch of chocolate chip cookies, I arranged them on a platter and placed them in the center of the kitchen table where she couldn't miss them.

I checked the time. Glenn Breckinridge, my best friend and head waiter, had agreed to meet me at the café. Although we had been sharing an occasional coffee during the construction, I missed seeing him every day. We weren't scheduled to meet for another hour so I dropped my phone into my bag and decided to pay a call on Sheriff Joe Wilgus.

The County Sheriff's Department was housed in a historic train depot at the edge of town. I parked my car at the café, popped in to make a cup of coffee, filled a to go cup, and walked the few blocks to the sheriff's office. A layer of gray clouds hung low in the sky, chilling the air, and muting the colors of the bursting fall foliage.

I found him at the front desk with his feet up, the swivel chair tilted so far back the springs complained. He was doing the crossword in the local paper. His lips rolled in as he studied the page.

"What's the clue?" I sat across from him.

"Five letters. Spring flower. Ends in a 'y.'" He looked up. "Does lily have one 'l' or two?"

"One." I set the coffee in front of him. "What's it start with?"

"Looks like it may be a 'p.' Pansy? No, that doesn't work." He frowned.

"If I tell you the answer, will you tell me how Kline died?"

He set the paper down and returned his feet to the floor. "Why do you want to know?"

"Bini Katz found him. She works at my farm. Tyler said it looked suspicious." I crossed my hands over my purse. "How?

"I guess you'll find out soon enough on your own." He pulled the lid from the cup. I removed two creamers from my purse and set them on his desk. "Coroner said the way the body was contorted and, well, the amount of vomit, that he would need to do some tests to determine the cause of death."

"And?"

He looked over at me, his face tense. "Ronnie Kline was poisoned."

"Poisoned? Oh, my. With what?"

"Some sort of plant. Lethal dose." He peeled the lid off the creamer.

"That's so awful." I stared at the floor then looked up. "Is it a painful death?"

"Based on his face, I would say definitely yes." A smirk appeared on his lips. "We found a bunch of muffins scattered on the porch. Katz had 'em in a basket. Now I wonder who could'a made em. Hm?"

"Wait, muffins? I had some in the freezer. Bini took muffins with her?"

"If she knew anything about Ronnie Kline she wouldn't have bothered."

He studied me. "We're testing 'em for poison, just so you know."

I pushed the small of my back into the chair. Here I'd been worried about *Bini* needing a lawyer. "I can say for certain you will not find a trace of poison in those muffins."

He shrugged. "We shall see. You think your farm hand might'a poisoned your neighbor?"

"Absolutely not. Bini is a very principled person. Honest to a fault, if you know what I mean. She must have taken the muffins as a way to soften him up."

"This is starting to get interesting." He leaned forward on his elbows. "Why would she be trying to soften up Ronny Kline? And why would anyone waste their time trying to do that?"

"Um, well, I'm not really sure. After all, he is a neighbor." I avoided his eyes.

"You're a lousy liar, Hart."

"Yes. Yes, I know."

"Why'd she go over there?"

I looked everywhere but at the sheriff. Gripping the straps of my purse, I finally met his eyes. "His nephew was getting ready to crop dust his winter wheat. We have a soil test coming up. Bini was going to ask him to wait until after the test."

The sheriff's eyes narrowed. He seemed to be thinking, which always made me nervous. "Why didn't she tell me that?"

My head reared back a little. "I have no idea." I tightened my grip and took a deep breath. Did I betray some sort of secret? No. He was going to find out one way or another. And someone had been murdered.

I swallowed hard and stood. "Try Peony. P-E-O-N-Y."

I walked back to the café and found Alessa outside the kitchen door. "Hey, long time no see." I smiled.

"I'm so excited I had to come over here as soon as I could."

"You have good news?"

"Remember when I mentioned my cousin was coming to try the wine?

Well, Rosalie, my dear, he has agreed to give you Italian cooking lessons."

"Wait, what? Are you serious?"

She nodded enthusiastically.

"I'm speechless."

"That's not like you." She winked. "You will have to pay him unfortunately. Maybe your brother?"

"Oh, no. Oliver has already done so much."

She tapped a finger on her chin. "I have it. You could invite other students. They can pay." She passed me a slip of paper. "Here is what he will charge you for five full days. And he will do the provisioning."

"Oh, my goodness. Are you sure he wants to do this?"

"Marco is a teacher. He has mentored many successful chefs."

"Marco?"

"Giovanelli." Those red lips curved into a wide grin.

"Can I faint now?" I tried to let it sink in. "Let me see what I can pull together. When does he get here?"

"Next week. The tourist season is over so he is traveling the states for a month."

We air kissed and I watched her walk away. The plastic yellow caution tape flapped in the breeze, breaking my flood of thoughts.

I found Glenn in the dining room dunking a tea bag in and out of a mug, his wire-rimmed glasses low on his nose.

"Hello, my dear." He peered up at me. "It seems someone has stolen the front steps."

"Mm. Yes they have." My brochure lay open before him.

"Did you see this place has a hot tub? It's heated with firewood. I've never heard of such a thing. And it's in Tuscany." He set the tea bag on a napkin. "When do we leave?"

"Haha. I like how you think. But I've got something better."

He nudged his glasses back into place. "Better than a wood-fired hot tub in the hills of Tuscany? This will be good."

I sat on the chair next to him. "I have no idea if I can make this happen, but Alessa's cousin is visiting and he has agreed to run a cooking school right here at the Day Lily. He'll give me five days. But I'll need at least five students in addition to me in order to afford it." I clasped my hands together. "Do you think I can do this?"

"Her cousin is a chef?"

I nodded. "He has three restaurants in Tuscany. Almost like an Italian Bobby Flay."

He leaned back in his chair. At seventy-two, Glenn had recently retired from his executive position at IBM and, after losing his wife, settled into a retirement community in Cardigan. He was an energetic, kind-hearted, elegant man. We became the best of friends when we realized we shared a curiosity for getting to the bottom of things, including solving two murders Sheriff Wilgus had failed to investigate.

"I haven't seen you in two days and all this has happened?"

"Oh, there's more. Are you hungry?"

"I'm meeting Gretchen at the Inn. Apparently she has some delicious leftovers from this morning's breakfast."

Gretchen was a lovely woman who started coming into the café on a regular basis not long after we opened, always seated at the bar drinking tea with a constant eye on Glenn. At first he rebuffed her, thinking he would never love another after losing his wife of over forty years. But then she invited him to her historic Bed and Breakfast for a cocktail and everything changed.

Turned out, Gretchen had also recently lost the love of her life. So instead of spending their first time alone together trying to avoid the subject of their previous spouses, they spent every minute telling stories, looking at pictures of grandchildren, weddings, vacations, and learning all about each other's previous love-filled lives. After that, they were free to move forward.

"Lucky you," I said. "I've heard about her chocolate scones."

"Mouth-watering." He took a sip of tea. "You said there was more to tell?"

"My neighbor was murdered yesterday. Poisoned, actually."

"Good, god, in Cardigan?" He crossed his arms tight against his chest. "I read the paper on line this morning. I didn't see a thing."

"Bini, you know, Bini Katz? Works at the farm?"

"Of course. She has been known to correct my knowledge of vegetables."

"Yes, me too. Anyway, Bini found him. He was just inside his front door."

"And our good sheriff is on the case?"

"Once he finishes his crossword. But, yes," Making air quotation marks, I said, "He's on the case."

"Why does that not comfort me?" Glenn stood and took in the room. "The recent progress is stunning. It's coming together beautifully." He rubbed his chin. "What's this chef's name?"

"Marco *Giovanelli*," I said with a flair.

"That name alone makes me hungry." Glenn picked a piece of lint from his corduroy pants. "Rosalie, how about if I hang around and do the dishes, that sort of thing during the class. Keep the kitchen running. I don't think I want to miss this."

"Are you sure?"

"More than sure. When have I ever not signed up for one of your adventures?"

"You're on."

"Well, then, we have work to do. Meet you here tomorrow?"

Chapter Five

I spent the rest of the morning cleaning the café, taking down the plastic partition, scrubbing the windows, anything to make it sparkle. Once I had nothing left to clean, I sat at the bar with a fresh espresso and my notepad.

Students. That was key if I was going to make this happen. I posted a notice on *Cardigan Life*, the Facebook group open to all Devon County residents. I followed with a post on the Day Lily Café Facebook page, twitter, and Instagram.

Next I thought about people I knew who might be interested. Marco's visit would coincide with Oliver's. Perfect. Having something for us to do together could ease us back into a relationship. I shot him a text and set my phone on the counter. And then I immediately knew who the next student should be.

A bell rang when I entered the *Four Seasons Florist Shop*. Kevin Edwards stood behind the counter snipping mums and asters. He was dressed immaculately, as always. Small in stature, he could pull off just about any outfit. Today it was a silky gray shirt and slender cream pants.

"There's my cutie," he said as I stepped in the door. Kevin, and his partner, Jake, were two of my best friends.

"That's a gorgeous arrangement," I said as I approached.

"Are magnolia leaves too Christmasy?" He gazed down critically at the work in progress. "Because I think their glossy finish would give this some texture."

"I love it." I waited for him to look up, unable to suppress a wide grin.

When he at last lifted his head he said, "Good grief, girlfriend. You look like you just popped Tweety Bird in your mouth. Now dish."

"I'm hosting a cooking school with a chef from Tuscany. And I want you to be one of the students."

"Get out." He placed his hands on his hips. "How did you . . ."

"Alessa's cousin. We start a week from Monday. He charges a fee. Two hundred-fifty per student." I placed my hands together as if in prayer. "Please say you can get some time off."

"So he's Italian? How *booshy*." He walked over to his calendar, tracing a finger over each day. After thinking for a moment, he said, "I am so in."

"Yay!"

Kevin frowned. "I'm going to have to do some shopping."

When I arrived home later that afternoon, I was happy to see Tyler's truck still in the drive and even happier to see Bini had gone home. Maybe Tyler and I could have a little time together. A gust of wind slammed the door into my leg as I got out of the car. I had to fight against the continuing blasts to get inside the house. The front door closed with such a force, Dickens let out a gruff bark.

After taming my hair and putting on a little lipstick, I opened Alessa's bottle of wine and sliced a yummy block of aged cheddar cheese. I set a basket of delicate crackers on the kitchen table and filled two glasses. I noticed the plate of chocolate chip cookies had been reduced to a few crumbs.

I was seated at the table with an empty glass by the time Tyler arrived.

"What's all this?"

"I thought we could catch up. And I've missed you." I nudged his glass toward him. "Alessa has a new vintage. It's going on the wine list."

He eyed my empty glass.

"She said it needed to breathe."

He took a sip. "This is pretty damn good."

"My thoughts exactly. Can you sit for a bit?"

20

"Of course." Tyler scrubbed his hands and sat down. His denim shirt sleeves were rolled up, revealing his defined arm muscles. After taking a longer sip, he looked over at me. "Goat barn already has one coat of paint on it."

"That was fast." I rested my chin in my hand. "How's Bini?"

"Sheriff wants to ask her some questions tomorrow morning." He gripped the stem of his glass.

"Did he say why?"

"Someone told him why she went to Kline's." One eyebrow lifted. "Anyone you might know?"

I cleared a catch from my throat. "I was surprised he didn't already know why."

"He never asked, so we never told him."

"Oh."

"When did *you* tell him? I thought the café was still closed."

I frowned. "You know it's still closed." Sitting a little straighter, I said, "I stopped by on my way into town. I wanted to know how Kline died."

Tyler finished his wine. "Did he tell you?"

"He was poisoned."

After popping a slice of cheese in his mouth, Tyler hopped up and retrieved the wine bottle. He refilled our glasses. "Then Bini will be fine. He was already dead when she got there."

"I agree." I clinked my glass against his and sipped. "Maybe someone else didn't want him to spray his crops. What's on the other side of his farm?"

Tyler shrugged. "Not much. He bought up the small farm that used to be next to him. Pretty much bullied the guy to sell. Family went broke after that. Next to that property is the bird sanctuary."

"Could someone from the sanctuary also have been trying to stop him? They wouldn't want those pesticides any more than we did."

"You mean like a crazed ornithologist?" Tyler said. "Anything's possible."

"What's Kline's family like? Wife? Kids?"

Tyler slugged back his second glass. The corners of his mouth turned down. "Don't do it, Rosalie Hart."

I lifted my chin. "Aren't you curious who might have poisoned our next door neighbor?"

"Nope." His eyes had a unique ability to laser beam through my heart.

"Well, there's no need to worry. I have too much to do to start looking into Ronnie Kline's murder. I never even met the man." I took a small bite of cracker to try and stop my stomach from flipping around.

He continued to stare over at me. "Did the sheriff tell you anything else? Does Bini need a lawyer?"

"I told you before, it's never a bad idea."

"What did he tell you?"

"Nothing more." I tucked my legs underneath me. "Why are you interrogating me?"

Tyler's shoulders fell. "I'm sorry." He took a deep breath. "Thank you for the wine."

"This is all pretty crazy, isn't it? Our neighbor poisoned. Bini finding him."

Tyler emptied the bottle, keeping the portions even between our glasses. He put two cheese slices on a cracker and munched loudly. Washing it down with another sip of wine, he said, "You look very pretty tonight. And this wine and cheese is a good idea. Sometimes I forget to slow down. You help with that, ya know, Rosalie?"

"I do?"

"Oh, yeah. I can get pretty wrapped up in this place, like everything has an urgency to it, get it done on time and get to the next task. And then I stop and take you in, and it's like, oh, now she's a good idea."

My heart warmed.

"A very good idea." He gave me a crooked grin.

"Tyler? How would you feel if I hosted a cooking school for a week. At the café. Alessa has this cousin. He's a chef."

"Hasn't that always been your dream?"

"You remembered."

"It sounds incredible. Do I get the leftovers?"

"Always. You sure it won't take me away from the farm too much?"

22

"You still gonna come home at night? Maybe bring some more bottles of this wine?"

I giggled. "Of course."

Tyler flashed me a warm, relaxed smile. "Hey, did you notice the wind?"

"How could I not? I barely made it up the steps."

"Be careful, Dorothy. Little gal like you could end up in Kansas."

"I felt a little like Dorothy. Why did you ask about the wind?"

Another cracker with three slices of cheese and he smacked his lips. Our eyes met. He paused, his gaze intense. I held my breath.

"Wind's coming from the south east."

"The south? You mean . . . ?"

He nodded. "Bini was right. Those chemicals would be all over our farm right now."

Chapter Six

G lenn rubbed his hands together as he came into the café. "I thought I'd go through our supplies. Who knows what we need? Soap, paper towels, and you certainly don't want to run out of toilet paper." He removed his jacket, keeping a Burberry plaid scarf around his neck.

"Great idea. And so far I have three students. Me, Oliver, and Kevin. We only need three more."

"Excellent." Glenn looked out at the street and frowned. "I believe number four may be outside the window."

A young woman stood at the glass peering in, her hands cupped around her eyes.

"Do you really think?" I said.

"Social media is a powerful thing."

As I headed toward the door, I stopped and looked over my shoulder at Glenn. "Could she really . . .?"

Glenn sat down. "Seems there's only one way to find out."

I opened the door. "Can I help you?"

"Are you Rosalie Hart?" she called from the sidewalk. "I saw your post on Cardigan Life. I . . ."

"Come around to the back. It seems someone has stolen my steps." I smiled at Glenn on my way to the kitchen.

The young woman followed me into the dining room. "Howdy," she said. "I'm Joanne, but please call me Jojo. I want to sign up for your cooking class if you still have room." She looked to be in her mid-twenties with short brown hair and perfectly round blue eyes. She was my height, which means she was short, and wore capri leggings and a loose sweatshirt. I noticed a tattoo of Sanskrit letters traveling up her index finger.

"That's wonderful news, Jojo. Yes, we definitely have room."

She walked up to Glenn in slip-on sneakers that gave her a little bounce in her step. She extended her hand. "Who are you?"

"I'm Glenn. The dishwasher."

"Coffee?" I said.

"Sure." Jojo sat next to Glenn. Her legs dangled from the bar chair. "With cream, please."

"So what brings you in?" Glenn said.

"I saw the notice about the class yesterday. I have some money set aside and thought this would be the perfect way to spend it." She smiled a sweet smile and I found myself liking her already. "Up until two days ago, I wouldn't have been able to do it."

"What's changed?" Glenn said.

"My Uncle Ronnie died."

"I'm so sorry." I thought for a moment and frowned. "Did you say Ronnie? As in Ronnie Kline?"

She nodded.

"He was my neighbor."

"Really? You probably never met him, did you?"

"No." I filled a mug with coffee. "How did you know?"

"Because he was an anti-social, bully." She rolled her eyes. "Not to speak unkindly of my dead uncle, but that's just how it was." Jojo poured a heavy dose of cream into her mug and took a long sip. She frowned at the cup. "This is really good. Anyway, I've been working for him. Or should I say *slaving* for him. I cooked his meals, food shopped, cleaned his toilets. He'd been having some health issues, so he paid me to take care of him. If this class would have come up while he was alive, he never would have given me the time off." She stared out the window, shaking her head. "Life is so weird."

"Yes," Glenn said. "I concur."

I caught Glenn's eye and he gave me a quick wink.

"Have you learned how he died?" I asked.

"Well," she set her mug down, "Looks like someone poisoned him. Can you believe it? Someone *killed* my uncle. In Cardigan."

"It's very hard to believe," I said. "How are you holding up?"

She shrugged. "This would be a whole lot easier to take if my mom were still alive, but she passed a couple of years ago from the cancer. That's why my brother, sister, and I helped my uncle out so much. We were all he had. Although I don't think he ever appreciated it. At least he paid me enough so I could save up some money. And I have my own little apartment and a vehicle. I guess I should be grateful for that."

"What about the farm?" Glenn said.

"The lawyer said there's a will. I don't have a clue what it says. Barty has been working the farm, but the lawyer said we should all stay away until the will is read." She tucked her hands under her thighs. "My goodness, I think it's safe to say the caffeine has kicked in. I think I just told you my entire life story."

"Rosalie's coffee will do that to you." Glenn smiled. "Any idea who the farm will go to?"

"Maybe Barty because he does all the farming now. It sure would be nice if he left each of us at least a little something."

I heard a rap on the door to the kitchen. "I'll be right back." When I saw Tyler on the stoop, I waved him in.

"I needed paint. Thought I'd stop in and see the place."

"Glenn is here. Come on in." We exchanged a quick kiss. "Say, what happened with Bini and the sheriff?"

"He told her not to leave town now that he has a motive." Tyler looked around. "This kitchen is amazing. Look at the stove. And two refrigerators?"

"Wait until you see the rest."

"Is that Miss Charlotte's kneading board? I didn't know you still had it."

"That board is what eventually led me to open the café." I always liked knowing Tyler had a close relationship with Aunt Charlotte before I ever met him. She was the one to encourage him to farm organically. In fact, he

26

was with her when she passed from a stroke, while I was stuck in traffic on the Chesapeake Bay Bridge trying to get to her in time.

He followed me into the next room and stopped when he noticed Jojo. "Hey, Joanne. What are you doing here?"

She hopped off the chair and picked up her keys. "I'm going to enroll in the cooking school. I'm super pumped."

Tyler scratched his jaw and looked at me. "Didn't you just tell me about this class last night?"

I smiled. "We have four students so far."

Tyler extended his hand to Glenn. "Good to see you, buddy."

"Always good to see you."

He gave his head a small shake. "Let me start over. Jo? I'm sorry about your uncle."

"Thanks, Ty." She looped a large handbag onto her shoulder.

Fists on his hips, he said, "So I guess your brother will get the farm?"

"No clue." She smiled at me. "So, I'm in?"

"The class? Absolutely."

"Can I bring you a check that morning?"

"Of course, Jojo. I think you will be an excellent addition."

"Cool. I'll be here right on time. I wouldn't miss this class for the world." She headed for the door but stopped. "I want to be a famous chef. Like maybe have my own TV show." She giggled. "A girl can dream."

Once we heard the back door close, I said, "What a coincidence. Ronnie Kline's niece will be in the class."

Glenn smiled. "That, my dear, would be an understatement."

I nudged Tyler. "You okay? You look a little dazed and confused."

"And that," Tyler said, shaking his head again, "would *not* be an understatement."

Chapter Seven

I passed by the Grande Hotel on my way home and decided to pull over. I had been in search of a bar tender for when we reopened, and remembered Doris Bird told me about a young man who was looking for more work. He bartended at the Grande, she had said, but only a couple of weekdays. In no hurry to get home knowing Tyler had already left for the day, I decided to stop in and meet him.

I pulled my suede jacket tighter around me. The first cool breaths of fall were upon us. I noticed a Carrera parked at an odd angle along the street. The red Porsche the sheriff had asked me about. There it was.

Worry for Bini nagged at me as I headed toward the hotel. Ronnie Kline was poisoned. A murderer was out there. And now the sheriff had a suspect with a motive. I looked back at the Porsche. It showed up a few days before Kline died. I stopped and shook my head. And yet there was a chance the sheriff could charge Bini with murder. I was permitted to be a little bit curious.

The shops in town were shuttered up for the night. Was the owner of the car inside the hotel? I continued up the wide tiled steps. I'm just looking for a bartender, I told myself.

At four stories, The Grande was one of the tallest buildings in town, bested only by an Episcopal Church whose steeple was the pinnacle of Cardigan's modest skyline. The Grande had been a bustling hotel in the 1700 and 1800's, hosting presidents and dignitaries when Cardigan was an important inland seaport. Recently it had been restored and now boasted Cardigan's only upscale restaurant and a small cocktail lounge.

The lobby was empty, so I peeked into the lounge. Ceiling fans spun lazily overhead while a bartender dried a glass with disinterest. A soft, jazzy riff sounded on the speakers. The only patron was a woman seated at the bar. Her fingernails clicked on a champagne glass, her chin rested in the other hand.

There were summer nights when The Grande was at full capacity with boaters and tourists, but on an October Wednesday evening, even one patron was a bonus and a reason to stay open.

The bar hosted four tall chairs. I left one between me and the woman and sat down, tucking my skirt beneath me.

She looked over, eyes narrowing. "Glad you could find somewhere to sit."

I smiled. "Busy place, right? I'm Rosalie by the way. And you?"

She blinked those dark eyes that took up most of her face. "Why did you just ask me that?"

My mouth dropped open a little. I gazed over at her. She was in a bohemian-like short black dress with tassels at the end of the ties, and a pair of velvet slippers embroidered with a Versace logo. She was gorgeous.

"I'm sorry, I didn't mean to be bold. I'll allow you your privacy."

"The last thing I need is to sit here alone. How about a glass of champagne? It's very expensive and I bought the whole bottle."

"Oh, my. Champagne would be lovely." I sat a little straighter. "And thank you."

"Oh, Sexy," she called to the bartender. "Is my champagne still nice and cold?"

"Got it on ice for you, Miss Sonja."

"How about another glass for my new friend?"

The bartender approached with a champagne flute and a bottle of rosé champagne. He filled it expertly, stopping just before the bubbles spilled over the rim. "I know you," he said to me. "Day Lily Café, right?"

"That's me."

He leaned in and lowered his voice. "I hear you're expanding. Nights? Bigger bar?" He looked at me expectantly.

"Sexy is good at what he does," the woman said. "He's good at *everything* he does."

His cheeks flamed red. "Name's Nathan."

"Doris Bird mentioned you. That's actually why I'm here. And you're free on weekends?"

"Oh, yeah. Not because I want to be. My student loans are strapping me."

I slid a business card over to him. "If all goes well, we reopen in three weeks."

"Awesome." He dropped the card into his shirt pocket and walked away.

I sipped the champagne and stared at the glass. "Oh, my. You have excellent taste. Miss Sonja, is it?"

"It's easy to have taste when you have a lot of cash."

I eyed her. "You also have a very nice car."

She took me in. "Why bother buying a Porsche if it isn't red?"

I gave her a half smile. "That's an excellent point."

"There's a reason Louboutin shoes are red on the inside strip of the heel. A woman crosses her legs, and there's that flash of red. Makes men think of lipstick. And more importantly, kissing."

"I never thought of it that way." I took another sip. It tickled going down. I licked my lips and let the aftertaste do its magic. Mm. A perfect medley of effervescence, fruit forward, yet dry and crisp. I placed my hands on the stem of the narrow flute and appreciated how the crystal caught the color of the champagne, tinting every facet the shade of a pale pink peony. There's that word again, peony.

"This champagne makes me think of Italy," I said dreamily.

"It's French, darling."

I stifled a small burp.

"So you own a restaurant? Is it any good?"

"I think so." I took another sip. "I'm going to study with a Tuscan chef for a week. We start class in a little over a week."

"I've never done anything like that. I like to cook. But it's a waste of time because I don't really eat."

"Sonja, do I detect an accent?"

"Russian. But you already know that." She tilted her head and smiled.

"Why so coy?"

"I'm sorry?"

"Surely you know who I am."

"Nathan called you Sonja. I know that much."

"Hello? *The Battle for the Highlands?*"

"Oh. I've never seen the show. I guess that's why I didn't recognize you. I'm sorry. I didn't intend to be rude."

"Darling, I was on the cover of *In Style* magazine two months ago. And my show won a Golden Globe this year for best ensemble cast. Highest rated HBO series ever?"

"I have a very small television."

She pouted. "I'm the beloved Queen Lorelei. And they killed me. That's one of the reasons I came here. I needed to get away."

"Did you say they killed you?" I took another long sip.

"They poison me. The end of the scene is the goblet rolling away on the floor."

I choked on my champagne. "Who poisoned you?"

"I'm the season ender shocker. No one will know I'm dead until the beginning of next season. And I'm telling you because I don't know why. But if you tell another soul I'll sue you." She drained her champagne. "I'll need your last name. *Then* I'll sue you."

I glanced around. Nathan was in the corner studying his phone. "When did they tell you this, Sonja?"

"On the set a few weeks ago. They didn't even give me a script. No words. The show ends with me sprawled on the floor. Well, I'm on the floor. They actually made me look pretty hot."

"You said that was one of the reasons you're in Cardigan. There are a lot of places to go to get away. Aruba, for one. And I hear the Greek islands are spectacular. So why did you choose Cardigan?"

"So many questions. Why are *you* in Cardigan?"

"Long and uninteresting story. Would not make a popular series." I dropped my hands in my lap. "I'm forty-five. Husband moved on. I got out of Dodge as fast I could. And now I'm here." I finished my champagne. "I don't regret it. This is a really nice place to live."

Sonja gazed at my empty glass. "Oh, Sexy—"

Nathan looked up from his phone and filled our glasses. "You ladies want something to eat?"

"We're good." She patted his hand. "But don't make me ask next time. You're supposed to notice when our glasses are empty. That's why I pay you the big bucks."

Once Nathan was out of earshot, I said, "Why would they kill you off if you're the beloved queen?"

"It's a thing. Surprise everyone. They wouldn't kill *her*. She's a fan favorite." She rolled her eyes. "They are going to regret it. My followers will be furious."

I sat back. "So what will you do next?"

She leveled her eyes with mine. "Too many questions, Rosalie. And what is your last name?"

"You're not the first person to tell me I ask too many questions. And the last name is Hart." I placed another business card on the bar. She tucked it in her bag and combed her hands through those luxurious locks. "You have great hair."

"Extensions," she said impatiently. "No matter how good you look, the directors will convince you it's not enough. I already had great hair. But they insisted on improvements. Eyelashes, too. So far I've kept them away from my boobs. Padded push up bras seem to suffice for now." She looked at me. "It must be nice living here. People like you don't need to look their best every minute of every day. No need to alter yourself to please some gross director."

"I'm sorry?"

"Let me put it this way. I haven't eaten dinner in over a year. Get it?" She blinked those wide eyes. "Nobody does in this business. It's a thing." Sonja emptied her glass in one gulping swig. "Champagne . . ." she flashed me a smile . . . "it's what's for dinner."

I laughed. I could see why she was successful. Despite her abruptness that bordered on insulting, there was something charismatic about her. "Your accent—is that part of your role?"

"My parents were born in Russia. We spoke Russian at home. I can drop it if I want, but I think people find it intriguing." She stared off for a moment. "Or, perhaps not."

"Are your parents actors, too? Anyone I might know?"

"No." She looked up. "My mother died when I was four. My father raised me. He was a very successful businessman. He threw lots of parties. I got noticed at one of them. Did some ads when I was a kid." She frowned. "How do you not recognize me? Wait, do you remember the commercial with the little girl who handed out popsicles to people for free on the sidewalk on a hot day?"

"Oh, my gosh, yes! My Annie was obsessed with that ad. She tried to do it herself on a July day in DC. They all melted. It was a mess and a half."

"Finally. Thank you for remembering."

"That girl was adorable."

"Agreed." She gave me a thin-lipped smile.

"Sonja, you said 'was' when you mentioned your father. You used the past tense. Has something happened to him?"

Sonja clutched her hands together. Her knuckles whitened. "You're intense, you know that, Rosalie?" She stood and lifted her bag from the hook under the bar. "I think it's time I collapse into bed."

Chapter Eight

On the following Thursday afternoon, the day before my brother Oliver was due to arrive, I was at the café sipping coffee and checking my list. I had just finished making a batch of my seasoned salt. It was easy to prepare and twice as tasty—fresh herbs, chopped garlic, lemon zest, and a cup of sea salt. With just an occasional stirring, the salt dried the herbs and garlic and it would be good to go for class on Monday.

I had spent the past week collecting supplies and organizing the café. But until yesterday, I was still down two students. I had upped my social media postings and put a flyer in Doris Bird's shoe store. And it finally paid off. A prospective student was due any minute.

I let him in through the kitchen, still no front steps, and he ducked to get in the doorway.

He straightened a pair of black-framed glasses. "Are you Rosalie Hart?"

"That's me."

His hair was dark and thick and a full mustache framed his upper lip. "I saw your notice on Facebook. I think it was in the group, Cardigan Life. You're hosting a cooking class?"

"You bet. There are two slots left. Would you like some coffee?"

"Yes," he said. "That's a good idea." He followed me into the restaurant and sat at the bar. He was dressed in khakis and a button-down Oxford topped with a leather jacket. A satchel made from the same weathered brown leather draped across his body. "My name is Brandon Preston Hitch. I'm a professor of ancient history at John Adams College."

34

I started up one of the Mieles. "And you like to cook?"

"I like to know things."

I frothed some heavy cream and set a cappuccino in front of him. "What kind of things?"

"Everything I can. I'm in Mensa and I just qualified for Jeopardy last week. I fly out to California next month." He picked up the cup. "My run will be epic."

I thought for a moment. "I like to know things, too. I guess we have that in common."

"Interesting." He sipped his coffee.

"So what appeals to you about the cooking class?"

"It's Italian. And I'm not. I'm the opposite of Italian." He finished off the cappuccino. "This is delicious. How did you know I would like this?"

"My staff call me a coffee whisperer. Did I get it wrong?"

His eyebrows dipped. "No," he said in a hushed voice. "This is perfect." He set the cup in the saucer.

"Thank you, Dr. Hitch."

"You may call me Brandon." He frowned. "This Italian chef. He's the real deal?"

"He owns three restaurants in Tuscany."

Brandon studied me. "You met him?"

"Not yet. But I am good friends with his cousin. I guarantee he's authentic."

He looked away, a wistful expression softened his features. "I've never been to Italy. But it calls to me like a Mediterranean siren. Just like in the classics."

I wasn't quite sure what to make of this man, but I had often stared at nothing while dreaming of Italy. And then of course, there's my budget. "Well, this is your chance, professor. A chance to get a taste of Italy. Literally."

He returned my gaze. "You have four other students?"

"Yes. You're number five. One more and we're good to go."

"You know, Rosalie, I moved here to start over. And so far it just feels like the same old act, only the setting has changed. Too much certainty can make a man dull. And I started out being dull. Plus I could use some new friends." He pushed the empty cup toward me. "That was good. Best coffee I've had in a very long while." He pursed his lips. "I can feel it kick in. It's as if my eyes have opened a little wider."

I smiled. "I believe they have."

"I'm in." He slapped his palms on his thighs. "Shall I write you a check?"

"Yes, please."

Chapter Nine

I arrived home the next day filled with an excited anticipation that class would be starting on Monday. But the best part was imminent. My big brother, Oliver, was due to arrive that evening. Just three years older, at forty-eight, Oliver was ridiculously handsome and had yet to marry. With his big job in Manhattan and a large rent-controlled condo on the upper west side, it was safe to say his life couldn't be any more different from mine.

I walked toward the house, juggling a basket of rolling pins of various shapes and sizes per Marco's request. I had toured Cardigan borrowing from friends and neighbors all afternoon. Heavy gray clouds swirled angrily overhead. A strong breeze kicked up my skirt and I tried to hold it in place with my free hand. A loose hair clung to my lipgloss as I made my way up the steps.

I found Tyler at the sink taking the last bite of an apple. "How excited are you?"

"Oh, my goodness," I said, slightly out of breath. "Beyond excited. I haven't seen Oliver in over three years."

"You sure don't talk about him very much."

"I don't?" I set the basket on the table. "Well, I adore him."

"You know, I'm glad your brother is coming. Getting to know him may clue me in on you a little better."

I tilted my head. "You don't need Oliver. I'm an open book."

"Oh, yeah? Well, I'm barely through the first chapter. And I'm a pretty fast reader."

"I guess I can see your point. I learned a lot about you when your brother was in town last summer."

He eyed my basket. "That's a lot of rolling pins."

"Marco asked me to have them on hand. I don't know why. Maybe pizza dough?" I slipped out of my coat.

Dickens let out a hoarse ruff. The front door creaked open. I spun around. "Oliver!"

I met him as he closed the door. He immediately dropped his bag and spun me around. "Rosie, Rosie, Rosie," he said as if he'd just come home from a war.

I hugged him, hard. After losing both our parents and Aunt Charlotte within six years, our Finnegan family had dwindled down to just Oliver, my Annie, and me. "I've missed you," I said.

He set me down. "You know, I haven't seen you since your divorce from Ed." He sized me up. "But I must say, you look a lot better than I expected."

Tyler stood next to me. "I believe our Rosalie's been Italicized."

Oliver let out a hearty laugh. "You must be Tyler."

Tyler extended his hand. "Good to meet you."

Oliver shook it vigorously. "Really great to meet you. And just so you know? I already like you better than Ed." He clapped his hands together. "Now, what do you have to drink in this joint?"

Oliver sipped the four-olive Tanqueray martini I concocted and the three of us settled into the living room. Despite his insisting he wasn't hungry, he eagerly dipped crackers and crudités in the bowl of melted smoked gouda cheese I had set on the coffee table. He wiped his hands on a cocktail napkin and took in his surroundings. "I haven't been here since I was a kid. Doesn't look much different."

"The kitchen is the only thing that's been updated," I said. "The stairs still creak and the beds are even lumpier."

He pointed to a small mahogany chest with brass hardware. "I used to play with my Hot Wheels in that thing. Turned it into a multi-level parking garage." He shook his head and took another sip. "It feels pretty weird sitting in this living room again. Especially knowing it's yours."

"You like to cook?" Tyler said.

"Nah." Oliver looked over at me. "I just needed to get away."

"And see the café," I said. "Your investment."

"That too." Oliver smiled, but it quickly faded. His brown eyes looked as tired as a basset hound's. A touch of gray streaked his hair and he seemed thinner. Oliver swam the butterfly in college and normally his broad shoulders barely fit into his shirt.

A tug of worry formed in my gut. I noticed he had drained his glass. "Another?"

"Oh, yeah. And skip the vermouth."

Tyler and Oliver chatted while I freshened Oliver's drink. Their deep baritones resounded in the high-ceilinged room. It made me smile to have my two favorite men getting to know one another.

As I poured the chilled gin through the strainer, I heard footsteps on the front stoop. It was already after eight. I couldn't imagine who it could be. I started for the door but it opened before I got there. Janice Tilghman, one of my favorite Cardigan friends, strode into the foyer.

"Janice." I started to give her hug.

"Keep your distance, Rose Red. I have another student for you."

"That's fabulous. Who?"

"Me. Who else?" She tucked her short, stylish blond hair behind an ear. "When do we start?"

"Monday and that's wonderful news."

"I'll give you a check tomorrow. I hired Betty Larkin to drive the boys around and told Trevor he's on his own for lunch and dinner. They should be fine as long as Betty can keep track of her readers."

I leaned in to hug her again and she stepped back.

"Please stop that, Rose Red. Take a chill pill."

"Okay, I'm just grateful you'll be taking the class. And I thought Oliver's arrival was the best news I would get tonight."

"Oliver's here?" Janice smacked me on the arm. "Get out of town. Really? Oliver?"

"Oh, so we can hit, but not hug?" I rubbed my arm.

"You didn't tell me he was coming. Signing up for this class just got ten times better." Janice charged through the house calling, "Oliver Finnegan, where the hell are you?"

I followed her into the living room. She stood, hands on hips, taking in the scene. "Holy cow, Oliver *and* Tyler." She grinned broadly. "Somebody sign me up for this brodeo!"

Oliver hopped up and embraced her warmly. "Jani, it's great to see you."

I smiled at their encounter. Oliver and I were friends with Janice as children. She grew up on the farm next to Aunt Charlotte's, on the side opposite Windswept Farm. We spent hours making up games and chasing each other, Janice always running a little more slowly in hopes Oliver would catch up. From the first day she and I met, we had nicknames for one another from our favorite fairy tale, Rose Red and Snow White.

"Man, oh, man. My old buddy, Oliver. You look good but I'm pretty sure I could still out run you. Do you remember how lousy you were at freeze tag?"

"I've never been good at sitting still. Ask any of my teachers." He laughed. "Remember my pants splitting during a game of spud? Didn't I slink against the house until Aunt Charlotte rescued me?"

"I think that was during your *Flock of Seagulls* phase."

"I had a very fashionable hairstyle." Oliver laughed again.

"How about a cocktail, Janice?" I said.

"I'm having a second martini," Oliver said. "You in?"

"Most definitely." Janice walked over to the sofa and plopped down next to Tyler. "Oliver and I are buds."

"You don't say?" Tyler finished his beer.

Once I delivered her beverage, I sat across from Janice. She took a long sip and smacked her lips. "Say, did you hear about your neighbor biting the bullet?"

"We did." I checked Tyler's reaction. His brows dipped but he continued to listen to Janice.

"Well, the word around town is," Janice's eyes danced as she paused to savor the opportunity to share fresh gossip, "Bini Katz scared him to death."

Chapter Ten

The next morning I found Bini at the kitchen table with her coffee and the local newspaper. She didn't look up.

"Bini, I've been meaning to ask you, how did it go with the sheriff? Tyler said he told you to not leave town."

She continued to look at the paper. "That's right."

"But why? Kline was dead when you got there."

She eyed me. "I'm his number one suspect."

"That makes no sense." I crossed my arms. "On what grounds?"

"You should know." She stood and carried her mug to the sink. "He now believes I had the perfect motive to kill Mr. Kline. Thank you for suggesting that to him."

"Oh." I combed both hands through my hair. "Good grief, Bini. He asked me why you were at his house, and I told him. I'm sorry this has caused so much trouble." I thought for a moment. "Maybe I should talk to the sheriff."

"I'm *sorry*?" She shook her head. "I think you've said enough."

Footsteps sounded from above and we both looked up to see Oliver reach the last step of the stairwell dressed in a pair of silk paisley boxers and nothing else. His thick brown hair was uncombed, an afternoon shadow darkened his face. He stopped abruptly when he saw Bini.

"Sorry, Rosie, I didn't know you had company."

"I'm not company," Bini said. "I work here." She sized up Oliver, a slight blush colored her cheeks. "You must own that 700 series black Beamer out there. New York plates?"

Oliver flattened a palm on his toned stomach. "That's correct. I'm Oliver,

Rosie's brother." He dipped his head. "I apologize for the choice of clothing. I live alone." He gave her a half smile. "And I'm usually the guy in the suit."

She narrowed her eyes. "Temperature's dropped this morning. You don't want to catch a chill." And she was out the front door.

"Hm," Oliver said. "Did that go as poorly as I think?"

"It's not you." I approached Mr. Miele. "Bini has a very direct manner." I glanced over my shoulder. "And she has a lot on her mind. You hungry?"

"Coffee will suffice."

He sat at the table just as Tyler walked in. "What happened with Bini?"

"I didn't know there was a Bini," Oliver said. "Thus the boxers."

Tyler's mouth curved into an amused smile.

"The gist of it is she blames me for the sheriff making her a suspect." I carried Oliver's coffee over to him. "I need to make this all go away."

"It will go away on its own." Tyler looked at me directly, as if to warn me to stay out of it. "She's also worked up about the chance Barty Bennet might dust those fields."

"Tell her there's a will," I said. "Jojo made it sound as if no one has a clue who the farm will go to. Anyway, he can't do anything until the will has been read." I folded the newspaper. "And please tell her to not go over there again."

"I will definitely tell her that." Tyler scrubbed his hands. "We're getting the straw and feed delivered today. Goats arrive tomorrow afternoon." He tossed a dish towel on the counter. "What are you two doing today?"

I glanced at Oliver. "I was hoping to show him the café."

"Nice." Tyler kissed my forehead. "Hey, Oliver, I'm glad you're here. Maybe we can grab a beer later on."

"Never said no to that."

Tyler made his exit and Oliver brought his mug to his lips with both hands. On cue, Sweeney Todd leapt onto the table and chin-bumped his mug, sloshing coffee over the sides and onto the table.

"What the . . .?"

"I should have warned you." I tore off several paper towels. "Sweeney's also very good at opening bathroom doors, by the way. His timing is impeccable."

"I'll remember that next time Bini is in the house." Oliver set down his mug and wiped his hands. "Speaking of Bini, what's the deal around here? Do people just walk into your house whenever they please?"

"Pretty much. But I like it that way." I sat across from him. "The first time I met Tyler, after an awkward introduction, I decided to invite him in for coffee. Since that day, I've had a pot ready for him every morning."

"Anyone else I should be expecting?"

"Maybe Janice. She pops in now and then." I smiled. "Refill?"

He shook his head. "I should probably put some clothes on just in case."

"You know, this isn't the first time this has happened to you."

Oliver frowned. "What do you mean?"

"Don't you remember? One summer you and I were here with Aunt Charlotte and you came down to the kitchen in nothing but your tighty whities. Aunt Charlotte was hosting Garden Club that afternoon."

Oliver dropped his forehead in his hands. "I think I blocked out that memory." He looked up. "There were like twelve women in here."

"Twelve women and you. Aunt Charlotte also had an open-door policy."

"Well, I guess there's nothing wrong with a healthy dose of humility now and then." He scooted his chair back. "I'll be getting dressed now." He stood. "And by the way, I would love to see the café this morning."

Chapter Eleven

After a late brunch of a mushroom, garlic, and muenster cheese omelet, toast, sautéed potatoes, and fresh cantaloupe, Oliver and I loosened our belts and headed into town. "I'm glad you got a chance to sleep in this morning," I said as I down shifted onto the main road.

"I've been up since five."

I shot him a concerned look. "Is the bed really that lumpy?"

"No. I was working. China and Europe start their days a lot earlier than the East Coast. There is always something to do."

I slowed behind a tractor that took up most of the road. "I thought you said you needed a vacation. A *real* vacation." I glanced over at him and noticed small bags under his eyes, crow's feet in the corners. At least he had shaved.

"I know I need it. I've tried, but I can't seem to do it." He powered his seat back. "Did I ever tell you I've been seeing someone for a while? Going on four years."

"You mentioned her. Sylvia? I'd love to meet her."

"You won't. I messed it up. I thought we were a good match for a lot of reasons. One of them being Sylvie loved her job as much as I love mine. She's a senior accountant with one of the big firms." He shrugged. "So I asked her to marry me. We both wanted children. We were super compatible. She said yes, on one condition."

"I'm curious . . ."

"She asked that I go one day without working. Just one day to see if we could make this happen. She didn't want to end up being a single parent,

44

sacrificing her career so that I could work eighty hours a week. She needed to know if her kids would have an involved dad.

"I was all in. We had a fabulous Saturday." Oliver smiled at the memory. "We started at the Guggenheim, then had a kir royale at the Plaza. You know, touristy stuff. Those royales cost fifty bucks each, by the way. We walked in the park and sat on a blanket in the grass. I even put my head in her lap and she combed her fingernails through my hair for forty-five glorious minutes."

"Sounds amazing. I want to have a day like that."

"We had dinner at an intimate place in the village, low lighting, candles, a jazz piano in a corner. She got up to go to the bathroom." He stopped.

The tractor waved me past. I shifted gears and darted around him. "Did something happen to her?"

He looked at me. "What do you do when someone goes to the bathroom while you're out to dinner?"

I thought for a moment. "I usually check my phone. I'm always hoping for a text from Annie."

"Ah, Anna Banana. I sure miss that kid. Anyway . . ." He huffed out a sigh. "Ding ding ding. You got it right."

"You checked your phone while she was gone? That doesn't necessarily mean you worked. Does it?"

"I was answering an email to a client. I didn't even notice she had already sat down. The email wasn't important. I had posted an away message. But I couldn't not do it. My fingers were typing before I could let it all register. I honestly don't know how long she had been sitting there."

"Oh, Oliver. What happened?"

"By the time I looked up, the tears had reached her chin. She said, one day? She just wanted one day. And I couldn't do it. She said she loved me. But she wasn't my priority. She said she felt wretched and she didn't deserve to feel wretched. Sylvie tossed five twenties on the table for her part of dinner and left me in the wake of her perfume." He leaned back onto the headrest. "It was a really nice perfume."

I parked on the street and stood next to Oliver as he took in the café. The blue awnings piped in white flapped in the breeze. The gold script Day Lily Café logo on the front door twinkled in the sunlight.

"It's perfect," he said quietly. "I would want to eat here."

"You really like it?"

"I had no idea what to expect." The caution tape snapped in another wind gust. "So how do we get inside?"

"Come with me."

When we reached the back door, I noticed a large, beat up cardboard box wrapped in copious tape on the stoop. I read the return address. "Florence, Italy. Oliver, this is the box Marco said he would send. What do you think is inside?"

He bent over and hefted it onto his shoulder. "Let's find out."

Once in the kitchen, I held the door open to the dining room so Oliver could set the box on the bar. He wiped his hands on his dark wash jeans, and took in his surroundings. "More perfection. You go about your business, Rosie, I just want to experience this place." He walked over to the hostess station and selected a menu.

I did as he suggested and gathered the mail and turned up the heat. After emptying the dishwasher and scrubbing the sink, I had delayed my gratification long enough. I was ready to open the box. I picked up a knife and noticed Oliver in the sunniest corner of the café. The menu lay open before him, but his gaze was fixed out the window, a contemplative expression on his face.

I set the knife down and decided to text Kevin. A fellow foodie, I knew he would be excited about its contents, too. In less than a minute he wrote, *be right there!!!*

I looked up to see Oliver standing next to the bar. "You got anything to drink in this place?"

"Just wine and beer for now. But I think I found a bartender for the reopening."

"Red wine sounds perfect." He sat on one of the high chairs. "You haven't opened the box."

I reached for a wine glass. "I'm almost ready." I thought for a moment and selected two more glasses. "How about a nice Sangiovese? Oh, and maybe some *Bocelli* on the speakers."

Kevin arrived soon after. He pushed through the doors and said, "Thank you, thank you, thank you for including me." His styled brown hair was slightly askew. He was dressed in a navy cashmere v-neck and creased khakis.

I handed him a glass of wine. "Kevin, I'd like you to meet my favorite and only brother, Oliver Finnegan."

"Charmed." Kevin shook his hand.

Oliver smiled. "I'm always happy to meet one of Rosie's friends."

We clinked our glasses and after a large gulp, Kevin said, "I didn't know there was a brother."

"That's because Oliver's been busy going places."

Oliver stopped mid-sip. "Whoa, what a blast from the past. That's what our parents used to say about me, isn't it?" He shook his head. "What did that even mean?"

"You don't know?"

"Not really." He frowned. "But hey, you have a box." He hesitated. "From an Italian chef, I should add."

Bocelli crooned in the background as I started the laborious task of cutting away the tape. Kevin rocked up and down on his toes.

When I at last lifted the flaps, a strong earthy scent met our noses. "Girlfriend," Kevin said. "I think there are fresh truffles in here."

"Do you think? Oh my goodness." I lifted out a large block of cheese.

"Look at the size of that thing," Kevin said. "Parmesan?"

"From what Marco's told me, this is going to be strictly Tuscan cooking." I read the label. "This is a *Pecorino Toscano*," I said in the best Italian accent I could muster.

Kevin reached for a large tin jug. "Olive oil. This is the good stuff. Extra virgin. First press."

"Oh," I said as I picked up something wrapped in a floral cloth. "This must be the truffles."

"Let's see." Kevin leaned forward as I peeled the cloth away. "White," he said. "Look at those babies. They smell divine. They still have dirt on them."

"This is truffle season in Italy," I said. "They must be about as fresh as you can get in the US."

"So this is all stuff he knew he couldn't get here." Kevin took a sip of wine. "What will we make with the truffles? Maybe creamy pasta with shaved truffles on top? My mouth is watering. This is incredible."

"Semolina flour?" I removed the bag and set it on the bar. "He asked me to get rolling pins. I'll bet we're going to make fresh pasta. Don't you think?"

"Absolutely," Kevin said. "Mama Mia."

"This is so awesome!" We embraced in a spontaneous hug.

The rest of the box contained porcini mushrooms, *saporito*, an Italian sausage unique to Tuscany, a long narrow wooden rolling pin, and chickpea flour. I lined everything up and Kevin and I stepped back to take it in.

"Did I tell you Alessa is bringing wine? Prosecco, too."

"If you can believe it," Kevin said, "I am without words."

"Why don't you sit next to Oliver so you can finish your wine."

Kevin picked up his glass and walked around to the other side of the bar. After refilling Oliver's wine, I sat on the other side of Oliver.

Kevin's fingers clutched the stem of his glass. "He's going to want fresh herbs from your garden. Maybe eggs from your chickens, too."

"I should let him know what I have. He and Alessa will be shopping this weekend."

Oliver leaned back and crossed his arms. "You guys are making me hungry."

"Agreed," Kevin said. "I'm famished."

I inhaled a deep breath. "This music, the wine, those truffles . . ."

"So this is definitely happening, right?" Kevin said. "Please tell me this isn't a tease. You have six students?"

"Just got my sixth yesterday. Say, a professor from the college signed up. You might know him. He teaches history. Brandon Hitch?"

"That name sounds local." Kevin took a sip.

"Really? He said he moved here from DC. Maybe Jake knows him." I said to Oliver, "Jake is Kevin's partner. He's the lacrosse coach at the college."

"Um, partner, and soon to be husband." Kevin's eyes danced.

"You're engaged?" I gasped.

"Mazel tov." Oliver lifted his glass. "I look forward to meeting him."

After we clinked glasses, Kevin took another sip and said, "Not sure that's going to happen." He sized up Oliver. "You're just his type. I finally get the guy to propose and then I have to introduce him to all this? Nope. Not happening."

I laughed. "This is wonderful news, Kevin. Can I be your best man?"

"Hello," he said and stood. "I'm the bride." He finished his wine and pushed in his chair. "I need to get back to the shop. And yes, you can be my bride's maid." He walked over to the truffles and took a long, dramatic sniff. "Keep these covered in a cool place. But don't refrigerate." He tucked the cloth beneath them. "Okay, I'm outies. And I will see you both on Monday." He blew us a kiss and was out the door.

When the door stopped swinging, I glanced over at Oliver. He was still leaning back, arms crossed, but a small smile had formed on his lips. "What?" I said.

"It's good to be here, Rosie. Really good."

Chapter Twelve

Oliver decided to head out for a walk around town. After cleaning up and putting away the goodies from the box, I decided to pay another visit to the sheriff. Bini had asked me not to. But I couldn't sit idly while he solidified his case against her. So I filled a carryout coffee cup and dropped two chocolate zucchini muffins into a small bag.

As I walked through the Sheriff's department parking lot, I passed a VW beetle with eyelashes over the headlights, alerting me the sheriff's secretary had showed up for work.

Lila sat at her desk in the small front room. Although she could have retired years ago, she liked the fact she could keep her own hours. She also liked to be up on the latest in town and had been known to hold court at the country club bar sharing the latest gossip, such as how fast Joe Rudy was traveling on route 19 and that Frank Buckley got a DUI over the weekend. Again.

My problem with Lila was on the days she showed up for work, she viewed herself as the sheriff's guard dog.

"Good afternoon, Lila. I'm here to have a chat with the sheriff."

"He's busy."

I looked through the open door into his office. "No, he's not."

"If I say he's busy, he's busy."

"I can see him. He's cutting his fingernails." I frowned a little. "At his desk."

She fluffed her bright orange curls and said nothing.

I held out the bag. "Chocolate zucchini. Don't tell the sheriff I gave them to you."

Hesitating, she said, "Don't overstay your welcome."

I walked past her and into the office. The sheriff's glasses were low on his nose as he studied the next fingernail. "What, Hart?" He didn't look up.

"Is it too late for coffee?"

"Never."

I sat down and waited. "Are you almost finished?"

"One more."

After the last click, he tossed the clippers on his desk, and reached for the cardboard cup. "Thanks for the bribe." He popped off the top. "You know I'm on to you."

"Are you complaining?"

"Just because I like your coffee, doesn't mean I want your help."

"I was wondering if you've found any evidence that points to Bini other than a motive?"

"It's a pretty good motive."

"Are you even looking for evidence?"

"Prints at the farm all belong to Kline and the nieces and nephew. But who says she had to go inside?"

"Have you determined what the poison was?"

"Water hemlock. Pretty common around barns in these parts." He stirred his coffee.

"Well, I know there wasn't any hemlock in the muffins." I sat forward. "So how did he ingest the poison?"

"I don't have to tell you any of this." He slugged back some coffee.

"But they're good questions." I tucked my hair behind an ear. "You don't really think Bini could have killed Kline, do you? That's a pretty big deal. Bini's a local. You must know her family. They live the ten commandments." I paused. "Including the sixth one."

"Look, I haven't ruled her out. And, yeah, it's a very big deal. Someone was murdered in my county. That's bad for reelection."

"They're reading Kline's will pretty soon. That could produce some more suspects."

"Nobody knows what's in it, right?"

"Maybe someone did." I thought for a moment. "And they wanted to be sure he didn't change it. Hm?"

His eyes narrowed. I assumed he was considering my words. But that was never certain when it came to the sheriff. He was more likely trying to come up with an insult of some sort.

"Poisoning is premeditated," he said. "She knew he was about to dust those fields. Pretty big motive. With plenty of time to plan it." He smacked his hand on the desk. "And that's my case. We done here?"

I held his gaze. "Thanks for talking with me. You know, I feel pretty bad about telling you why Bini went out there."

"You think I wouldn't have asked her myself?" He said in a louder voice. "Don't give yourself so much credit."

"Ahem." Lila cleared her throat from her perch at the desk.

I glanced over my shoulder to try and make eye contact, but she was unwrapping the second muffin. I looked back at the sheriff. "I met the woman driving the Carerra."

"You don't say. I hear she's an actress."

"The Battle for the Highlands. That's pretty big."

"Why the heck is she in Cardigan?"

I shrugged. "I think she wanted to get away."

"Nobody comes here who doesn't have a reason to."

I frowned for a moment. "That's actually pretty astute, Sheriff Wilgus."

"What else do you know?" He tossed his cup into the trash.

"My brother Oliver is visiting from New York. He drives a 700 hundred series BMW. He's a good guy. Please don't pull him over just for fun." I stood and adjusted my skirt. "Good luck with the investigation. Let me know if I can help in any way."

He shook his head. "Nope."

"What if I told you Jojo Bennet is taking my cooking class. I'll be with her every day for a week."

"Why would that kid take your cooking class? She's like twenty-five or something."

52

"She might need to vent after the will reading."

He leaned forward, elbows on his cluttered desk. "Let me know every-thing."

"If you ask nicely."

Chapter Thirteen

When I got back to the café, I found a note from Oliver. He was going to the Grande to have a beer with Tyler. I considered joining them but thought better of it. This was a chance for them to get to know each other. Hang out. And hopefully grow to like one another.

The house was dark when I arrived home, the only light coming from the faint glow of a violet and indigo streaked sky, the muted colors mirrored in the river below.

It was close to seven. Sweeney serpentined through my legs, almost tripping me several times. He really was well-named. I switched on some lights and heard the sound of a truck door slamming. Soon after, Tyler and Oliver strolled into the room. Tyler's work shirt had come untucked and his hair was windblown. Oliver's eyes glistened with an alcohol glaze.

I crossed my arms. "What's up?"

Tyler kissed me on the lips. I detected the slightest trace of beer on his breath. "We went into town for a drink."

"Did you have fun?" I said tentatively.

He leaned back against the counter. "Oliver met someone."

"I did." Oliver plopped down into a kitchen chair.

"You went to The Grande? Let me guess. Sonja Volkov?"

They exchanged a look. "How the heck did you know that?" Oliver said.

"I met her. And apparently so did you two." My stomach tightened knowing they were spending time with such a striking woman—the complete opposite of me.

Tyler flashed me a warm smile. "How was your day? I heard there was a box."

"There was." My shoulders relaxed. Why did I immediately go to feeling insecure? Why did I assume he would eventually stop loving me? It never ceased to amaze me how my divorce created so much self doubt. I thought I had gotten past it, but testing the waters with Tyler was stirring up all kinds of crazy feelings. "She's pretty famous, apparently. Do you watch the show, Oliver?"

"Yeah, right." He laughed. "In my spare time. But I might check it out. She comes across as a very good actress."

I smiled. "You liked her, Oliver?."

"I didn't say that. We didn't talk to her for too long. She had already finished one bottle of champagne. I think she was on number two." He propped his feet on an adjacent chair.

"Everyone in town is trying to figure out why she's in Cardigan. Especially when she could afford to be hiding out somewhere exotic." I glanced at Tyler. "She sure is beautiful though."

He inched closer and whispered, "She's not the only beautiful woman in Cardigan." He traced a finger up my arm, giving me chill bumps.

I elbowed him. "I like you having a couple of beers."

Oliver removed three Heavy Seas Amber Ales from the refrigerator. He held one out to me. "You in?" I nodded. He handed the other to Tyler and twisted off the cap with a hiss. "I've had a very good day. Best day in a long time." Oliver dropped the bottle caps in the trash. "Say, aren't the Orioles in the playoffs this year? Want to watch the game, buddy?" He looked at me. "Where's your TV, anyway?"

"The armoire in the living room."

"It's a lot like watching TV on an iPad," Tyler said, causing Oliver to laugh.

While Oliver headed out to the living room, Tyler said, "Is it okay that I'm here?"

"It's more than okay." I reached for his hand and squeezed.

"Hey, Rosie," Oliver called. "You got any popcorn?"

"Very good idea. I love your popcorn." Tyler picked up his beer and went into the living room.

I pulled out my special popcorn pot, a dented relic that made the best batch because a little steam escaped from where the lid didn't quite fit. The cheers of a crowd filled the next room. I took a slug of beer, and found it refreshing. I grinned when they both chanted, *"Let's Go Ooooooo's!"*

Chapter Fourteen

L ate Sunday afternoon, the day before class was to start, I stood in
my bedroom, paralyzed with indecision about what to wear. I was
scheduled to meet Marco at last. We were to get together at the
café and plan the week to come. A loud *'woo hoo'* sounded from the living
room. Tyler and Oliver were cheering on another game.

I weighed my choices. We were just having a casual meeting. And yet,
Marco was an authentic Italian chef. Famous in the Tuscan region, if not
the entire country. I wanted to impress him, show him that I knew my stuff,
that I was equal to the task. My shoulders fell as I exhaled.

The only item I was certain about was my mother's pearls. I placed my
fingers over the strand and channeled her love. Both my parents had always
stressed the best approach to life was equal doses of humility and self-belief.
Even to Oliver, although he was going places. I took it in. It was a good
lesson. I didn't need to impress Marco. I needed to be myself. So I decided
on my café uniform: A white blouse, sleeves rolled up to the forearm, above
the knee black skirt, the pearls, of course, and black tights. I fluffed my hair
and spritzed on my go to perfume, Coco Channel Mademoiselle.

I stood before the mirror, the glass hazy and pocked. It had been in my
mother's family since the mid-eighteen hundreds. When I was a child,
Charlotte used to let me dress up in her hat, gloves, and matching shoes
before this very mirror. I would imagine being a grown up, stylish and
important, as I clomped around in the low pumps, lifting a pinky finger for
flair. Charlotte loved Oliver and me as the children she could never have
after the love of her life was killed in Vietnam. And for six weeks every

summer, we were hers.

Just two years apart, Charlotte and my mother had been close their entire lives. Every Sunday afternoon, my mother would percolate a cup of coffee and sit on the stairs talking with Charlotte for hours. I liked to eavesdrop on those conversations, often getting a hint of my mother's opinions of me, Oliver, her husband, her dreams.

How different my life would be if they were both still alive. I touched the pearls again. "Thanks for keeping me humble, Mom." I smiled. "Oliver is here. Not sure if you know that." This was only my second day with my brother. "I think he needs me, Mom. No, wait, I am sure he needs me. I don't know how or if I can help, but I'm going to try." My eyes welled. I blinked several times, willing my mascara not to run. God, I missed her. And I prayed I could be of some help to my brother.

I slid an index finger underneath each eye, rolled my shoulders back, and clicked my black wedge shoes together. I had a meeting with Marco Giovanelli. I could do this. I smoothed my hands over my skirt and glanced back at the mirror. Lipstick would definitely be required.

The café sparkled. I had done everything possible to get ready for the class. Having shaken off my self-doubt, I decided to make a little nosh for us. I smashed some coriander and allspice seeds and simmered them in olive oil with crushed garlic, orange peel, bay leaf, and red pepper flakes. Once the flavors were infused into the oil, I poured it over a wedge of goat cheese. The warm spicy oil melted the cheese into a creamy spread. Next, I toasted some baguette slices and rubbed them with a raw garlic clove. I dimmed the lights and arranged it all on the counter with napkins and two red wine glasses. I sat at the bar and gazed out the front window. The sun was low in the sky, igniting the changing leaves on the maples lining the street. I folded my hands into my lap and waited.

I jumped up when I heard a rap on the back door. Marco wore a broad smile as he entered the kitchen, a bottle of wine in one hand, a weathered briefcase in the other. He brought wine, I thought. We were on the same page.

"Ciao, *Rosalia*. We finally meet." He set the wine on the counter, took my hands in his, and kissed my cheeks, one, then the other. He smelled divine.

"Ciao, Marco! I'm so happy you are here." I glanced around the kitchen. "Where do we start?"

"Do you have a corkscrew?" His almond eyes were warm and kind. He was definitely taller than me but his frame was trim, his dark hair wavy around his head, slight graying at the temples, his jeans, low on his hips. "I see you have a Vulcan range. That will do nicely." He smiled as he took in the rest of the kitchen. "Is that aromatic salt drying over there?"

"Yes."

"That was a good idea. We will be using that in everything." He clapped his hands together. "Where is the wine opener?"

"Come into the dining room." I motioned him through the swinging door and held my breath while he looked around the room. He was still smiling.

I stood next to the bar. "This is where we'll do the prep work. What do you think?"

"It is *perfetta*." He handed me the bottle. "But let's you and I sit with one another. Shall we?"

I filled our glasses and Marco sat at the bar, immediately slathering a baguette with the cheese. He took a bite and wiped his mouth. "I want your recipe."

"Really?" I sat adjacent to him and squeezed my hands together. "It's yours."

He lifted his glass. "*Rosalia*, to our new adventure."

"To us." My face flushed. I was so excited I had to suppress a squeal from working its way up my throat.

And then we got down to business. Marco removed a notebook from his briefcase. It was already full of notes, but he needed more information. We talked for almost an hour about who the students were, who should be paired together, what ingredients we still needed. He explained his methods, disciplined but always with an allowance for spontaneity and creativity. I scribbled my own notes and took a deep breath. I was already learning from this man. From the day I decided to open a café, I wanted to study with a professional chef. I knew I had good instincts, but this man was going to take my cooking to a whole new level.

Marco closed his notebook and topped off our wine. He put his chin in his hand and took me in. "Why did you open this café, *Rosalia?*"

"Well, I was making coffee for everyone I knew. And I had started selling my homemade bread anywhere that was willing to sell it."

"And why were you doing that?"

"That's what I do. I found myself with no one to cook for. That had never been my life circumstance before."

"Yes. I understand this."

"You do? Because sometimes I feel a little crazy."

"We cook because we must. It is what we do."

"Yes. That's exactly it. I have a friend who's a writer. As much agony as it may cause her, she says she can't not write. It's in her DNA." I crossed my legs and straightened my skirt. "Is that true for you? I know you are a very successful businessman. But is the cooking still a part of it for you?"

"It is everything." He studied me. His eyelids lowered. "Everything."

"Yes. I get that."

Marco finished his wine and hopped up. He winked and said, "I think this is the beginning of a beautiful friendship." He gripped his briefcase. "Until tomorrow, Rosalie."

I watched him go and slugged back the rest of my wine, fanning myself as I drank.

Chapter Fifteen

Monday
Day One of Cooking School

Menu
Antipasti/Appetizers
Fiori di zucchini ripieni / Stuffed zucchini blossoms
Rosalie and Kevin

Pesto di Pomodoro Bruschetta / Tomato Pesto Bruschetta
Janice and Oliver

Uova alla Diavola all'Italiana / Italian Deviled Eggs
Joanna and Brandon

"Cooking is a little Minx"
-Artusi Pelligrino

G lenn and I watched while Marco wrote the menu on the café's chalkboard. His handwriting was exquisite, each letter perfectly formed.

I nudged Glenn gently. "I've always wanted to make stuffed zucchini blossoms."

"Now's your chance." He smiled. "I can't believe this is all happening. *Brava*, my dear."

Marco brushed his hands together. "I spy an espresso machine."

"I'm on it." I headed over to the bar. "Have you had your tea?" I called over to Glenn.

"Not yet."

"Glenn," Marco said. "You are an engineer, is that correct?"

"Yes. But I believe the past tense is in order."

"Once an engineer, always an engineer." Marco put his hands on his narrow hips. "And I will always be a chef, even if I am too old and feeble to slice a tomato." He looked around the room. "We should put the cutting boards out."

Glenn tied a white apron around his waist, the Day Lily Café logo embroidered on the top corner. "I'll get to it. Keep the orders coming."

I set the frothy espresso on the bar. "The students should start arriving soon."

Glenn pushed through the swinging door carrying a case of wine. "Alessa has brought us a present."

"Ah, my cousin said she would do this," Marco said. "I hope she included the new red blend. I had some last night. It is *delizioso*."

"There are two more cases in the kitchen." Glenn dotted his forehead with a handkerchief.

Oliver appeared behind Glenn with a second case in his hands. "It's starting to look a lot like a cooking school in there." He set the case on the floor and walked over to Marco. Shaking his hand, he said, "Oliver Finnegan. Rosalie's older brother. Or should I say, her lesser half."

"*Ciao*, Oliver." Marco pointed to the chalkboard. "You will be making bruschetta today."

Oliver pushed his hair from his forehead. He lifted the flap of the box of wine on the counter and removed a bottle of prosecco. He looked at me. "Are mimosas permitted in cooking class?"

"Marco?" I said.

"*Assolutamente!*"

By 9:00 AM we six students had gathered around the bar, each with a mimosa in hand. Marco stood at the helm with a second espresso. "There is an apron courtesy of our hostess. I suggest you put it on." His eyes danced. "Things will be getting messy."

I tied my apron behind my back. "This is a perfect time to introduce ourselves. I'm Rosalie, and when I was young, I had a best friend named Carly Calderone who had an Italian grandmother who cooked every day. The aromas in that kitchen alone caused me to fall in love with Italian food. I've dreamt of taking a cooking class ever since." I glanced at Marco. "And thanks to Alessa and Marco, my dream has come true." I grinned hard. "Oliver?"

Oliver's dark brown hair had fallen onto his forehead, his button-down oxford was untucked. "Well, all you need to know is I'm Rosalie's older brother, Oliver Finnegan. And I'm happy to be here, although I'm not much of a cook."

"Maybe that's about to change," Marco said.

"Okay," I said. "Who's next? Janice?"

Janice cleared her throat. She was athletically stocky and played field hockey in boarding school, and I'm almost certain she did some damage to the opposing teams. Her makeup, as usual, was flawless, with a tint of red lipstick and a manicure to match. The only sign of her Eastern Shore roots was the practical, no-nonsense pair of flip flops. "I'm Janice," she said in her trademark gruff voice. "But most of you already know that." She took a quick sip of her mimosa and smacked her lips. "I'm married to Trevor Tilghman and I have three boys who run me ragged. And I'm really looking forward to being here and not at home. There you have it." She pointed a finger pistol at Brandon. "Bang, you're up."

Brandon rolled his shoulders back. "I'm not sure what to say. Let's see. I am a professor with a doctorate in ancient history and I know a lot of things. I don't get out much so taking this class is a stretch for me. But I love all history, especially mythology and the classics so this could be fun, learning about Italian culture." Brandon adjusted the collar of his striped shirt. "Did you know the olive was one of the most commonly grown foods in ancient Rome? It also had a symbolic meaning. Olive leaves and branches represented peace, fertility, and prosperity." He lifted his chin. "Did I come to the right place, *Signor* Marco?"

"Most definitely." Marco unfolded his arms. *"Benvenuto, Signore.* Perhaps we should snack on some olives while we are cooking."

Jojo stood next to Brandon, barely reaching his shoulder. Her face was scrubbed clean and shone like a polished apple. Dimples framed her smile.

Brandon turned to face her. "I believe you're next."

"Okay. Peace, fertility, and, what did you say? Prosperity? May we all have those for the next five days."

Janice frowned. "Um, let's scratch the fertility, girlfriend."

"Fertility has many meanings," Brandon said. "For instance, there's a fertile mind—"

"No worries, Doc," Jojo interrupted. "I get what she's saying. Okay, first of all, I'm sorry to say I have to leave early today. They are reading my uncle's will this afternoon." She tucked her hair behind an ear. "But I'm really happy to be here. I was saving up my money for something special and when this class came along, boom, that's it. Oh, and I want to become a famous chef. But so far my only claim to fame is I am the only one in possession of my mom's secret crab dip recipe."

"My dear," Marco said. "Secret family recipes are as valuable as an heirloom gemstone."

Jojo faced Kevin. "Tag, you're it."

"Last but not least," Kevin said. "By the way, I already adore you, Jojo. Okay, I'm Kevin and the caffeine and champagne have kicked in at pretty much the same time, so look out."

Kevin placed his index finger on his cheek. "Hm. What else? Oh, I know. I'm engaged to Jake Francona, who is the love of my life and a hunk and a half. Just putting that out there." He flashed me a sincere smile. "And this woman saved our relationship not too long ago. And I wouldn't miss this class for the world."

"Way to go, Rosie," Oliver said in a low voice. "This is going to be awesome." He raised his glass. "I'd like to make a toast. To my sister, Rosie, for bringing us together in this magical setting. And to Marco Giovanelli for agreeing to teach us, your humble minions, to cook, and hopefully, get a hint at how to live like an Italian."

Chapter Sixteen

Marco stood at the end of the bar, palms on the marble. "Artusi Pellegrino, the author of the quote I have shared with you, wrote *La Scienza in Cucina* or, Science in the Kitchen, in 1891. He called it a cooking manual, the first of its kind. And it is largely responsible for what we now refer to as Italian Cuisine.

"In the next five days we will focus on cuisine unique to *Toscana*. But there are some basics to Italian cooking that I hope will influence the way you think about the art of preparing food. Because it is an art, when done with care, and most of all, passion." Marco looked my way. I hadn't stopped smiling since I woke up.

"There are 3 basic steps in Italian cooking: *Tagliato, Soffritto*, and *Insaporire*, in that order. They are the foundation of almost every Italian dish — pasta, risotto, soup, meat, fish."

I looked around the table wondering if anyone else was longing for a pen to write this down. I tucked my hand tentatively in the air.

"Yes, Rosalie?"

"I want to take notes."

"Ah. Of course you do." His eyes twinkled. "I like that about you." He laughed softly. "Not to worry. I have sources to share. And I highly recommend Marcella Hazan's *The Essentials of Classic Italian Cooking*."

"Chef?" Brandon said. "What do these words mean? How do they translate?"

"My eager learners. The first, *tagliato*, means literally, to strike." Marco cocked his head. "A better translation is to chop. *Soffritto*, or sauté, involves

66

cooking the ingredients you have prepared or chopped. The *insaporire*, which means bestowing taste, is adding the vegetables, which, make no mistake, are the foundation of Italian cooking.

"Shall we start with *il tagliato*?" His eyebrows rose and he looked at each attentive face. "*Si?*"

"Let's do it," Kevin said and winked at me.

"We start with an onion. Who would like to chop it?"

Oliver shrugged his shoulders. "I have no idea how to chop an onion."

Marco selected a fat yellow onion from a wooden bowl in the center of the counter that overflowed with onions and garlic bulbs. He tossed it to Oliver. "Then you shall learn."

Per Marco's instructions, Oliver cut off the end, and peeled away the skin. Next he sliced the onion almost to the bottom, stopping with just enough space to keep the allium intact. Then he turned the onion and made perpendicular slices.

"Next is the fun part," Marco said.

Oliver put the onion on its side and began to slice. The evenly-sized pieces fell onto the cutting board like dominoes. Oliver looked around the table, an expression of delight and surprise brightened his face. "This is kinda fun."

"Well done, *Signor*. So here we have *il tagliato*. Most recipes in America tell you to sauté your onions, garlic, and vegetables all together. But in a true Italian *soffritto,* you begin with the onion, sautéing it in olive oil until it is translucent, about five minutes. Then add the garlic and stir for a minute or two, or until it is just starting to take on color. Not until then do we have the addition of vegetables. When Rosalie and Kevin are ready to begin their zucchini blossoms, which starts with a *soffritto*, we shall join them in the kitchen."

"*Tagliato*," Brandon said. "That's a good word."

Jojo looked up at him. "That's the word you picked? To strike? What about flavor?"

"All right," Marco smacked his hands together. "Shall we begin?"

Marco distributed sheets of paper with the assigned recipes and the room filled with conversations as each pair discussed who would be responsible for what.

Jojo offered to take the eggs back to the kitchen to boil and suggested Brandon chop the anchovies since he was so into *tagliato*. She returned a few minutes later with a large basket of tomatoes and basil sprigs. "Bini Katz dropped this off a little bit ago. She harvested them from your garden and thought you might want to use them today." Jojo set them on the counter. "Bini used to babysit us. She was really strict. I don't think she ever liked me."

"She isn't too crazy about me either." Oliver lifted a beautiful ripe tomato from the basket.

Janice snatched it from him. "You chop the garlic, K? It takes days to get that smell off my hands."

"Fine by me." Oliver reached for a garlic clove and picked up his knife. "I don't mind getting a little smelly. And now I actually may know how to do this."

"Ah," Marco said. "That reminds me. Who knows the best knife to use?"

"I've done research on this," Brandon said as he opened a tin of anchovies. "Wusthof knives are by far the best. They're German and forged of stain-resistant high-carbon steel."

Marco grinned mischievously. "The best knife to use is a sharp one." He removed the cylindrical sharpener from the block in the center of the bar and held it out for Oliver.

"That wasn't fair," Janice said to Brandon. "He tricked you."

"It was actually pretty funny." Brandon smiled at Janice. "I wasn't expecting that. Do you ever find there are times when you take yourself too seriously?"

"Absolutely not," Janice said. "Never ever."

Brandon chuckled. "Now who's funny?"

Marco watched Oliver as he tried to peel a clove of garlic. "Smash it with the side of your knife first."

"Like this?" Oliver flattened the blade over the clove and pushed hard with the heel of his hand. The garlic gave way with a pop.

"Precisely."

Oliver glanced at Janice. "You're just standing there."

"I am? I thought that looked pretty cool. I buy my garlic in a jar."

Oliver gave her a half smile. "You're chopping the tomatoes, right? Any problem with that?"

Janice shrugged. "Can I get some prosecco first?"

"That's the only way to chop a tomato." Oliver flattened another clove. "With a nice dose of prosecco in your belly. Draw two, would you?" He looked down at the garlic. "This is pretty cool. Popping garlic." He looked up at Marco. "You barely need to peel them."

Jojo checked the timer on her phone. "Are you sure the eggs should only cook for seven and a half minutes, Chef?"

"We are preparing, how do you say in America, jammy eggs?" Marco smiled. "Be sure to immerse them in an ice bath as soon as they are finished."

Jojo returned to Brandon's side. "Jammy? That's a new one for me. It's hard to keep up with the trends. I just figured out how to pickle something and now that will be out of style in a couple of days." She frowned as Brandon dropped an anchovy in his mouth. "Uh, Chef Marco? Is the good doctor allowed to eat the ingredients?"

"Excellent question." Marco rounded the bar and headed for the kitchen. "There is something I have forgotten." He returned with a handful of spoons and dropped them handle side down into a coffee mug. "A good chef must always taste as he goes." He looked at Brandon. "Could you toss me one of those anchovies? You see, if they are too salty, you should rinse them in addition to reducing the salt in your recipe."

Oliver held up his hands. "Draw two, bartender."

Brandon tossed the small fish end over end, first to Marco, Oliver next.

Marco popped it into his mouth. "This one is perfect."

Jojo crossed her arms. "Flying fish and jammy eggs. Who knew?"

"Kevin," I said, as I studied our recipe. "How about I sauté the sausage. You want to start with the onion and garlic? I mean, *soffritto*?"

"*Chop, chop,*" Kevin selected a knife.

69

Marco handed him the sharpener.

I pushed through the kitchen door and found Glenn seated on a stool reading the *Devon County News*. He looked up. "Anything for me to wash? I've been quite idle back here so far."

"Not yet." I removed a heavy sauté pan from a hook over the stove. "Anything in the news?"

"You mean in the paper or from Birdie's shoe store?"

I swirled a little olive oil in the pan. "Definitely Birdie's."

"The hottest news is there's a woman driving a red Porsche around town. Apparently, she almost hit a pedestrian."

Chapter Seventeen

We had spent the afternoon assembling and then devouring the antipasti dishes, and now the students and Marco had gone for the day. Janice had offered to give Oliver a lift and I was looking forward to rehashing the day with my best friend.

"We're making homemade pasta tomorrow," I said as I brought the last of the dirty dishes back to the kitchen. "Remind me to bring the rolling pins."

"Don't forget the rolling pins." Glenn draped a dish towel over his shoulder.

"Always so helpful, my friend." I walked over to the counter and stirred the seasoned salt. I set the wooden spoon on the side of the dish. "Glenn, why don't we prop this door open tomorrow. I feel like you're missing out on all of the banter. Plus, when the students are back here, they'll be able to hear what Marco is saying."

"Excellent idea." Glenn set the towel on the counter. "I'll put a wedge under it right now. I think there's one in the bathroom closet."

I jumped when I heard a rap on the back door. I flipped on the outside light. Jojo was on the stoop, a tall brooding man behind her.

"Hey," I said. "Come in. Glenn and I were just getting ready for tomorrow."

"Rosalie, Glenn," Jojo said as she stepped into the kitchen. "This is my older brother, Bartlett."

Glenn shoved the wedge under the door and straightened. He nudged his glasses up his nose. "Why don't we sit in the dining room."

Jojo had changed into a conservative dark skirt and a striped blouse for the will reading. She followed me through the open door. Bartlett, who

71

looked to be around thirty, brought up the rear.

"Oh, my goodness," she said. "This place smells like heaven. Garlic and butter and all things nice." She closed her eyes and opened them. "How did everything turn out?"

"So good," I said. "We saved some for you." I picked up a platter covered with plastic wrap and set it in front of her.

Jojo looked over her shoulder. "This morning was incredible, Barty."

Barty wore a short-sleeved madras shirt that was buttoned tight around his neck, thumbs hooked in the front pockets of a frayed pair of khakis, his frown deep set.

Jojo looked back at me. "I begged Barty to stop here. I just had to see the finished products."

I peeled back the plastic. "Your deviled eggs are delicious."

Jojo lifted one off the plate. "Look, Barty, you have to try one. It has capers and anchovies in it."

"It's green." He crossed his arms tight against his chest.

"That's from the tarragon, silly." She peered down at the platter. "Oh my gosh, look at the stuffed zucchini blossoms. They turned out so beautiful. I can't believe they didn't fall apart when you sautéed them."

"You'll have to try the bruschetta, too," Glenn said.

"Oliver and Janice slow-roasted the tomatoes for almost an hour," I added. "They are to die for."

"Seriously, Barty, you don't know what you're missing." Jojo popped an egg in her mouth and brushed her hands together.

"She got everything," Bartlett said abruptly, stepping closer to the bar.

Jojo was still chewing. Her eyes grew wary of her brother's proximity.

He looked down at the platter of delicacies and shook his head. "Big day for you, little sis. Fancy cooking class. Inheriting the nicest farm in Devon County. Whatcha gonna do for an encore? Win the lottery?"

Jojo swallowed. "Stop it, Barty. If you don't mind, for now I'd like to pretend this never happened." She dabbed at a piece of egg on her lip with a napkin. "He left everything to me. I mean, everything."

"You didn't add that our uncle also put in his will that you can't share any of his estate with either of us. Now, I'm wondering, how exactly you got him to do that?"

Jojo's face reddened, eyes downcast. "Please. I told you, I want to share it with you guys. There has to be some way around that part of it."

I frowned. "I've heard your uncle wasn't a very nice man. Was his decision to give everything to Jojo a surprise?"

"Not nice?" Bartlett said, eyebrows arched. "He was a mean SOB. Always has been. Guy offered to take us for ice cream one time when we were kids, but when we got out of the car, he changed his mind. Said we were bad kids and stood there and ate an ice cream cone right in front of us. Triple decker. Slurped it all up while we waited in the 90-degree heat."

"Oh, my." Glenn shook his head.

Jojo wadded the napkin. "That's a true story."

Bartlett's dark eyes took in his surroundings. "I used to be a short order cook in this place when it was Brower's. Coffees with free refills were fifty cents. Bet it's a lot more than that now with all those fancy machines." His nostrils flared.

The back door opened and shut. A woman stepped into the room. She looked a lot like Jojo, but taller and paler.

Jojo's head reared back. "Um, Rosalie, Glenn, this is our sister, Phoebe Parker." Her eyes narrowed. "What are you doing here, Phoebs?"

Phoebe pulled her coat tighter. "I just needed to talk. Today was a total shock for me."

"You've been crying," Jojo said. "Look, it was a shock for me too. But this isn't the time or place."

"So, this is your cooking school." She wiped her nose with the back of her hand. "How much did it cost you to take this class?"

Jojo dropped her forehead in her hands. "Do you have to do this here?"

Bartlett walked over to Phoebe and grabbed her bicep. "Let's go. You need to get a grip."

"But Barty," she said trying to break loose. "This is wrong. I don't know what I'm going to do. He was supposed to divide it up." She looked up at her brother. Her face had begun that involuntary misshapenness that a major

73

cry brought on. It was only a matter of time before the sobs started to heave.

Bartlett turned to face us. "See what you've done?"

Jojo twisted her fingers together. "But I didn't do this."

"You were with him every day. How'd you do it? You put something in his food right after he changed the will? Oh, and here's another one for you. Where were you the morning he was poisoned? I thought he was paying you to take care of him? Nicely done, Jo." He shook his head in disgust and guided Phoebe out through the kitchen, his cowboy boots clicking on the floor.

I filled a glass with what remained of the prosecco and set it in front of Jojo. "Are you okay?"

"I don't know." Her hands trembled as she picked up the glass. "I didn't want for this to happen. I really didn't." She looked up. "It was so mean for Barty to say that."

"How could you possibly know what your uncle was going to do?" I said.

"No one knew." She pressed her back into the chair. "I didn't want the inheritance. I mean maybe a little, but certainly not all of it."

"Well, there's your answer," Glenn said.

Jojo's eyebrows dipped. "How so?"

"Maybe you were the only one not trying to manipulate him. You know, earn his favor. Maybe this is your reward for not being greedy."

I patted her hand. "I believe Glenn has made an excellent point."

A small smile appeared on Jojo's face. "At least I met all of you before this. I sure am glad I'm taking this class." She slugged back most of the prosecco. "What's on the menu tomorrow?"

"Fresh pasta," Glenn said. "And a gourmet meal to follow." He looked over at me. "Don't forget the rolling pins."

Jojo said good-bye and Glenn locked the door behind her. He returned to the bar, a frown on his face. "Where was she when her uncle died, Rosalie?"

"A most excellent question."

Chapter Eighteen

Tuesday
Day Two of Cooking Class

Menu
*Primi Piatte/*First Courses
*Ravioli al Burro e Salvia/*Ravioli in Butter and Sage
Rosalie and Kevin

*Spaghetti con I tartufi alla Spoletina/*Spaghetti with Truffles
Joanna and Brandon

*Fettucini con Panna e Saporito/*Fettucini with Cream and Sausage
Janice and Oliver

"For the Nonne, who have taught the world so much about eating"
-Matt Goulding *Pasta, Pane, Vino*

E veryone arrived early the next morning, eager to get back to cooking. Conversations hummed and the nutty aroma of brewing coffee filled the room. Kevin had brought his famous key lime bars and the plate was almost empty. Sun blazed in the windows, warming the room, and I smiled as I took in the scene.

Oliver sidled up next to me. "You still having fun?"

"Oh, my goodness, yes. I hope you are too."

He straightened his spine and rolled his shoulders back. "I think the country air is agreeing with me. And this is the quietest place I've ever been. I guess I never noticed before."

"We had a lot of cows growing up. And a rooster."

Oliver laughed. "My point is, I'm happy to be here with you, kid."

I noticed Glenn in the doorway, a nervous expression on his face. "Hey," I said. "What's up?"

He lost his footing for a moment as a woman pushed past him.

"Sonja?" I said.

"She was in the kitchen," Glenn said, and fixed his glasses back on his nose. "I was bringing in a few boxes from Marco's car and found her surveying the room."

"Why was she doing that?" I said.

"Hello? I'm standing right here." Sonja strode into the middle of the restaurant, hands on her hips. Black suede boots ended just above her knees. A strip of pale skin shone under her tight black mini.

"Rosalie? I want to take your class."

"You what?"

"I've decided to enroll in your class." She looked at me expectantly.

"You. Are. Fabulous," Kevin said.

Sonja gave him a pseudo shy smile. "Thanks, cutie. So are you." She sized him up. "Nice cashmere. Love the sky blue. It goes with your eyes." She looked over at me. "So? What do you say?"

"I'm afraid we're capped out at six. I'm really sorry, Sonja."

She looked around the room. "I don't see any famous Italian chef."

"He just got here," I said. "Can I—"

Eyeing Jojo, Sonja said, "Who are you?"

"Me?" Jojo looked surprised. "I'm Joanne. Jojo for short."

Sonja studied her, eyes narrowed. "Jojo Kline?"

"No." She side-stepped so that she was standing slightly behind Brandon. "Who is that?" she whispered.

Sonja walked back to Oliver. She removed the mimosa from his hand and finished it. "You and I could have had some fun in here." She wove her long fingers through his hair. "You're the most interesting thing in this town so far."

Kevin leaned in toward Janice. "You should get yourself some of those boots."

"No one wants to see that," Janice said flatly. "No one should *have* to see that."

Marco came into the room, his glasses low on his nose. "Are we ready to begin?"

Sonja's fingers were still looped in Oliver's hair. She stepped back. Her arm dropped to her side and she pouted a little. "Too much disappointment in this world."

We all watched as she exited back through the kitchen. She really had mastered the runway walk. I was surprised she didn't tip over.

"Wow," Kevin said. "Did that just happen? Do you guys realize she's Sonja Volkov? You know, Queen Lorelei in *The Battle for the Highlands?* I should have gotten a video. No one would believe it."

"It still happened," Brandon said. "So many of us minimize an experience if we don't catch it on video."

"Okay, so what is she doing here in Cardigan?" Kevin said, ignoring Brandon. "Do you think they're going to film the next season here?"

"Uh, Kev," Janice said. "We're like at sea level here on the Shore. You really think they'll film Battle for the, wait for it, *Highlands* here?"

I inched closer to Glenn. "What *is* she doing in Cardigan?"

Chapter Nineteen

Having recovered from Sonja's interruption, we gathered around the bar at last. Oliver was on his second mimosa. "You okay?" I said.

"Yes."

"Sonja remembered you from the other night."

"I honestly don't think she came here to see me. That was just an afterthought. Maybe she really wants to cook."

"Perhaps." I glanced at Jojo. Sonja had asked if her name was Kline. How would she know the connection? Glenn and I had work to do.

"Everyone," Marco said. "Our quote for today is 'thanks to the *Nonne*.' If you don't already know, *Nonna* is Italian for grandmother. Italian grandmothers have been making pasta for generations. As we will do today. Homemade pasta, if done right, is a delicacy, less chewy than dried pasta, and much more flavorful.

"We will start with each of you preparing your own batch of dough, then you and your partner will begin making your assigned pasta dish."

"Look at ours," Kevin said. "Ravioli in sage butter? I wonder what the filling will be."

"What about fettuccini with sausage and cream?" I pushed the sleeves of my sweater up to my elbows. "I'm already hungry."

Marco sifted semolina flour onto his cutting board. He passed the sifter to Janice. "You will need two cups."

As the students took turns with the sifter, Marco said, "Mold the flour into a mound like so. Then make a well in the center with your fist." Flour sailed through the air. "Next, crack open two eggs into the center." He smacked the eggs together. They broke simultaneously, not a stray piece of egg shell to be found.

We followed his lead and the sound of splitting eggs filled the room.

Oliver looked at my dough. "Rosie, shore up the sides. You're going to have a breach like the wall of *Rojan*."

"I'm trying."

Marco whisked the eggs nestled in the mound of flour gently with a fork. "After your eggs are blended, you will begin to integrate the flour a little at a time."

"Rats," I said as my eggs spilled over the rim onto the counter. I scooped them back into the flour but they spilled over the other side.

I glanced at Oliver's smooth mixture. He had already begun to knead it as Marco demonstrated. "What are you doing?" he said.

"I don't understand." I stared down at the lumpy mess. "I could make bread with my eyes closed."

"Based on that train wreck, I suggest you keep them open."

I looked around the room. Jojo already had a smooth round ball. Brandon stood next to her, flattening his with intense concentration.

"Rosalie?" Marco said. "I think you need to start over."

"Really?" I begrudgingly sopped up the mess with several paper towels and tossed my sorry dough into the trash. It hit the bottom with a heavy thud. Janice glanced over at me. She made an 'L' on her forehead with her fingers and mouthed 'loser.' I stuck my tongue out at her.

I started again, whisking my eggs more carefully until they were a uniform yellow. Then I tried adding the flour. "How are you doing that?" I said to Kevin who stood on the other side of me. His dough was already spread flat and wide.

"Hello?" he said. "Do I not make all the pastries for this place?" He stopped rolling. "What's going on, girlfriend? Add the flour from the edges but keep the rim solid. You'll get it." He set his roller down. "My phone hasn't stopped vibrating. I better check. Be right back."

I puffed out some air and added more flour just as Marco said. But it sat in my egg mixture like floating dumplings.

"Do we have to eat any of Rosalie's pasta?" Oliver said.

Marco smoothed his dough with the narrow wooden roller, the muscles in his forearms pronounced. He glanced over at me. "I know how to do this," I said, my voice cracking. "I've kneaded dough my entire life."

Oliver lifted his pristine concoction by the edges and flipped. It was so thin you could almost see through it, but there wasn't a single tear.

"That looks really good," I said.

"I'm enjoying myself. It's very therapeutic."

"We are making three types of pasta," Marco said. "Ravioli, spaghetti, and linguini."

Those words I'd heard my entire life sounded brand new and exotic, when Marco said them. The way he enunciated the t's in spaghetti, the inflection when he said the final 'i's'.

"I will demonstrate how to make each," Marco said, "and then you can partner up and begin preparing your dishes."

Kevin strolled in from the kitchen. "Is that your seasoned salt drying out there?" He sucked on a finger. "It's delish. But something is different."

"I don't think I changed anything."

"I'm almost out of the last batch," he said. "I hope I'm on your list."

Glenn followed him out of the kitchen and stood next to me. "How's it going?"

"Everyone is rolling out their pasta dough and it's all beautiful." Hair clung to the perspiration on my forehead. "Except for mine. My two attempts were a disaster and a half."

"Then you are doing an excellent job of making your fellow students feel special."

I smiled at Glenn. "How do you do that?"

"It's all in how you look at things. And just so you know, I think I learned it from you."

"Oh," Kevin said. "Oh my . . ." He burped and covered his mouth. His face had paled and beads of sweat dotted his forehead.

"Kevin," I said. "You look awful."

"I feel awful. Really awful. I . . ." He dropped to his knees and clutched his stomach.

Kevin's face was ashen. I grabbed my phone, punching in 9-1-1 as fast as I could. "Hello?"

Jojo knelt next to Kevin. "His forehead is cold. Someone get him some water." She placed her fingers over his wrist. "Oh, my gosh. His pulse is racing."

Glenn and I exchanged a quick glance as I finished my call. He dampened a dishrag and hurried over to Kevin. Placing it on his forehead, he said, "We are all here with you, son." He eased Kevin onto his back and propped his knees up. "Now try to slow your breathing."

"My insides are burning." His chest heaved.

"Where's the damn ambulance?" Janice threw open the door. Sirens grew louder and then stopped. "Get your butts in here," she bellowed. "Peter Cooper, this guy's a friend of mine." She held the door open as they wheeled the stretcher inside, climbing over the gaping hole and into the restaurant. "Do your best."

Glenn squeezed Kevin's hand. "Stay with us. Help is here."

"Oh my gosh," I said, a sickening thought entering my mind. "Peter? Tell the doctors he could have been poisoned." I placed my hand over my stomach. "With water hemlock."

"Good God," Glenn said as they lifted Kevin onto the stretcher.

Chapter Twenty

J ake paced, his bulk making the already small waiting room seem like a mouse house. He was an athlete, coach of the John Adams College lacrosse team, and I was pretty sure it was good he was moving. But I was starting to feel claustrophobic. He passed again. I tucked my feet as far under my chair as I could to avoid tripping him.

After assessing Kevin's critical state, the paramedics rushed him to the Devon County hospital. It was a small hospital, but there wasn't enough time for a helicopter to Baltimore. I glanced out the window. It was already the middle of the afternoon. We'd been waiting for an update for hours. My phone was on fire with the constant flow of texts from the cooking class.

"Can I get you something, Jake?"

"Maybe some information?" He rubbed his palms together so hard I thought they might ignite. "I don't even know if Kevin is alive." He looked up, his eyes framed with tension lines. "I should have pushed for Baltimore."

"They had to stabilize him." I shook my head. "I just don't understand what happened. One minute he was asking about my salt and the next he was clutching his stomach." I stared down at my lap, letting the sequence of events sink in.

Jake checked his watch. "He's been back there for three hours."

I looked up, surprised to see the sheriff enter the hallway outside the waiting room. "What is he doing here?" I stood as a doctor approached. She leaned in and whispered to the sheriff.

"Hey . . ." Jake burst into the fluorescent-lit hallway. "Since when do you tell him what's going on before me? Kevin and I have a domestic partnership.

I'm his power of attorney."

I hesitated before following him. I didn't want to hinder his ability to get the update he was desperate for. But then again, I had to learn what happened to Kevin.

"Hello, Jake. I'm Doctor Deerfield." She was a young woman who looked to be in her early thirties. She slid off her glasses and met Jake's eyes. "I was on my way in to update you. But there's been a complication that required me to call the sheriff."

"I'm sorry?" A deep red flush worked its way up Jake's neck.

"Looks like your boyfriend was poisoned," the sheriff said.

"Sheriff . . ." the doctor cautioned in a hushed tone.

"Oh, no." My shoulders fell.

The doctor clutched her clipboard. "We pumped his stomach and are giving him fluids. He's also on a respirator, but that's just a safety precaution. With hemlock poisoning you want to make sure he doesn't go into respiratory arrest." She looked at me. "Thanks for the tip to the paramedics. But what made you think he had been poisoned? And with hemlock of all things."

"Excellent question," Sheriff Wilgus said.

"You know exactly why." I steeled my eyes into his.

"What's the last thing he ingested?" the doctor said.

"Kevin had just tasted my seasoned salt."

"You don't say," the sheriff said.

"Look, Wilgus," Jake said. "This isn't about you." He faced the doctor. "Can I see him?"

"Yes, of course. I'll walk you to his room." Jake followed her down the hall. Her kitten heel pumps clicked on the glossy tile floor. "He's responding well," she said as their voices faded. "I think we got to him in time."

I watched them go. "Thank goodness he's okay."

"Did you poison him?" the sheriff said.

"I adore Kevin. I can't believe this happened."

"Who made the salt?"

"I did. But I know exactly what ingredients I used."

"Any chance someone else might eat your salt while you're standing here talking to me?"

"Glenn. He must be cleaning up." Chill bumps swept over my arms. I grabbed my purse and fished out my phone. He answered on the second ring.

When I finished our brief conversation, I turned to face the sheriff. "No one else ate the salt. Glenn's going to seal it in a ziplock for you." I dropped my phone in my purse. "I'm afraid he's already done the dishes. And I'm sure he's wiped down all of the counters by now."

"Where and when did you make that salt?"

"At the café. Last week some time. But it has to dry in the open air. It's been sitting on the counter next to the door."

"So anyone could have access to it."

I nodded.

The sheriff shifted his weight. "Doc said this hemlock could have shut down his organs."

I gazed up at him. I felt completely enervated. "So now what?"

"First we have to make sure it was the salt that poisoned him. Then we figure out who could have dumped it in there."

"Are you thinking what I'm thinking?"

He frowned. "That this has something to do with Kline?"

"Yes." I hugged myself. "What about my cooking school?"

"It's a crime scene."

"We can take precautions. My students paid a lot of money for this class."

"No class tomorrow. But tell everyone to be there so I can question them. And if you take precautions, as you said, maybe you can reopen. It all depends on what I learn tomorrow."

I studied his face. My eyes filled with gratitude that he wasn't using this as an opportunity to try and run me out of town. "This is two poisonings, Sheriff. We have to figure this out as quickly as possible."

Sheriff Joe Wilgus gazed down his nose at me. "Agreed."

Glenn sat at the bar. The Wall Street Journal lay open before him, but he was staring out the window, arms crossed. "Hey," I said as I approached.

"Rosalie." His eyes shot over to me. "How is Kevin?"

"Recovering. Doctor Deerfield said he'll be back to 100% soon, but only because we all acted so quickly."

"Take a load off," He patted the chair next to him.

"I think I need to stand, but thank you. And thanks for cleaning up." I dropped my purse on the bar. "I'm surprised you're still here."

"Marco stayed all afternoon and finished the pastas. There are trays of it in the refrigerator with damp cloths on them. He said it should last until Thursday if by chance we can reopen."

"That's wonderful." I rubbed my lower back. "Maybe I will sit down."

"So," Glenn said. "Were you right? Was he poisoned?"

I nodded. "Apparently this particular poison attacks the vital organs. We are so lucky they got to Kevin in time."

"And why was the sheriff so sure it was your salt?"

"That's the last thing Kevin ate. Remember? He was licking his finger. And no one else got sick. We were all making the same pasta. And Marco is adamant about us tasting as we go. It has to be the salt. Kevin even said it tasted a little different."

Glenn frowned. "And the sheriff thinks someone mixed the poison in the salt in order to kill who, exactly?"

"He's assuming Kevin, but you and I both know it could have been anyone in the class."

"Rosalie, I feel just sick. I left that kitchen unattended many times with the door wide open. I don't know how often I went to Birdie's or stepped outside to have a chat with Gretchen." He rubbed his forehead. "This is my fault."

"My dear, Glenn." I patted his shoulder. "The only way this is your fault is if you put the poison in the salt. And I know for certain you didn't." I closed his newspaper and folded it. "Besides, this is Cardigan. No one locks their doors, let alone worries about their food being poisoned."

He studied me. "I know you have already asked yourself this question."

I smiled. "Who was the poison intended for?"

"Exactly."

"Put your thinking cap on, Mr. Breckinridge. We have work to do."

Chapter Twenty-One

As I drove down the lane to Barclay Meadow, a pixie of hope danced in my chest that Tyler was hanging out with Oliver again and I would find them in my kitchen, foraging for food, laughing, and happy to see me. But when I rounded the circle, the only car in the drive was Oliver's. I killed the engine and fell back into my seat. Reminded of my fatigue, I resigned myself into believing it was for the best. And I had just been through one of the worst days of my life. Kevin had been poisoned at my restaurant. *My* restaurant. *My* cooking school. Was the sheriff right? Should I shut it down? But if someone wanted to murder one of us, closing the school wouldn't prevent that.

I stepped out of the car and shut the door. Kevin could have died. It was all washing over me like a rogue wave. I reached for my phone as I walked. I stumbled when I saw a text from Jake.

Kevin is stable. I'm so freakin' relieved I didn't lose him. I'll keep you updated. Love you!

I dropped my phone in my bag and exhaled. There was nothing more for me to do tonight and I could sleep with the knowledge that Kevin was going to be okay. I pushed open the heavy front door with a loud creak. The house was dark. I flipped on a light and scooped up Sweeney Todd. As I headed toward my bedroom, I noticed Oliver's door was ajar. I peered in but his bed was empty. "Where's Uncle Oliver?" I said to Sweeney as I scratched his ears. I gazed down the hallway at my own room, craving sleep, but knew I should check on my brother. That's what you do when it's family.

I passed through the house. The words safe and sound echoed in my head.

Where was he? I picked up my pace. All the first-floor rooms were empty. I stopped in the kitchen and began breathing again when I noticed an ember glowing in the dark off the back porch.

Oliver sat in one of the Adirondack chairs facing the river. He puffed hard on a crinkled joint and exhaled a steady stream of smoke.

"There you are."

"And glad to be." He knocked off the ember and pinched the end. "Care to join me? It's a beautiful night here in sleepy little Cardigan."

I sat in the adjacent chair and crossed my ankles. "Not so sleepy today. Did you see my text? Kevin was poisoned."

"That's pretty crazy, Rosie. Anybody figure out why?"

"No idea."

"Thanks for the texts. I hope Wilgus doesn't shut you down. You know, this cooking class is beyond anything I could have expected." He eyed me. "This Chef Marco?"

"Yes? What about him?"

"The man is enamored with you." He smiled as he stared out at the river.

"Enamored with a woman who can't make pasta dough? He must think I'm ridiculous."

"He never stops watching you."

"I just hope we can keep it going. The class, I mean." My cheeks warmed. I squeezed my hands together and looked at Oliver, studying his handsome profile, his rumpled hair and makings of a beard. "Especially because you haven't finished what you came here to do."

Oliver gazed at me, seemingly perplexed at my words.

"And," I said, "I don't want to let whoever did this succeed in intimidating us."

"Listen to you." Oliver laughed. "I thought you were a duck and cover sort of girl."

"That didn't work out so well for me."

Oliver continued to study me. "I'm sorry. For being such a rotten brother."

"That is the last adjective I would use to describe you."

"It's true. Life kicked you in the ass. First Mom dies, then Aunt Charlotte, and she leaves you this monstrous farm and old, outdated house, and then your butthead of a husband goes and saddles up on another . . ."

"Oliver." I swallowed hard. "Another metaphor, please?"

"Your husband destroyed your marriage. Better?"

"It was quite a trifecta."

"And I abandoned you."

"None of it was yours to fix."

Oliver looked away. It was a moonless night. The river now something you almost had to imagine, its presence revealed only by the lapping of the water against the pilings as the gray of the night and the distant landscape blended into one seamless hue. "Mom's death hit me hard," he said. "Harder than I expected."

"She was an amazing presence. Life has a little less color without her in it."

"That's not what it's about for me."

I tried to make out his expression. "What are you saying?"

"I've been thinking about this a lot. And I guess I feel like she died before I had a chance to make her proud."

"Oliver, you are a tremendous success."

"I make a lot of money. A lot. Don't be naive."

My chest tightened. "I am anything but naive, Oliver."

His head fell forward. "I'm sorry." He picked up his lighter and flipped it between his fingers. "You see? I do that crap. I say things that hurt, like barbs on an effing stingray, just to keep people from getting too close."

I wanted to placate him, point out his wonderful qualities, but he was working through something. I bit the inside of my cheek. I knew better than anyone, Oliver was the best kind of person. "So why do you think Mom wasn't proud of you?"

"Excellent question. And it's pretty obvious." Setting the lighter on the arm of the chair he said, "Rosalie, I'm pushing fifty. Mom was not so patiently waiting for me to find the right woman and raise a family. I think she worried I'd been seduced by the money and the fast lane. All that money you could at least have a couple of kids. Right? And truthfully, I always thought that would be around the corner. The next relationship would be the one. It was going to happen. Just not this one. For almost thirty years I told myself that. Then I met Sylvie. Right after Mom passed, so she never knew. But Sylvie was the one. No question." His shoulders fell. "And I've been sitting here watching this river flow by and wondering how in the hell I let her slip away."

We sat quietly, my hands folded in my lap. An owl hooted in the distance. The water lapped. "Oliver?"

"Yeah, Rosie?"

"Is there any weed left?"

I could barely make out his wide grin. "You sure?"

I gripped the arms of the chair. "After a day like today, I think it's a very good idea."

"And the last time was . . ."

"Oh, gosh. Definitely before Annie was born."

Oliver flicked his lighter and brought the joint back to life. I placed it between my lips. "Careful," he said. "A little goes a long way these days."

I nodded as I took a small puff. I held it in for a moment, and coughed it out. Passing it back to Oliver, I said, "Do you think I got enough?"

"Um, yes, methinks you did." Oliver took a slow drag. The glow of the embers illuminated his face in shadow and light. Once he exhaled, he dropped what little remained of the joint on the ground and stepped on it.

A light breeze carried the scent of pine needles and drying leaves mixed with a touch of earth and sweetness from Oliver's marijuana. I sat forward. "What's that sound? Are the chickens awake?"

"The goats arrived today."

"Oh, I totally forgot." I sat back. "Did you by chance see Tyler this afternoon?"

"We had a beer together then he headed out. I think he was waiting for you to come home."

"We haven't seen each other since Sunday." I combed my hair back from my face and licked my lips. I was feeling a little hungry. "How cute are the goats?"

"They're just little guys. And they have a lot of energy."

"Oliver? We need to pick names for them. There's five, right?" I drummed my fingers on the chair. "What do you name a goat?"

"Mr. Goat?"

"All but one are female." I hesitated. "And that wasn't very clever. Come on, help me."

"I live in the city. Maybe we can give them all cab driver names."

"That's not a terrible idea. But let's think a little more. Oh, I know. What if they all start with 'G'? We could have Lady Ga Ga. Oh, I like that. And, what else, how about Gilda Radner? And definitely Grace Kelly." I was a little startled how fast I was talking but I couldn't stop myself. "So far we have Gaga, Gilda, and Grace. I'll have to see them before I choose who is who. And . . ."

"Rosie?"

"Yes?"

"I have it." He folded his hands over his stomach. "The perfect name."

"Pray tell?"

"Cal Ripken."

I coughed. "Well that doesn't start with 'g'."

He shook his head. "Goat. G - O - A - T. You know, greatest of all time? We could have a Tom, a Michael . . ."

"That's actually pretty good. I like Cal."

We sat still for a moment. The goats had quieted. A sliver of a moon had risen over the water, its reflection undulating on the river before us.

"Rosie?" Oliver jolted forward. "Did you hear that?"

"No." I strained my ears. Branches cracked in the distance, then silence. "It's probably a deer or maybe a raccoon." Another snap of a branch. The shuffling of leaves grew louder. "Those are footsteps, Oliver. Someone is out there."

"Go!" He jumped out of his chair.

We speed-walked to the house, side by side, seemingly in a race. The screen door slammed behind us. I flipped on the outside lights and latched the door.

Once inside, I fell back against the wall. My heart pounded.

"Holy mother." Oliver's chest heaved. He looked over at me, eyes wild. "I haven't felt this exhilarated in years."

Chapter Twenty-Two

Sheriff Wilgus' SUV idled in front of the café as Oliver I rounded the corner into town. Oliver finished his coffee and set it on the floor mat. "Should be some fun, today, right, sis? Lots of levity. Good times with the sheriff interrogating all of us."

"A wise woman once said, it is what it is."

As I turned down the alley, Oliver said, "And you still don't have any front steps. All that renovating and you lose your steps."

I huffed out a sigh and parked the car behind the café.

It was a gray day without a hint of a promise of the sun poking through. Dried leaves crackled under our feet and there was a trace of woodsmoke in the air as we headed inside.

Glenn was at the door. He fiddled with something under the handle and let us in.

"You're here early," I said.

"I'm keeping the door locked. I installed a dead bolt. People are going to have to knock to come in." He began to re-lock the door.

"Maybe wait a minute," I said. "Sheriff Wilgus is already here."

Glenn stepped back. "I feel a bit like a prison guard."

I patted his arm. "You are doing exactly what we need to do if we are going to convince the sheriff to let us reopen tomorrow."

Oliver unzipped his jacket. "So why is he interviewing everyone here and not at the station? Shouldn't he be using a soundproof room or something?"

Glenn straightened his shirt collar under his sweater vest. "I believe it has something to do with your sister's coffee and cinnamon muffins."

"Cinnamon muffins?" Oliver's eyebrows arced. "Where might I find said muffins?"

"I'll put some out once I make the coffee." I glanced out the front door. The sheriff's vehicle sported dark tinted windows so I had no idea if he was inside. Then I noticed the gray exhaust puffing from the tailpipe had ceased. I braced for his arrival.

The wood floors groaned as he made his way into the center of the room. He eyed the array of tables, all adorned with white cloths. "I'll use that one in the corner by the windows." He dropped his hat on the bar. "Coffee ready?"

"Two minutes," I said. "I was just about to get the muffins." I held out a piece of paper. "I made a list of the students."

He eased himself on one of the tall chairs at the bar. "Let Glenn know my deputy should be here in a bit to pick up that salt of yours."

"Oh, good. And I told the students they all needed to stop in this morning. My brother, Oliver, is already here. Anything else?"

"That's more than enough before I have my coffee."

I headed back to the kitchen and noticed Glenn struggling with the deadbolt again to let Janice inside. "This lock is very hard to turn. Oof," he said as it at last gave way.

"Where's Oliver?" Janice demanded.

"He went for a walk." Glenn's glasses slid down his nose. "Maybe I should have hired a professional."

"Get yourself some WD40." Janice charged in. "I can't stay long." She slid her hands into the pockets of her navy pea coat. "I have a lot to do this morning." Her eyes narrowed, and she frowned a little.

"You okay, Snow White?"

Glenn eyed Janice with concern and picked up the plate of muffins. "I'll take these out front."

Once he was gone, I said, "Janice?"

Tears immediately filled her eyes. "Trevor is having an affair."

"That can't possibly be true." I handed her a tissue.

She dabbed under her eyelashes. "My makeup is going to get messed up." She sniffed. "Damn, I feel awful."

"Trevor adores you. What made you come to this conclusion?"

She wadded the tissue into a ball in her palm. "I looked at his phone yesterday afternoon. There was a thread of texts with Bonnie Tucker. I walked over to him, dropped his phone in his lap and asked what the heck he was doing texting with her, of all people, and he mumbled something about one of her kids and snatched up his phone. He kept it with him the rest of the day." She tossed the tissue in the trash. "He never does that. He hates phones. Sometimes he even asks me to answer his texts for him. Especially the ones from his mother."

"I don't think I know Bonnie Tucker."

"All you need to know is she just went through a divorce. Got it?" She shook her head. "I drove by her house on my way here. Guess who's Range Rover is parked right in front? Three guesses. First two don't count."

"There must be some sort of explanation."

"There's only one and you know it." She pressed her lips together. "I called a private detective. He's going to start parking on the street to get some live feed tomorrow."

"Oh, my." I brushed my hair from my face. "Can I give you a hug?"

She took a step back. "Nope. Now where's Joe? I want to get this over with."

"Table in the corner. I'll get you a coffee."

"Where's that prosecco?"

"Is that a good idea?" I said gently.

"Rose Red . . ."

I glanced out the door. "Here's Oliver now. I'm sure he'll join you."

She charged into the restaurant and almost collided with Glenn. After a long breath in, she exhaled. "I'm sorry. Are you okay?"

"I'm fine."

She shook her head as she made her way to the sheriff.

"Fill me in later?" Glenn said.

"Yes. Oh, and can you ask Oliver to bring Janice a glass of prosecco?"

"This is an odd day, my dear. Very, very odd."

Janice stood next to the sheriff's table as I poured the coffees, hands in her pockets again. I paused and waited to see if I could hear their conversation. It dawned on me that having the sheriff do the investigation here was a bonus if I could actually hear his questions. And more importantly, the answers. The sheriff's back was to me. I stood very still, hoping he wouldn't sense my presence.

Oliver came into the room with Janice's prosecco. I put my finger to my lips, signaling him to be quiet.

"Are we eavesdropping?" he whispered.

I nodded.

"But they can't build them there, Joe," Janice said. "Two tennis courts behind all those homes?"

"That's the country club's business, not mine." The sheriff sat back and crossed his arms.

"They're putting lights on 'em. Can you imagine? Putting your kids to bed with a bonk, bonk, bonk in the back yard? Holly's biting mad. I'm with her. Those houses are on the seventh hole. It's the prettiest hole on the whole damn course. Now they want to tear it up? Those house values are going to plummet."

"Let me guess, you're starting a committee?"

Janice looked away. "I know I should, but I got other things on my mind."

"They'll never do it," the sheriff said. "Nobody plays tennis anymore. Now, maybe they should put some of those pickle ball courts in. I'd like to try that."

"I'm going to head out." Janice stared off. "Like I said, I got stuff to do." After a moment she looked back at the sheriff. "You down with that?"

He waved her away.

Janice stopped next to us and picked up the champagne glass. She swallowed it in one gulp and let out a dainty burp. "Thanks, buddy."

"Janice," I said. "Did the sheriff ask you anything about Kevin?"

"Kevin? Um . . . no."

"What about yesterday? Did he question you at all about the poisoning?"

"Nope." She shook her head. "Not a peep."

A small smile appeared on Oliver's face. "And you are free to go?"

"Um . . . yup. Listen, shoot me a text if we have class tomorrow." She fished for her keys. "You're going to catch this guy, right, Rose Red?"

"Wait," Oliver said. "Why did you just ask her that?"

"Because it's her thing. This isn't the first time she's solved a murder." Janice lowered her voice. "Joe Wilgus may not know it, but he's never going to find this guy without your sister."

The sheriff called from his perch by the window. "What makes you so sure it was a guy?"

Janice turned to look at him. "It's the kind of thing a man would do. No woman in this town would try to poison Kevin. This I know." Her lips quivered. "Okay, hopefully I'll see you both here tomorrow." Janice hurried through the door.

Glenn set her glass in a dish bin. "He certainly conducted a thorough interview."

"He didn't ask her one thing about Kevin."

"Can we go back a few paragraphs?" Oliver said. "Did Janice just say you solved a *murder?*"

Glenn stepped aside while Brandon entered the room. He was dressed in his usual khakis, this time a pale blue oxford, all topped with the worn leather bomber jacket and cross body satchel.

He took in the room. His eyes stopped on the sheriff sitting at the table in the corner, staring out the window. The sheriff was waving to an older woman who stood outside on the sidewalk. She cupped her hands around her mouth and called through the glass, "Is she finally open?"

The sheriff shook his head and she continued on her way, making an abrupt detour around the frayed caution tape.

"That's him?" Brandon said.

"Janice has already been here," I said. "He let her go pretty quickly."

"I have no problem talking to this man. And maybe I'll have something helpful to say." He strode over to the table.

Oliver, Glenn, and I stood behind the bar paying close attention.

Brandon extended his hand, but the sheriff kept his arms crossed.

"And you are?" Wilgus said.

"Brandon Preston Hitch."

"Well, that's a mouthful." The sheriff looked down at the list of students and back up at him. "Am I supposed to know you?"

"I'm a professor at John Addams College."

"I've never heard of you."

A smug smile appeared on Brandon's face. "I keep a low profile. And unless you are a student of ancient history, I doubt our paths would have crossed." He gripped the strap of his satchel. "Now, I understand you have some questions for me."

The sheriff grunted. "Not before I have another coffee."

"Well, it seems we agree on something. I'll fetch one for us each. Same cup?"

The sheriff nudged his empty mug over with his knuckle. "She knows how to make it."

"Oh, yes." Brandon smiled. "I know this much is true." He looked over at the three of us lined up behind the bar. "Sheriff Wilgus?"

Another grunt.

"Shouldn't this interview be conducted in private?"

"This is the best table in the place. And I was ready for that coffee ten minutes ago."

Once Brandon reached the bar I said, "I'm really sorry. I'll make the coffee and the three of us can wait in the kitchen."

"No need. It was just a matter of protocol. I thought it should be brought to his attention."

"You have a point," Glenn said. "Technically you aren't required to speak with him at all."

I started the coffee. I looked over at Brandon, trying to hide the worry tightening my eyes.

He nodded. "If I don't allow the interview, then we might not be able to reopen the class." He passed me the sheriff's empty mug. "And none of us want that to happen."

I realized I was holding my breath. "Thank you, Brandon." I started his cappuccino.

He studied me. "You're curious, aren't you Miss Rosalie? About what I'm going to say."

"I'm a very curious person." I glanced at Glenn. "But this is no surprise to anyone." I set the coffees on a tray and refilled the muffin basket. I held the tray out for Brandon. "The muffins might make him less grumpy."

"That would be a refreshing change." Oliver snatched one up. "But you see, Brandon, not only is my sister curious, she's also an optimist."

Once they had finished their coffee in silence, the sheriff tucked his thumbs through his belt loops and stared out the window again. Glenn had gone back into the kitchen to watch for Jojo. I wondered if he was uncomfortable eavesdropping on what was technically an attempted murder investigation.

Oliver yawned. "It's like waiting for Judge Clarence Thomas to move."

I giggled.

The chair creaked as the sheriff shifted his weight. He looked over at Brandon at last. "Do you know Kevin Edwards?"

"Only from the class. Up until Monday, I'd never seen him before."

"You know his boyfriend? Coach of the lacrosse team?"

I listened hard. Was the sheriff actually doing his job?

"I know of him. Jake Francona. Kevin mentioned him the first day. I believe they are now engaged."

The sheriff leaned forward, elbows on the table. "You play on their team?"

Oliver pinched my arm.

"I have no idea what you're referring to." Brandon stroked his mustache.

"Sure you do." He waited a moment. "You know. Do you like *men*."

"Are you asking me if I'm gay?"

Wilgus shook his head. "Took you long enough."

"No, sir, I'm not." Brandon's body had tensed.

"You got anything against 'em?"

"No."

"Hitch . . ." the sheriff said. "That's a local name. You from around here.?"

99

"I'm from Washington DC."

"Come here in the summers as a kid?"

"We were an Ocean City kind of family," Brandon said. "What are you getting at?"

"Did you know anyone in this class before Monday?"

"I met Rosalie once. No one else."

Wilgus leaned back again. "Any altercations with the other students?"

"No. I'm rather fond of everyone here."

The sheriff picked up a muffin and peeled back the paper. Two empty wrappers were on the table in front of him. "Ever know a man named Ronnie Kline?"

"No."

After finishing the muffin and brushing the crumbs from his hands, the sheriff said, "So why'd you come here, anyway? Small town like this."

"I was hoping to find some peace and quiet." Brandon removed his glasses and polished a lens with a napkin. "And Washington DC had run its course for me."

Wilgus leaned in. "You hiding out?"

"I was hired by the college to do my job. And I am quite good at it, I might add." He slid his glasses over his ears and gripped his satchel again.

"What's with the purse?" The sheriff scowled. "You think you're Indiana Jones or something?"

Brandon shook his head slowly. "I believe we're finished here." He stood, scooting his chair back. He picked up his cup and walked over to the bar. "That man is ridiculous," he said in a hushed tone. "Miss Rosalie, would you mind if I sit for a bit? Maybe at the table on the other side of the room?"

"Of course not. Let me know if you get hungry."

"What was that all about?" Oliver whispered.

"I have no idea." I rolled my lips in. "You okay? You must be getting bored. Do you want me to ask the sheriff to talk with you next?"

"After that? I can't say. Part of me wants to blast him." Oliver gave me a crooked smile. "The other half is intimidated. I honestly don't think I've ever met a sheriff before. Let alone a guy like him."

I wiped my hands on a dishtowel. "I'll be right back."

Sheriff Wilgus tossed his muffin wrappers onto the tray. "How many more?"

"Muffins or students?" I sat down across from him. "You have a list. Jojo and Oliver are left."

"Oliver. Is that the brother you told me about?"

"Yes. He's right here waiting to speak with you." I looked down at the table. The coffee mug had made several rings on the list of students. "Are you taking notes?"

"Haven't heard anything interesting yet."

"Why were you so rough on Dr. Hitch?"

"I don't like him. He thinks he's better than me."

I looked up to see Jojo coming through the door. Her hair was still wet from a shower. She looked around the room, smiled and waved when she saw Brandon. He returned the wave. I wondered if he had been waiting for her.

"What's wrong with you, Hart?" the sheriff said.

"Jojo's here, is all."

When she arrived at the table, she said, "Hey, guys. What's happening?"

My mouth dropped open as I watched Sheriff Wilgus' face break into a smile. Had I ever seen him smile before? A smirk, for sure, but a smile?

"How 'ya holding up?" he said with what seemed to be genuine concern.

"I dunno." She shrugged. "So much has happened. And I miss this class. It was really fun."

I stood. "Let me know if you need anything."

"Thanks," Jojo said. "But I'm good." As I walked away, she said to the sheriff, "Do you need to ask me stuff?"

"How are your siblings handling this?"

"Not well." She picked at a nail. "Barty and Michael, Phoebe's husband, are steaming mad. They've been hanging out together trying to figure out a way to get the farm."

"Your uncle did the right thing. You're the only Bennett with any sense."

"Thanks. I wish everyone else in town could see that." She glanced over at Brandon.

"Just don't let them bully you."

"Easier said than done."

"Look, kiddo," the sheriff said. "I don't need to ask you anything, just so you know."

"Really? Well, okay. Maybe I'll go say hi to the doc."

Jojo approached Brandon who was reading from a Kindle. They spoke with their heads together, and she left. A few moments later she passed by the front windows.

I returned to the sheriff. "That's it? You realize Jojo was taking care of her uncle, don't you? She was there every day."

"So?"

"Why wasn't she there the morning he died?"

"Must have had a good reason. It's probably better she wasn't. Woulda been a tough thing to see." He rubbed his chin. "You got anything to eat?"

"Of course. Would you like some more muffins?"

"I have a hankering for some egg salad. No mustard, though."

"I put curry in my egg salad. Just a pinch."

"Curry?" His face looked as if he'd just bitten into a lemon.

"Okay." I combed my hand through my hair. "I'll make egg salad of all things."

"Hart?" the sheriff called after me. "Don't put any of that seasoned salt in it, K?" I could hear him chuckling to himself as I walked into the kitchen.

After the sheriff had taken his time eating two sizable sandwiches, he finally summoned Oliver. He had been questioning him for quite a while. Brandon was still at the table reading, a third cappuccino in front of him. I stared at the back of the sheriff's head, the sheen from his hair products catching the midday sun.

Glenn emerged from the kitchen, a library book with 'Civil War' in the title tucked under his arm. "Is he asking Oliver about the woman in the Porsche?"

"I heard him say the name Sonja the last time I topped off their coffees.

But he stopped talking until I walked away. He still hasn't taken any notes."

"And he thinks she poisoned the salt?"

"It's not too far of a stretch. She was here yesterday morning. Remember?"

"Who could forget?" Glenn studied me. "But you are not very convincing."

"Oh, it could definitely be her. There was someone behind my house last night. Scared Oliver and me to death. Plus, she arrived in town a couple of days before Kline died."

"But for now, there is no possible connection between that woman and the Kline clan. At least not yet, that is." Glenn wiped his mouth with a wadded napkin. "That egg salad was delicious. Did you pickle the shallots?"

"I did. I'm glad you liked it."

He tossed the napkin into the trash. "We are spinning our wheels a bit, aren't we. Do you still think the poison was meant for Jojo?"

"That's my guess. An obvious guess, but a guess still the same."

"Rosalie," Glenn said, lowering his voice. "What if Jojo did indeed kill her uncle. Then she could have poisoned the salt as a distraction. To make it look like someone was going for her."

"That's an excellent theory. She certainly had the most access to her uncle and the café. But she seems so bewildered." I frowned. "Who are our other suspects?"

"Only people I can come up with are Jojo's siblings. If it's not them, then we will have to widen the circle of the investigation quite a bit."

I glanced around the restaurant and stopped at Brandon who had kicked off his loafers and propped his feet on an adjacent chair. "We don't really know anything about Brandon, do we?"

"He seems to be a nice gentleman."

I considered him. "Still waters run deep. And for all we know, he either poisoned the salt, or, the poison was meant for him." I frowned. "But I can't even think about that. He would have to know Ronnie Kline somehow and he's a newly arrived college professor."

"True. And from what I hear, Kline spent his only time off the farm at the Cardigan Tavern."

"What, Hart?" I looked up to see the sheriff standing before us. Oliver had put his head down on the table they had shared. I thought I heard a small groan.

"I'm sorry?"

"You know something. I can read your face like a bad book."

Glenn straightened his spine and checked my reaction.

"We're just wondering what you learned today. And if you have a suspect."

"That wasn't what you were thinking, Hart. Now spill."

I played with a stack of cloth placemats, debating what to tell him. "We were saying we think the poison might have been intended for Jojo. After all, they had just read the will the day before. I'm sure the whole town knew by sunset that she inherited Windswept Farm."

"Jojo? Well, whoever did it wasn't too careful about making sure she ate it."

"That's an excellent point." I gave him a small smile. "Maybe it was to scare her? It was definitely a large dose. But not lethal enough that Kevin wasn't able to recover."

"Still sounds pretty far fetched."

"Sheriff," Glenn said. "I'm curious about something. Why are you so certain it was neither Janice nor Jojo? You didn't ask them a single question."

"You wouldn't understand. You're not from here."

"Well, I've certainly heard that enough since moving here," Glenn said in a friendly manner. "But, please, I'm genuinely curious how things work around here."

"Or, perhaps, don't work?" I said, eyebrows raised.

"I'll give you the short version." He shifted his weight to the other foot. "But I still don't think you'll get it. Ya' see, both those women are landowners. Their families own some of the most important farms in this county. And they have for generations. They are the reason some things get better, and some things stay the same. And things staying the same ain't a bad thing. That's why you won't see a big box store in this county. These people are influencers. They have money and smarts and loyalty. They aren't gonna go kill one of their own. No matter how mean a man he was." He narrowed his eyes at Glenn. "You getting this?"

Glenn frowned. "I believe so, it's just—"

"Look—" The sheriff stood. "I'll keep it simple. You don't shit in your own bed. Got it?"

"Well if you put it that way," Glenn said, "Rosalie would also be a part of this Devon County elite. She owns a farm that has been in her family for almost two hundred years. Doesn't she deserve this respect you're referring to?"

The sheriff narrowed his eyes at me. "She's more like a squatter."

"Of course, I am," I said. "Thank you for the enlightenment. So now what? Anyone could have poisoned the salt. Anyone who passed through that kitchen. Other than Jojo and Janice. At least according to you and your job."

The sheriff scowled. "I'll ignore that last comment. So, who else was here? Narrow it down."

I thought for a moment. "Alessa. She delivered wine."

"That woman wouldn't poison a tick. Who else?"

I could tell by Glenn's furrowed brow he was trying hard to remember too.

"Bini," I said. "Didn't she drop off the tomatoes and basil for the bruschetta?"

"She was in the kitchen?"

"Yes. The morning before Kevin got sick. That's certainly not the only time she's—"

"Were you with her the whole time?" The sheriff said to Glenn.

"No. I went out to her truck to unload it."

"Maybe you're right, Hart."

"I'm sorry? Right about what?"

"She was at both crime scenes. She already had a motive. Now she had access to a second crime."

"Sheriff, there were other people here," I said. "Not just Bini. Why, Sonja was here, right Glenn? We still don't know why she's in town."

"And Jojo's siblings," Glenn said. "They—"

"I have everything I need. She's the only one confirmed to be at both crime scenes." He shoved his hat back and scratched his head. "I think I'm going to toddle over to your farm and ask Bini Katz a few more questions. Maybe read her her rights."

"Bini would never do such a thing," I said, feeling exasperated. "And, like I said, other people had access to the salt. We were just getting started."

"She didn't want Kline to spray his crops. You told me that, Hart. Now Jojo has the farm. What's to stop Jojo from spraying the crops? Get it? Ba-da-bing. Ba-da-boom. Slip her a little poison." He hitched up his belt. "You organic types are so darn militant about things. Always taking it too far."

"Sheriff Wilgus, please don't jump to conclusions. You don't have any evidence."

"Feels a little like my birthday." He looked around the room. "Sun's finally shining. This is a good day after all. Maybe I can do a little fishing this evening." He started to walk away but stopped. "Don't go warning your little employee. I wouldn't want my murderer to skip town." He tipped his hat. "That could be bad for business."

Once the sheriff had left the building, Oliver slumped into a chair at the bar. "I feel like I was just in a Cohn brothers' movie."

"Sort of like being run through a wood chipper?" Glenn said.

Oliver smiled his crooked grin. "Exactly. What's with that guy, anyway? He was trying to implicate Sonja for driving a Carrera." Oliver thought for a moment. "First of all, I barely know the woman. And does he think she's the perp because she's not from Cardigan? Are people around here that paranoid?"

"We just had a little lesson on why he would suspect her as opposed to people who actually knew Ronnie Kline." Glenn chuckled. "But the sheriff wasted your time. He's since concluded Bini Katz is the murderer."

"Bini? Here we go again." Oliver shook his head. "Woo-ee she is not going to take this well. The word cyclone comes to mind." Oliver drummed his thumbs on the bar. "I think maybe I'll wait a bit before I go back to your place, Rosie."

"I can't imagine how this will hit her. I wonder if I should get over there to help. And maybe I should warn Tyler."

Oliver smacked the bar. "Then you are crazier than her. Look, it's five o'clock somewhere. Maybe we should try some of Alessa's chianti and lay low for a bit."

"I'll get the glasses." Glenn hopped up.

While Oliver poured, I glanced at Brandon. "Can you grab a fourth glass?"

After texting Tyler the sheriff was on his way to question Bini, I picked up two glasses of wine and approached Brandon. He slipped his feet back into his leather shoes and snapped his Kindle shut. "Did the sheriff learn anything worthwhile?"

"He thinks so. But the man has a tendency to jump to conclusions. I believe we have a long way to go before we find out who poisoned the salt."

"So it was the salt?"

"Yes." I set the wine before him, noting Oliver's heavy pour, and sat down. "Who are his suspects?"

Surprised at Brandon's interest I said, "He only needs one and then his work is done. He's accused a woman who I know couldn't have done it. So, as it stands now, whoever really did this, is walking around freely and could easily do it again."

"And you are trying to figure this out?"

"Kevin almost died." I swallowed a catch in my throat. "I can't believe how you are all willing to continue with class after this. I mean, we are on lock down and will do everything we can to keep people safe, but your commitment to this class is really touching. All of you. No one is backing out. Not even Marco."

"It's a good class. And I like that you are going to solve this mystery. Let me know if you need any help." Brandon smiled and lifted his glass. "*Grazie, Signora.*"

I held mine up. "A day and a half of cooking school and you're already speaking Italian?"

"I like to know things." Our glasses clinked together. "*Alla Vita.*"

I watched him over the rim of my glass. His eyes were closed as if savoring every nuance of the wine. He opened them. "I detect a touch of cherry and a hint of tobacco leaf. You?"

"Maybe a little pepper? It has a nice zing like a good Zinfandel." I set my glass on the tablecloth. "What did you think about your interview with the sheriff?"

"No comment."

"I think he was intimidated by you. That always brings out his mean side." I gazed over at him. "I'm curious why you stayed. None of the others did."

"I find this all fascinating. Remember when I told you my life had become dull? Well," he smiled, "I certainly can't say that anymore." He took another sip of wine. "Are we having class tomorrow?"

"I'm hopeful." A large gust of wind flapped the awnings. The rare southerly winds continued to wreak havoc. "Are you and Jojo getting along? I believe Marco is going to keep us in the same pairs."

"She's an interesting young woman. She's told me some of what's been happening with her uncle. How her brother and sister are so angry with her. She has a resiliency about her. As if no one can take her down, no matter how hard they try." He paused. "People handle grief in very different ways."

"So, Brandon, do you have a family?"

"Not at the moment." He swirled his wine. "This is a very tasty Chianti. Do you know the year? Is it a Sangiovese?"

I laughed. "I don't mean to pry."

"No. My life isn't very interesting. I moved here to try and change that."

"I did the same. I moved here because my marriage had fallen apart. Turns out it was a good decision."

"Thank you for being so forthright. I did the same. I was living in DC. As was my ex-wife." He took another long sip. "Enough said."

"Rough divorce?"

"Oh, my, yes."

"I get that. Why you moved, I mean. I've walked through that seemingly endless tunnel myself. But you have to get to the other side. Otherwise, you are standing in darkness breathing in carbon monoxide."

"My goodness—" Brandon almost choked on his last sip. "Can I borrow

108

that metaphor?"

"Of course." I smiled. "I'd be honored. So, what went wrong in your marriage?"

He removed his glasses and set them on the table. "The first time I saw my wife, she was crossing the room at a party. It was as if a spotlight followed her path. Everyone noticed her. Men and women alike. She exuded confidence and charismatic energy."

"Did you know her?"

"People like me don't know women like her. At least that's what I thought. But later on she caught my eye and gave me one of those desperate pleas for a rescue from the guy next to her. I'd had a couple of gin and tonics and so I did. I couldn't believe I had the guts to do it. Did I mention the gin and tonics?"

"What happened?"

"For a while, her lens zoomed in on me. She found me to be quirky, a little goofy, but I think she felt a safety with me. She made me feel as if I were the most important man in the world. It lasted long enough for her to marry me."

He seemed blissful at the memory, and then pain immediately tightened his eyes.

"What went wrong? If you don't mind my asking."

He frowned. I waited until he lifted his head. "The sun is a fickle thing. Planets spin and orbit and eventually those warm rays are illuminating someone else while the others grow cold."

I placed my hands on the stem of the glass. "Well put. I'm very sorry."

"I wasn't surprised. Although my ego was a little bruised, I had to get out of there. Find something or somewhere to ground me. Something familiar. Something I knew. When I was offered this job, it all seemed to fall into place." He leaned back in his chair.

I thought for a moment. "Something familiar? What's familiar about Cardigan?"

"Not Cardigan. Teaching. I had been doing mostly research at George-town. Teaching grounds me."

I pressed my back into the slats of my chair. "Can I ask you her name?"

He frowned. "Why would you want to know that?"

"I think names are interesting. And how people treat them."

"I'm intrigued."

"My husband only called me Rose. I mean, Rose is a beautiful name. But it wasn't mine."

"Ah." Brandon smiled. "It was as if he wanted you to be a different person from the start."

"Who knows? But I agree with you. It has significance." I glanced over my shoulder. Oliver and Glenn were laughing together. I looked back at Brandon. "Oliver calls me Rosie. And Janice, Rose Red. Now those names are playful."

"Endearing."

"Exactly. And my guy? He never calls me anything but Rosalie. I'll never forget the first time he said my name."

"Her name was Lily." He finished his wine. "And she only called me Brandon. But then again, that's my name. Although I always wanted to be named Murray."

I smiled. "I'm very glad you're here with us. Thank you for sharing. I hope this class will be the tonic you need."

"Thank you, Rosalie. It is already having that effect."

I studied him. There was no pretension. He had been completely open. I found myself feeling quite comfortable with him. Safe, like his ex-wife. "You're most very welcome."

Chapter Twenty-Three

Once the okay came from the sheriff to reopen the class tomorrow, Glenn and I prepped the café. Oliver had decided to go the Grande in order to avoid Bini's meltdown. I wondered if he would see Sonja again. And if that was his intention.

Glenn entered the kitchen with a bin full of dishes and wine glasses. "We should be finished once I load these."

"Glenn?" I said as I stacked the cutting boards. "I've been texting with Jojo."

"And?" He set the bin next to the dishwasher.

"The sheriff told her he suspected the poison had been meant for her."

"Why would he say that so prematurely?"

"I guess he talked to Bini and solidified his case."

"Bah." Glenn crossed his arms. "He's flying by the seat of his pants. And why stir things up with Jojo?"

"Agreed. And now her lawyer is concerned about her siblings' behavior so he told her to retrieve some things from the house. Things like Kline's check book, bank statements, oh, and a safety deposit box key. Thing is, she's scared to go there alone."

Glenn smiled. "And you offered to go with her?"

"Want to join me?" I checked his reaction. "Maybe she'll let us look around a bit."

"Search for clues?"

I nodded. "This all started with Ronnie Kline. Maybe we should start there too."

Glenn placed the last of the glasses in the dish rack. "When do we leave?"

"She's on her way there now. But I'd understand if you're too tired. It's been a long day."

"Ha," Glenn said. "I've done nothing but sit and read my book. I'm as bored as a gourd."

He started the dishwasher. "I'll get the lights."

Glenn and I climbed into my car and buckled our seat belts. I switched on the heat and backed out of the alley.

"What exactly are we looking for?" Glenn buzzed his seat back as far as it would go and extended his legs.

"I don't have an agenda. I just want to look around and see what we see."

He gazed out the window. "I like the sound of that. We'll do a walk through. Notice what looks out of place."

"And what isn't out of place." I rounded the bend and headed out of town. It felt strange driving the route I always took home, only this time we were on our way to a crime scene. I squeezed the steering wheel. "I hope we find something, Glenn. We don't have much time before things could get a whole lot worse."

After a few minutes, Glenn lifted his chin and pointed. "Look, Rosalie. There's the sign. Windswept Farm, circa 1748."

I turned onto a narrow lane lined with tall, gnarled Cypress trees. After at least one hundred yards of being assaulted by limbs, the view opened up to acres upon acres of pristine fields. I tapped Glenn's arm. "Check that out."

A wide expanse of early growth crops spread out before us. The setting sun lit the field and the nitrogen-rich green of the budding spikes glowed as if under a spotlight.

"Is that the infamous winter wheat?"

"Yes." I stopped the car.

"And Barclay Meadow is just over that line of trees?"

"He was going to crop dust. With the way the wind has been blowing, it would have contaminated our test for certain." I shook my head. "Bini was right."

"From my experience with Bini, I would say she is almost always right," Glenn said. "But it would be easier to take if she wasn't quite so sanctimonious about it."

"Oh, Glenn," I said as I continued down the lane. "You just said a mouthful."

I drove around a small S curve and the house came into view. With two-story pillars, it stood grand, with commanding red brick and floor to ceiling windows. A widow's walk surrounded the rooftop punctuated by two looming chimney stacks.

I parked the car and shut off the engine. "It's like a fortress."

"And now it all belongs to Jojo." Glenn frowned. "She certainly doesn't seem to be embracing the idea."

I looked over at him, a stitch forming between my eyebrows. "Are you still wondering where she was the morning her uncle died?"

"Most definitely." He continued to stare at the house. "Rosalie, I know we have both grown very fond of our Jojo, but we need to keep in mind what we said earlier, that she could have easily murdered her uncle. And here's her motive sitting right in front of us."

"Easily, is right." I thought for a moment. "She cooked and cleaned for him. She could have poisoned him a dozen different ways."

"Maybe she waited for the right timing. It's like Barty suggested. She's in the will, boom, drop a little hemlock in his morning coffee."

"According to Tyler, Kline had resorted to drinking Maker's Mark in the morning. Little hair of the dog. At least that was the rumor."

"You don't say?" Glenn rubbed his chin. "So why the salt?"

"Like we said before. To make it look like someone is going for her. It certainly convinced the sheriff." I dropped my hands into my lap. "I hate thinking this. I really do like Jojo."

"She hasn't had an easy life, by the sounds of it. Who knows what she's been through with an uncle like that."

"Glenn, I'm feeling the need to take a step back. It's like I'm tunnel visioned about this. Why does someone murder? Who resorts to that?"

He frowned. "Other than a person who is criminally insane, I'd say, someone who is desperate. Who sees no other way out."

"I keep thinking of the seven deadly sins. The three that pop out are greed, envy, and wrath."

"You're right to think this way," he said. "Motivation is our key here. But these poisonings may or may not have been out of passion. They could have been carefully premeditated."

"You just gave me the chills." I pushed my sunglasses back on my head. "Ready?"

"Ready as I'll ever be." Glenn braced his hands on the door and gingerly pulled himself out of the car.

"It's not the easiest car to exit." I rounded the hood and took his elbow. "I'm sorry. Once the café is up and running again, I'm in the market for a different car."

"I rather like this one," Glenn said as he stretched his lower back. "Maybe next time I should drive." He gave me a little wink.

Chapter Twenty-Four

I heard voices and looked over to see Jojo and Bartlett in front of a brightly-painted red barn. A pacing black Lab in the back bed of Barty's truck announced our arrival. Jojo was huddled next to a white Hyundai, clutching the top of the open door.

Barty scowled as we approached. "What are they doing here?"

"They're helping me."

"Helping you do what exactly?" One side of Bartlett's mouth curled into a sneer.

Jojo gazed at us, a small pout on her lips. "They're helping me with everything."

"Hello, Bartlett," I said. "How are you?"

"What do you care? I don't even know you."

"A better question young man," Glenn said, "is why are you here?"

Bartlett pulled a heavy set of keys from his front pocket and twirled them around his finger. "Someone needs to take care of this place." He shook his head. "I can't believe it all went to you. None of this makes any sense."

"Barty, our uncle was murdered. How are you not upset about that?"

He narrowed his eyes. "How'd you do it, little sis?"

"Bartlett," Glenn said. "I really don't think this is the time for that kind of behavior."

"Butt out, old man." He looked back at Jojo. "And *she* needs to take care of this farm. We have to get the fields dusted and *she's* not doing anything about it." He kicked at the dirt.

"Stop it, Barty," Jojo said. "This all just happened. I haven't even been inside yet. That's why we're here today. I couldn't do it by myself."

"You don't have a freakin' clue what you're doing." He snapped his hand around his keys. "How'd you get him to change the will?" He leaned in. "Huh?"

"I told you, I don't know."

His face was close to hers. "Well, I think you do."

Glenn took a step toward them. "Young man—"

Jojo's shoulders fell as her brother at last headed for his pickup. Glenn and I bookended her and waited in silence as the truck skidded down the drive. "Are you okay?"

"It's getting worse by the minute, Rosalie. Barty just told me he hired a lawyer and do you know what? The lawyer said if something happens to me in the next thirty days, he and/or Phoebe will get the farm."

"You mean if you die?" Glenn did a double take. "Your brother just said that to you?"

She slammed the car door shut. "Among other things."

"I'm glad we got here when we did." I patted her back.

"Barty won't hurt me. He may be angry and a little bit shocked, but he won't hurt me. He's never laid a hand on me. Not ever." Jojo sunk her teeth into her bottom lip and stared off at the billows of dust left in his wake. "He sure is upset. I've never really seen him like this."

"Jojo, would you mind if Glenn and I look around the house? Maybe we can find some sort of clue about what happened to your uncle that morning."

She nodded. "That's a really good idea."

Glenn stared at the house. "This is quite a place, Jojo. Must have a fascinating history. Has it always been in your family?"

"Almost. That's why Uncle Ronnie was insistent one of us kids got it."

"Such a big house and farm," Glenn said again. "Did your ancestors own slaves?"

"I don't know anything about that," Jojo said. "All I know is Uncle Ronnie always used those migrant workers when it was time to harvest. My guess is Barty was going to do that, too."

"I see." Glenn frowned.

"Ready to go inside?" I said to Jojo.

She nodded. "This is going to be super weird."

"Has anyone else been here other than Barty?"

"Phoebs came over the morning after. Nobody told her not to because we didn't know that our uncle died of unnatural causes. She scrubbed the place clean, emptied the fridge and freezers, took out the trash, and hauled it all to the dump."

"Has the sheriff been out other than the day your uncle died?" I asked.

"No." Jojo hugged herself as she walked up the steps on the toes of her sneakers.

When we reached the ten-foot double doors, I said, "Shall we?"

Jojo sifted through her keys, a large hummingbird charm connecting them. "I still can't believe he was murdered. I could deal with a heart attack or something. This is so awful." She unlocked the door and pushed it open. A gust of cool, stale air met us as we stepped inside.

Jojo switched on the chandelier illuminating the foyer. A dark circle on the wood floor indicated a rug had recently been removed. That must have been where Bini found Kline's body. I wondered who removed the rug and where it was. All the evidence would be right there.

I gazed around the space. From what I could see, the house looked pristine. I doubted we would find anything useful if Phoebe had already cleaned.

Jojo walked up to a thermostat. "I never thought about turning on the heat. It's been pretty cold though. I don't want the pipes to freeze." She spun the dial and turned to face us. "What exactly do you want to see?"

"Do you mind if we start looking around?" Glenn said.

"What will you do if you find something?"

I pulled my jacket tighter. The house was uninviting, the chill in the air felt as if Ronnie Kline's spirit was trying to evict us. "We'll show you. If you want to know, that is."

She shrugged. "I kind of doubt it. Like I said, I'm still in shock." She rubbed her arms. "I keep waiting for him to come down those stairs."

"This is your home, now," I said. "At some point you will be ready to bring it back to life. Honor your family's legacy." I smiled. "Believe me, I know it takes a while. When you're ready to start, the first thing we should do is bake some bread. From scratch," I added. "I'll help you."

"I like bread." Jojo twitched her lips to one side. "But for now, I'm just going to gather his things. I'll wait for you guys in the kitchen." She headed for a closed door off the foyer and stopped before an oil painting of a family seated on a sofa, the background dark, their faces unsmiling. "I'm twenty-five years old and I have the weight of generations of Klines on my shoulders." A tear made its way down her cheek. She continued walking. "God, I miss my mom." I knew exactly how she felt.

Once Jojo disappeared through the doorway, I looked around the wide foyer and then at Glenn. "Where do you want to start?"

"Upstairs?"

"Okay. I'll look around down here." I scanned the space, trying to decide where to begin.

Glenn gripped the banister. "I'm not going through any underwear drawers."

"That's why people hide things in them." I smiled. "Think like a detective."

He started up the stairs. "This place is giving me the willies."

I passed through an ornate dining room with wallpaper covered in vines and tropical flowers, and out to a back room with three walls of windows. Two easy chairs faced the water, a small table between them. A pipe nestled in an ashtray. I walked over to a brass bar cart and inspected the bottles. I noticed a bottle of Maker's Mark. Not a speck of dust on it. His nieces and nephew would know that was his drink of choice. I was tempted to take it with me but that could very well end badly. The sheriff was being more civil to me lately, but I knew better than anyone how thin that ice was.

I found my way to a formal living room with several groupings of more arm chairs and sofas. The fabric was threadbare and there were no ashes in the fireplace. A layer of dust coated the books on the rows of shelves, and I guessed the last people to enjoy this space were not of Ronnie Kline's generation.

I walked through another doorway and arrived at a mudroom at the back of the house. I noticed a closed door and suspected it was a closet. But my curiosity was piqued and I opened it. Several musty-smelling overcoats hung from a small pole. An array of boots were lined up on the floor. It all seemed disappointingly normal. I looked up at the shelf overhead. Other than a faded felt Stetson, it was empty. I started to close the door but noticed a tiny pinprick of light coming from somewhere over the shelf.

I shoved away the coats and felt around the back of the closet. My fingers hit a small crack indicating some sort of opening. I continued to explore the edges and sure enough, discovered a key hole.

My heart pounded. If I were Ronnie Kline and I had a hidden room, where would I keep the key? I searched the pockets of one of the coats. Nothing. After going through three more, I tried the boots. Empty. I looked up at the shelf. Standing on my tiptoes, I pulled the cowboy hat down.

It was surprisingly dust free. I flipped it over. The hat was lined with an expensive beige silk. I ran my fingers across the smooth fabric and stopped when I felt the outline of a key. After finally discerning a slight opening in the seam, I worked the key out of the hat.

The door opened into a small space with one octagonal window high on a wall. A leather-topped desk and a swivel chair sat firmly in the middle of the room. I switched on the green banker's lamp and rounded the desk. After perching on the chair, I steadied myself, and studied the array of drawers.

I tugged on the center drawer until it opened with a squeak. Once I regained my composure, I pulled my phone from my purse and snapped photos of each page of the document I had discovered. I returned it to the drawer and shut it carefully.

I found Glenn and Jojo in the kitchen, a bottle of Pusser's rum on the table, and a tumbler of dark cloudy liquid in front of each of them. Jojo's was almost empty. I hesitated, wondering if I should say anything. If Jojo truly was a suspect, would I be giving her what she needed? But this was her home now. It wasn't my secret to keep.

I joined them at the table and crossed my legs, trying to stop my foot from jiggling.

"How did it go?" Jojo said.

"This house is fairly empty," I said. "Was that your uncle's lifestyle or was it Phoebe's cleaning?"

"For the most part my uncle lived a sparse existence."

"Other than owning hundreds of acres of land." Glenn sipped his rum.

"How about you?" I said to Glenn. "Anything interesting?"

He smacked his lips. "There is a gunroom. It's quite immense. And there is a very large arsenal of weapons." He set his glass down on the table with a thud. "Did you know this, my dear?"

"Yeah," Jojo said. "He was super proud of that room. There are a bunch of antique guns in there. Pretty valuable stuff."

"There is also an AR-15." Glenn leaned back in his chair.

"I know." Jojo sipped the rum. "Uncle Ronnie was in the army for a while. Spent most of his time in Eastern Europe."

"And now all those guns are yours," I said.

"I've never owned a gun before." Jojo tucked her legs underneath her. "This just keeps getting weirder."

The floors began to vibrate and a loud groan generated from below. "Oh my goodness," I said. "What is that?"

"The beast." Jojo smiled. "It's an oil heater. It's in a dark scary corner of the basement. Whenever we had to stay the night, my uncle would tell us we better be good or we would have to sleep down there."

"Aptly named." Glenn studied Jojo. "Did he ever follow through with that threat?"

"Only once. Barty was eleven. He had started up the tractor and taken a joy ride around the farm. He didn't get hurt or anything, but Uncle Ronnie was steaming mad." She exhaled heavily. "Who do you think killed my uncle, Miss Rosalie? Did that woman who works for you do it?"

"I was just about to ask you the same question," Glenn said to Jojo.

She gazed down at the glass. "If it's Phoebs or Barty, I don't want to know. I'd rather they just got away with it." She looked up. "Enough has already happened to my little family."

"Wills can bring out strange behavior in relatives," Glenn said. "I suggest you take it one day at a time."

"Jojo," I said, "why weren't you working here the morning your uncle died?"

She blinked a few times. "Um, that was Monday, right? Sometimes on Mondays I do a yoga workout in my living room. I have some music I play, a good mat, that kind of thing."

"And your uncle didn't mind? I thought you said he never would have let you come to cooking class, that he expected you to be here every day."

"He docked my pay whenever I did my yoga. Other than that, he didn't seem to mind." Jojo avoided my eyes.

"Did your siblings know about the yoga?"

"Phoebs did. Sometimes she'd do it with me, if Michael let her, that is. But that wasn't very often." She finished her rum. "Rosalie, surely someone else could have killed my uncle other than my siblings."

I studied her, noting the subject change. "We are doing our best to find that out. And I hope we do soon." I recrossed my legs. "For everyone's sake."

She tapped her fingernails on the glass. "You found something, didn't you?"

"Yes."

"Do you know who killed my uncle?"

"No."

"Okay, let's leave it at that." The beast's rumbles slowed to a deafening silence. Jojo dropped her feet to the floor. "You ready to get out of here?"

"How was the underwear drawer?" I asked Glenn.

"Full of boxers and only boxers."

I switched on the headlights. "Any evidence he had a lover?"

"Not that I detected. No feminine products in the bathroom. No extra toothbrush. Only one pillow indented." Glenn exhaled a long sigh. "Spill, my dear. What on earth did you find?"

"Ronnie Kline had a contract to sell the farm."

"Sell the farm? To who?"

"A Russian company."

Glenn's breath materialized in a puff of condensation. "Ronnie Kline was about to sell his farm to a Russian company? I thought he wanted to keep it in the family."

"Glenn?"

"Oh, my," he said. "Let's hear it. I know it's going to be good."

"Sonja is Russian."

Chapter Twenty-Five

After dropping Glenn at his car, I was happy to be on my way home at last. Clouds blocked the setting sun and a spattering of rain had begun to fall. I downshifted as I rounded the overgrown shrubs in the center of my circular drive.

The musty, cat-spray scent of the boxwoods met my nose as I got out of the car. I was happy to see Tyler's pickup. We made a habit of ending our days together. It was a requirement of sorts. We led busy lives with off kilter schedules and needed to make the time to be with one another, or it would never happen. But we agreed it was too soon to talk about moving in together. We were taking it slow, testing the waters with just a toe tip after having both gone through brutal and unwanted divorces. Tyler's was years ago, but he was still bruised and hesitant to give it another try. Mine more recent, so I was definitely on board with his need to keep the pace slow, and I hoped, steady.

Sometimes we shared a cup of tea after work, discussing our days, concocting grandiose plans for the café and the farm that would help combat global warming and nourish the world with organic fare. Other times it was just me arriving home late, passing off the day's special for his dinner, and Tyler's appreciative lovely kiss on his way out the door. But the best nights were when we reserved a block of time, just for us. Weather permitting, we'd sit out by the river, narrowing our world to only the two of us, no one to save, no one to feed, no one to conquer, just languishing in our good fortune to have found one another. And of course, finishing the evening with more delicious kisses.

I closed the car door with my hip and hitched my purse up on my shoulder. I was eager to get inside. Maybe Tyler and I could squeeze in just a few moments of loveliness. I could use some tenderness after the past two days.

"Rosalie," Tyler said from the stoop. His barn coat was buttoned up tight, his hands stuffed in the pockets. "You certainly took your time getting home."

"Hey." I smiled. "Well, I'm happy you're still here." The rain fell harder, my hair already popping into corkscrews. "Can we go inside? I sure could use a hug." I studied his face. There were no twinkling eyes. No happy-to-see-me smile. My stomach began to plummet. "Is something wrong?"

"The sheriff was here this afternoon."

"I know. I texted you."

"Why did you know before we did?"

"He was at the café asking questions about the poisoning. Look, the whole thing with Bini is ridiculous. I'm sorry you had to deal with him." The wind kicked up another notch. I tried to shove my hair back from my face. "Any reason we can't go inside?"

Tyler descended one step. "Bini's parents hired a lawyer."

"Okay. That's good." I thought for a moment. "Yes, better to be proactive. Who did they hire?"

"What difference does that make?"

"Who, Tyler?" My purse slid down my arm, the yank on my shoulder a little painful.

"Jack Morris." Tyler frowned. "Sheriff said this was your idea—that it must have been Bini."

"That's not true." Icy wind had begun to numb my cheeks.

"You sure?" Tyler shifted his weight to the other foot. "Then where did he get the idea?"

I stepped back. "It's complicated. He was asking who had been at the café—"

"Thanks to you, Bini has been accused of both murder and attempted murder. You said something the day it happened. You asked me if either of us were involved. You still believe it was her, don't you?"

124

"That's not true. I know Bini didn't do any of this. Are you going to let me explain?"

"I'm pretty confused right now." Tyler pulled his collar up. "I love you, Rosalie. But I have never understood your need to nose around in other people's lives."

My shoulders fell. "You aren't even listening to me."

"I can't believe you did this. Bini could go to prison."

"No, she won't. I'll figure this out." I searched his face. "I love you, Tyler."

He hesitated, then trotted down the last few steps. "I need to think." He brushed past me and opened the door to his truck. Dickens, who was still on the stoop, let out a small whine. Tyler took the stairs two at a time and scooped up his arthritic dog. I stared after him until the red glow of his taillights were swallowed up by the cedar trees.

Chapter Twenty-Six

Early the next morning I stood in the kitchen and focused on Mr. Miele, willing him to brew a little faster. I was relieved there was no sign of Tyler or Bini. I was pretty sure Tyler hadn't had enough time to 'think,' as he put it. And I was almost certain he was still in 'jump to conclusion' and 'blame your girlfriend' mode. The emotions swirling around in both my head and stomach were making me dizzy.

Once the last of the coffee trickled into the steel carafe, I filled my travel mug and started for the door.

Oliver stood before me, fully dressed in an untucked oxford and comfortable jeans. "You leaving me behind?"

"There's a note. I thought maybe you could drive yourself today."

He gazed out the window. The sun was just a faint glow behind a curtain of clouds. "Class doesn't start for three hours."

"I have a lot to do."

He walked over to the coffee pot and filled a mug. "Then I'll help."

"Okay," I said, noticing the tension in my jaw ease as I unclenched my teeth. "Yes, I'd like that, Oliver." I dropped my purse on the table. It felt familiar and unfamiliar at the same time that my older brother just offered to help me through a difficult time. I let it sink in and decided I liked it. A lot. "Did you by any chance hang out with Tyler last night?"

"He was working when I got home. I waited for a bit but then headed up to bed. I had some emails I'd been ignoring."

"Really? Good for you, ignoring emails. I think this vacation may be working."

Oliver studied me. "Did *you* see Tyler when you got home?"

"Yes." I nodded quickly.

Oliver considered my response but said nothing. He held up his mug. "I'll drink this in the car."

The rain had finally stopped at 3:00 AM. I knew this because I was wide awake. In its aftermath the temperatures had dropped leaving a chilly, unfriendly morning. Oliver and I climbed in the car as the day brightened to a dull gray.

Oliver took a long sip of coffee just as I took off down the gravel lane. A large dollop sloshed onto his lap. "Uh, sis. Think you could slow down a little?" He wiped the drip on the cup with his thumb. "I really don't think we're going to hit traffic."

"Sorry." I gripped the steering wheel.

He took another long sip. "What happened with Tyler?"

"What makes you think something happened?" I stared hard at the lane, trying to avoid the divots and pot holes.

"You don't have to tell me, but I think you'll feel better if you do."

I hesitated. Maybe he was right. Maybe hearing Oliver's thoughts on the matter would be a whole lot better than the desperate dark places my mind was going. "The sheriff told him I think Bini killed Kline and poisoned Keven."

"And Tyler's upset with you about this?"

I nodded. "Very." I turned onto the main road that echoed the Cardigan River's bends and headed into town. "He wouldn't let me explain. There's no possible way I think she could have done any of it."

"Let me guess, because you may not have gone here yet, but, hm, you now think you are unworthy of being loved?"

I coughed out a laugh. "I think I reached that conclusion at around one this morning." I flipped on my low beams as we hit a patch of fog. "Thank you for asking. I feel better just blurting it out."

"It's a Finnegan thing, you know."

"What is?"

"A need to know. Everything. Whether it's good for you or not." Oliver finished off his coffee and dropped the mug into a cup holder. "I wasn't going to let you get away without telling me. Did we get that from Mom?"

"She was almost clairvoyant that way." I clutched the bottom of the steering wheel. I thought about our mother, our family, nostalgia tugged at my heart. "She knew Petey Wilson was going to kiss me before I did."

"And how exactly did she do that?"

"She had a feeling. When I got home from the ninth grade dance, she asked me if it was a pleasant kiss."

"Pleasant?" Oliver said.

"She said kisses should be lovely. If they are forced or messy, you should find another boyfriend."

Oliver smiled. "She never told me that."

"Ah, so that's why you never married." I returned his smile.

"If a kiss was all it takes, I'd have grandchildren." He laughed and gazed out the window. A wide view of the river appeared along the road. "Hey, Rosie, check this out."

An Osprey flew low over the water alongside us, a large fish struggling in its talons.

"How fast are you going?" he said as the osprey kept pace with the car.

"Thirty-five."

"Punch it up a little."

I pressed on the gas and inched the car up to forty.

"He's keeping up. Holy crap, this is awesome." Oliver continued to watch the osprey. "Nice catch, buddy," he said and laughed. "Look at that fat fish." He eyed my speedometer. "Try forty-five."

My Mercedes accelerated. So did the osprey.

Oliver shook his head. "I swear he's watching us. This guy is having a little fun. Or showing off that fish." He chuckled again. "Or both."

It was another half mile before the trees reappeared and the osprey was no longer visible. Oliver faced forward. I turned on to High Street and stopped behind a pickup allowing a pedestrian to mosey across the road.

"Rosie," Oliver said.

"Yes?"

"Did you really solve two murders?"

"With Glenn's help."

"And you're trying to figure this one out, too."

"I am."

"Why?'

I turned down the alley and parked. The car was quiet. Just an occasional faint tick of the engine. "That's a good question." I exhaled a long sigh. "I guess the short answer is, after my marriage fell apart, I couldn't grasp how it happened. What went wrong? When and why? Now I have a need to understand why bad things happen. After we solved the first one, I realized I had helped someone by finding the answers. It felt good. And it gave me hope that there is such a thing as closure."

Chapter Twenty-Seven

Glenn struggled with the lock while we waited. "Sorry," he said once he managed to get it open.

"Thanks, buddy." Oliver strolled into the restaurant.

"The WD40 didn't help. And it made quite a mess."

Oliver poked his head in the door to the restaurant. "Janice is already here."

She was seated at the bar, her Stella McCartney handbag puddled on the counter. She stared at her phone.

"Good morning, Snow White." I headed over to the coffee machines.

She clicked something on her screen and frowned.

Oliver stood next to her. "Everything all right?"

Janice's eyes tensed as she continued to stare at her phone.

"Jani?" Oliver looked at me and I shrugged.

I started the first batch of coffee as Janice leaned forward on her elbows, still starting at her phone. Oliver sat at the bar and played with a sugar packet.

Glenn sidled up next to me. "Any news on Kevin?"

"They're discharging him today. Jake is excited to get him home."

Glenn rubbed his chin. "Any more thoughts about what you found?"

I dumped the used grounds. "Only whether or not I should tell the sheriff. It might take him off Bini's trail."

"What else is on your mind?" Glenn said. "I have the impression something is vexing you."

"You can't be any good at poker, Rosie," Oliver said as he stuffed the sugar packet back in the container.

"Tyler blames me for the sheriff charging Bini." I tried to avoid Glenn's steady gaze. "And that's all I'm going to say about that." I tied my apron around my waist. "Except, can I ask you guys something? Do you think I'm a busybody?"

"In the best of ways," Glenn said. "You have a unique talent to part the fog when the answers are hard to see." He smiled.

"Maybe. But it isn't winning me any popularity contests."

"Not yet. But it will."

Janice looked up. "People say I can be difficult. That I'm hard to be around sometimes."

"Snow White, that's the craziest thing I've ever heard you say. Everyone loves you. Including all of us." I studied her. "You okay?"

"How about a Prosecco?" Oliver hopped up. "And I saw some lemon muffins back there."

"Not really hungry," she said. "But yes, definitely, to the Prosecco." She stared back at her phone. "Make it a big glass."

I stood next to her and peered over her shoulder. "Is that the P.I.'s feed?"

"Trevor's vehicle is there again. Right out front."

I squeezed her shoulder. "There has to be an explanation."

"I'm a little buggy, girlfriend. Please don't squeeze my shoulder."

Oliver set a glass down in front of her. "Wilgus isn't coming back today, is he?"

"No, why?"

He just walked by. I was afraid he was going to come in. I would like a day without that man."

"I'll be right back."

"Sheriff Wilgus—" I called when I reached the sidewalk.

He slowed until I caught up to him. "What, Hart?"

"I was out at Windswept Farm yesterday." I realized I still had a dish towel in my hands.

"Let me guess, it was Miss Scarlet in the conservatory?"

"No, actually it was the butler." I peered up at him. His eyes were masked by his aviators but I could see he was fighting a losing battle to suppress a smile.

He put his hands on his hips. "Spill."

"We both know Phoebe already threw out all of the food, but the liquor is still there. It's in, well, if you must know, the conservatory."

"So?"

"There's a bottle of bourbon. Maker's Mark. It's been opened. Wasn't that his drink of choice?"

He lifted his chin. "You touch it?"

"Of course not. That's your job." I smiled, relieved he wasn't about to lose his temper.

"And you think that could be the murder weapon? Think it's full of poison?"

"It's worth a shot."

"That another joke?" This time he let the smile come.

"Good one." I started to leave but stopped. "I found something else."

The smile faded.

"Kline had a secret room." I twisted the towel. "There was a desk inside containing a contract to sell the farm to a Russian company."

The sheriff stood motionless. Not even a twitch.

"I can tell you where it is. I don't think even Jojo knew about it." I peered up at him wishing I could read his eyes. "Well?"

After a long pause, he said, "Is Jojo here yet? I'll need a key."

"No. She should be here soon."

"Hart?" The sheriff swallowed. "I'm sorry about yesterday. It's just, well, these people who move here and think they know everything really get under my skin."

"You called me a squatter."

"No offense, but that's what you are." He put his hands on his hips. "I'm serious about this."

"How am I a squatter? I own this business. I just expanded."

He shook his head. "You aren't the first one. But folks like you, they start a business, put out a shingle, think they are going to change things. But then they get bored. The small town gets to them and they pack it all up and go back to where they came from. Happens all the time. So you may want to dig in here, be a part of things, but it's hard for folks here to trust you'll see it through."

"Oh. I didn't realize." I took a step back. "Thank you for explaining. It actually makes some sense." I looked past him, squinting at a hint of sun. "Jojo."

"What about Jojo?"

"She just rounded the corner."

He looked over his shoulder. "I'll call you when I get there. You can direct me to this . . ." he made air quotation marks . . . 'secret room.'"

Once he and Jojo were in a conversation, I exhaled the air I'd been holding in my lungs. He took me seriously. And he's actually going to follow through. I put my arms over my head and did one small pirouette.

Chapter Twenty-Eight

Thursday
Day Three of Cooking Class

Menu
Primi Piatte/First Course
Ostriche al Forno con Pancetta/Baked Oysters with Italian Bacon
Janice and Oliver

Pasta/ Pasta
All students will complete their pasta dishes from Tuesday

Secondi/Meat, Fish, Poultry, and Game
Pesce en Crosta di sale/Fish baked in a crust of salt
Rosalie

Dolci/Dessert
Mousse al Cioccolato all'Italiano/Italian Chocolate Mousse
Joanna and Brandon

A tovola non si invecchia/
At the table with good friends and family, one does not grow old
-Italian Proverb

P romptly at nine we were gathered around the bar, aprons secured, mugs and glasses filled.

"Good morning." Marco rubbed his hands together. "Rosalie has done an excellent job keeping our pasta fresh and ready to eat this afternoon. So today we will be preparing dishes to augment the pasta course. And this afternoon, after you take a nice *pisolino*, Rosalie, Glenn, and I will present you with an authentic, four course, Italian *cena*."

I glanced around the bar at my fellow students. Janice was looking at her phone again, her forehead deeply furrowed. Oliver flashed me another puzzled expression. I stood alone, Kevin's absence more prominent than ever now that we were back to cooking. Brandon stood next to Jojo looking tailored and pressed. Jojo bounced up and down nervously in her slip on sneakers.

Marco finished his espresso and set his cup in a dish bin. "My friends, I have shared with you on the chalkboard, an old Italian proverb. 'At the table with good friends and family, one does not grow old.' I hope you take this to heart this evening. We are preparing a four course Italian meal. I think once you are seated and take in the moment, you will embody this proverb."

Janice put her phone down and mouthed, 'I'm sorry,' to Oliver.

"Janice and Oliver will be preparing the appetizer. Oysters *alla Italiana*. During my free time yesterday, I found some of your famous Chesapeake Bay oysters." He rubbed his hands together. "We Italians love our oysters." He wiggled his eyebrows. "You know what they say about consuming oysters and the bedroom?"

Janice stared at the bowl of oysters on ice Marco had set on the counter. "Who's going to shuck them?"

"Why, you are, *Signora*."

She looked back at her phone. "I've got a guy. He works all my parties." She scrolled through her contacts. "I'm sure he could stop by for a bit."

"I think we got this." Oliver leaned in. "You can scratch it off your bucket list, Jani."

"Brandon and Joanna will be making chocolate mousse for the dessert course."

Jojo looked up at Brandon. "You like chocolate, doc?"

"Who doesn't?" he said, not admonishing her for the 'doc.'

"And Rosalie? You and I are going to do something amazing with a rockfish I also discovered yesterday in my shopping travels. *Si?*"

"Yes," I said. "Yes, of course." I stood straighter. Marco and I were going to cook together. I glanced at Oliver and he gave me a thumbs up and a warm smile.

An hour into class, the air was saturated with the aromas of roasting garlic, grilled pancetta, and melting butter and cream.

"There's one oyster left," Oliver called to Janice who was sautéing the topping.

"You people are relentless." She switched off the stove and placed the pan on a trivet. After topping off her prosecco, she walked into the café. All eyes were on her. "I read an article once," she said. "It was about who are the happiest people."

"I know this," Marco said. "The happiest men are the ones who make more money than their brothers and fathers."

"That actually sounds about right," Brandon said, and sipped from a glass of chianti.

"Nope," Janice said as she stood next to Oliver. "The happiest people, men *and* women," she shot Marco a look, "are the ones who pay people to do the things they hate to do."

Oliver placed the shucker in front of her. "Happy people eat oysters."

"Janice," Jojo said. "It's not as hard as you think. My Uncle Ronnie used to make me do it all the time. You have to twist the shucker. Try it. It will pop right open."

"You people don't get it," Janice said. "I know how to do this. Are you kidding me? My family is pre-bridge." She propped the shucker between the shell halves and snapped it open with one twist. She checked her nails for damage. "I just think they taste a lot better when someone does it for me."

"*Brava,*" Marco said. "Well done. How is the pancetta?"

Janice rolled her eyes. "It's resting while I check my phone."

"I think the sugar and butter are ready," Jojo said to Brandon. "Did you chop the chocolate?"

"*Si.*"

I peered over Janice's shoulder. The camera was focused on a small house with a white picket fence lined with yellow chrysanthemums, Trevor's Range Rover by the curb.

"Trevor told me he was going up to Wilmington for a Costco run this morning. He lied. You see? He's probably bopping Bonnie right now." Her voice caught in her throat. "You got an explanation for that?"

"There must be one. Do her children go to the same school?"

"Really, Rose Red?" She shook her head. "I can't decide if I want to cry or go over there and...and..." Her shoulders fell. "I can see why people do that stuff. You know, catch 'em in the act and do something you'd see on Law and Order." She peered up at me. "This is bad." Her raspy voice cracked. "I've never felt like this before."

"I'm here for you, Snow White. One hundred percent," I said as a tear travelled down my cheek.

Marco and I stood side by side. He had placed a large rockfish on a cutting board in front of us. Although the fish had been cleaned, the head was still attached. Glossy, blank eyes stared from its sockets.

"This is a nice piece of fish," I said.

"Alessa knew exactly where to find it. Seems a friend of her husband goes out on the river every day."

"He's a waterman," I said. "And a good one at that. So, what do we do?"

"We are going to prepare an Italian salt encrusted fish. But first we must stuff it with an herb and lemon zest mixture." He eyed my window boxes bursting with herbs. "What would you suggest?"

"Well, I've been reading a lot of Italian cook books lately. And I saw a tarragon sauce where you soak some crusty bread in vinegar. It had garlic, olive oil, a little basil. Does that sound familiar?"

"Ah, *si*! I know this sauce. And it is unique to Toscana. It is perfect for this fish." Marco clasped his hands behind his back.

"So we could put some tarragon in the herb mix. And maybe rosemary? Too strong?"

"Never, *Signora*." His grin was wide, his eyes bright. "You harvest the herbs and I'll retrieve the other ingredients."

As I returned from snipping the sprigs, I glanced over at Janice and Oliver. Her phone was nowhere to be seen. Oliver stood close by as they topped their oysters with the grilled pancetta mixture. "I liked what you said earlier," Oliver said to her. "About paying people to do what you hate. It's what makes the world go 'round in a way. For instance, I absolutely despise doing laundry. And nothing makes me happier than picking up a stack of neatly pressed clothing from Mrs. Lee. Now that I think about it, I'm pretty sure I whistle the entire way home."

"Thanks. You're a nice guy, Oliver." Janice pushed down lightly on a strip of pancetta. She shifted an oyster so that it was perfectly aligned on the broiler pan. "These are going to be good," she said and sniffed.

"Maybe I'll run out and get some real champagne to pair it with before we have our feast."

"I'll buy."

"Then let's get two." Oliver nudged her.

"Yeah, like that's happening on my credit card, Oliver Finnegan, New York jet-setting kabillionaire."

Marco returned from the kitchen. "Your friend. She's smiling."

"The magic of Oliver."

"It runs in the family," he said.

"I think that quality is unique to Oliver." I spread the rosemary out on the counter. Its garden-fresh scent filled the air.

"*Signora.* You have work to do."

"Yes, I know. I'll zest the lemon. Did you—"

Marco stepped closer. I could smell the faint trace of his cologne. "Why do you think I agreed to do this?"

I resisted the urge to take a step back. "I don't know. Why?"

"Because my cousin told me about you. About your passion for what you do. And now that I am here, I see what she sees. You are observant, you catch things others miss. And you are an excellent cook. It takes instinct to be good. And I see that in you."

I took in his words and nodded. "Thank you."

"Do you know what Anthony Bourdain said, God rest his soul?"

"Not sure. But I'm a fan."

"He said, food is power."

I held his gaze and tilted my head. "Yes," I said. "I believe that is true. Which explains a lot about both of us."

Chapter Twenty-Nine

Once we stuffed the fish with half of the aromatic mix, Marco and I whipped up egg whites, salt, and flour, and added the rest of the herbs. We spread half of the salt mixture on the oven dish, placed the fish on top, and encrusted the rest of the fish from top to bottom, head to tail.

"Nice shape on this fish," Marco said.

"He's a little plump." I brushed my hands together. "But who am I to judge."

"You have a nice touch, Rosalie." Marco caught my eye. "I like how you move. You're very, how do you say, adept?"

My heart did a little flip. Was Oliver right? Is Marco flirting with me? "You are adept yourself, Chef. You have very nice hands."

"Ah," he said and picked up a dish towel. "You noticed."

When I returned from setting the fish to rest in the kitchen, Janice and Oliver were sipping coffees, heads dipped in conversation. We were all waiting for Brandon and Jojo to finish their dessert. Marco had promised the students a break so that he and I could complete the four-course meal. It was already two o'clock. Our meal was to start at five.

"Finally," I said to Glenn in a low voice when Jojo began dropping chunks of dark chocolate into the warm cream and sugar mix. She picked up a whisk.

"Stir continuously," Marco said. "Keep it as smooth as possible."

"Are they actually cooking?" Oliver said.

Janice looked up. "'Bout time. What's the big deal, anyway. Get on with it.

140

We're supposed to have a break."

"You mean a *pisolino*." Oliver smiled.

"I know it sounds odd coming from me," Glenn said, "but I think they are trying to savor this experience." He frowned. "That did sound odd coming from me. I think I'm getting a little woozy from all the aromas in here. The air is thick with garlic and butter, and what is that? Rosemary? Who can think straight?"

Oliver crossed his arms. "With that kind of atmosphere, one can only use their senses to navigate."

"Listen to you two," Janice said. "Now you're poets or something?"

"Look at that," Brandon said as he wiped the last of the chocolate from his hands. "Smooth as velvet." He took a long sip of wine.

Jojo stood on her tiptoes and peered into the pan. "Oh, my gosh. It is."

"You know the rules." Marco stood before them with two spoons. "Taste as you go."

Brandon accepted a spoon and dipped it into the sauce. He lifted it as a small stream of chocolate fell from the bottom. He held his other hand under it and faced Jojo. "Ready?"

"You gonna feed me that?"

"Open up." Brandon slipped the spoon into her mouth.

Jojo closed her eyes. "Mm," she groaned. "I have died and gone to heaven." She opened her eyes and picked up the other spoon. "Your turn, doc."

Janice sat up straighter. "What the—"

Jojo inserted her spoon into Brandon's mouth, leaving a small dab on his mustache. Brandon's groan was longer and louder than Jojo's. Oliver pressed his lips together, stifling a chuckle.

Brandon grabbed a second spoon and had another taste. He picked up his wine glass and sipped. "Oh, my, you have to try this, Joanne. Have a taste of the chocolate then sip your wine. That's how they do it in Napa." He passed her a spoon.

She slid the spoon from her mouth and Brandon held his wine glass to her lips. "Oh," she said and stomped her foot. "Whoa. That's amazing."

"I think I would like to try that," Glenn said.

"Hello," Janice called out to Jojo and Brandon. "There are other people in this room and we are getting uncomfortable."

"Oh, Brandon," Jojo said, seemingly oblivious to the rest of us. "I can't believe we made something so good together."

"It was all you, my dear. I just added the chocolate."

"You sure did," she said.

Janice nudged Oliver. "Should I tell them to get a room?"

Oliver looked over his shoulder at Marco. "You're pretty good at this."

Marco smiled and lifted three more spoons from the mug. He dipped them into the chocolate and handed one to each of us in turn. "This," he said as I inserted the spoon in my mouth, "will soothe your soul."

Chapter Thirty

Glenn and I pushed two tables together and covered them with a delicate white cloth. For the finishing touch, I lined several votive candles down the middle and dimmed the lights of the café.

"I want to know more about Phoebe," I said to him as I added extra chairs. "She cleaned out the house. Why would she be so willing to do that if it had been Jojo's job?"

"To erase any evidence?" he said while sweeping the floor.

"And she knew Jojo wasn't going to be there the morning Kline died." I smoothed a wrinkle from the tablecloth. "I want to go to her house."

"On what pretext?" Glenn leaned the broom against the bar and wiped his forehead with the back of his hand.

"I'm working on that." I studied him. "You didn't get a rest. Why don't you sit down and I'll bring you something. Glass of wine?"

"Yes. I'll take you up on that."

I placed a glass of ice cold Chardonnay on the bar. "I told Sheriff Wilgus about the secret room. I also suggested he test the bottle of Maker's Mark."

"Did he threaten to run you out of town?" Glenn took his first sip.

"Nope. And you know what else? He texted me the bourbon tested positive. It was loaded. Enough to kill him almost instantly, unlike the salt."

"We need to know more about both of Jojo's siblings. Today is Thursday. Maybe a visit to the Tavern tomorrow evening?"

"We always find out something at the Tavern."

As the students began to arrive, the first thing that struck me was they had dressed up. Janice had changed into a shift dress and a cardigan sweater,

Jojo wore a short little black dress with dangly earrings and some lipstick; Brandon had donned a bow tie, and Oliver a navy cashmere v-neck sweater. I looked at Glenn. We had been cooking, cleaning, and moving furniture for hours. "I feel like a dust mop."

"We dimmed the lights."

"Yes. Thank goodness."

Oliver presented us with a bottle of Moet Chandon. "For the oystahs," he said in his best New York accent.

"Shall we sit?" Marco said. He had insisted that I be a guest at the feast, that he and Glenn would serve each course before they sat down to join us. While Oliver filled the champagne glasses, Glenn entered the café with a large tray, the oysters crackled and popped as he set the dishes before us.

When we were all seated Oliver raised his glass. "To a wonderful group of people. I am having a heck of a good time." He paused. "And to my sister, Rosalie Finnegan Hart, may I never stay away so long again."

I sipped my champagne and raised my glass. "I'd like to add to that."

"Let's hear it," Oliver said.

"To Kevin."

"To Kevin," they replied in unison.

Oliver slurped his first oyster and smacked his lips. "Damn, these are good."

The pasta course was paired with an Italian chardonnay. As we devoured the small portions of ricotta and sage-filled raviolis, spaghetti with freshly shaved truffles, and the fettuccini with cream and sausage, our voices grew louder, our faces animated. At one point Marco tapped his glass to gain our attention.

"How is the pasta?"

Groans of delight resounded in the room.

"I don't know how you Italians do it," Janice said. "If I ate like this every night I'd be as big as a house."

"Ah, did you know," Marco said, "That Sophia Loren once said, 'Everything you see here, I owe to pasta.'" He smiled. "And remember, my friends, what I said about eating good food with friends and family. You don't age and you don't get fat."

"Well then," she said. "What's next?"

When Marco returned with the rock fish, it was to a standing ovation. He had previously brushed away all of the salt crust, and what remained was the most tender and moist fish I had ever tasted.

I wiped my mouth with my napkin and said, "I don't know about the rest of you, but I feel as if I'm dining in a piazza in Florence."

"Here, here," Jojo said.

"But may I remind you," I continued, "that every morsel of food in this meal was prepared by us."

As the whooping and cheers began, I glanced over at the door and startled when I realized Phoebe was staring in. "Jojo," I said. "Phoebe's here."

The room fell silent.

"What the heck?" Janice said. "Why is she here, Jo?"

Jojo's back was to the door. She turned to see her sister and faced forward again.

"You can't just ignore her," Janice said. "She knows we see her."

Jojo tossed her wadded napkin on the table and pushed back her chair. Glenn hopped up to open the lock. A whisper of fear breezed down my back.

"Glenn," I said. "What if?"

He stopped when he reached the door and looked out at Phoebe. He wiggled his hands in the air and pointed at her. She frowned but eventually realized what he wanted and pulled her hands from the pockets and opened her palms.

"Pockets," Glenn called through the door.

Jojo watched closely.

Phoebe pulled the lining of her pockets inside out. A set of car keys tumbled onto the sidewalk. "Okay?" she said as she bent over to pick them up.

Glenn nodded and unlocked the door.

Jojo held her hand out for her sister so she could climb over the hole in the ground that was once my steps. "Careful," she said, and shut the door.

"Phoebs, what are you doing here?"

"I have to talk to you." She sniffled and wiped her nose with the back of her hand. "I've been texting you all day."

"I don't have any answers to your questions." Jojo glanced at us, eyes wary.

"Why did he do it?" Phoebe said, her throat tight with tears. "Why did he change his will?"

"First of all, I don't really know how you and Barty are so sure he changed it. I'd never seen the will before in my life. But either way, we'll figure this out."

"No." Phoebe shook her head several times. "It's too late."

"Look, I'll call you tomorrow. Maybe we can get a coffee after class."

When Jojo reached out to touch her arm, Phoebe shrugged her away. She gazed over at the candle lit table. "Wow."

Jojo grabbed the door handle. "You need to go. I'll call you. I promise."

Phoebe jammed her hands into her pockets. She looked down and said, "spider." Glenn, who stood behind her waiting to lock the door, started to step on it.

"Wait!" She knelt down and coaxed the spider into her cupped hand. She covered it with her other hand and stood.

"*Signora*," Marco said, "perhaps you would like to join us for dinner. We have more than enough food to share with you."

My heart warmed at Marco's kind gesture. But that was the Italian way, all inclusive, the more mouths to feed the better.

"Um, no, I have to go." Phoebe ducked her head. "Michael told me to come straight home after I talked to Jojo." She started to go but stopped. "Thank you, sir. For inviting me to dinner."

I stood and hurried over to her. "Phoebe? How about if I bring you some of this food tomorrow. We have so much. If you need to get home, I'll share it with you tomorrow. I'll stop by in the morning?"

"No. Don't do that. Don't come to my house. You mustn't."

"Ok," I said. "No worries. Look, let me take you out the back door. I don't want you to hurt yourself." She followed me into the kitchen, her hands still cupping the spider.

Once everyone returned to their seats, Brandon said, "That woman is a walking oxymoron.First she's making demands and then she rescues a spider."

"Something tells me that spider was pretty content where he was," Oliver said.

"My uncle used to smash every spider he saw," Jojo said. "Phoebe hated it. She would pull a tick off the dog and carry it outside. She rescues every living thing she finds. Mammals, reptiles, insects—"

Oliver smiled. His face glowing in the candlelight. "And the tick would jump back on the dog the next morning?"

Jojo's shoulders fell. "Yup. Exactly."

"Your sister?" Brandon said. "She's married?"

"Yes." Jojo pressed her napkin back into her lap. "To Michael."

Brandon leaned forward, elbows propped on the table. "I can tell you four things about that man and I'll bet I'll be right."

"No way," Oliver said. "What's one?"

"He either gambles or has a drug addiction or both."

Jojo's mouth dropped open. "He gambles. On the Internet. And he's terrible at it. He also sells drugs. But I don't think he uses them."

Brandon glanced around the room, a proud smile on his face.

"Two," Janice barked. "Let's hear it."

"Okay, um, oh, I know, he hates his father."

"Does he?" Oliver said.

Jojo's mouth dropped open. "They haven't spoken in years. Do you know Michael, Doc?"

"Nope. These are just educated guesses." He rubbed his chin. "Ah, he was once at the top of his game, maybe in high school, homecoming king or something. And now he's a bit of a bully."

"Jojo?" I said.

"He was the quarterback of the football team. He got kicked off for cheating on an exam. And, yes, he rules their roost. I think that's why Phoebe doesn't want kids."

"You googled him," Janice said.

"No, I didn't," Brandon said. "It's just a fun little game I like to play."

"You said four," Oliver urged.

"Okay, how about this. He drives a pickup."

"Bleep," Janice said making the sound of a buzzer. "That *so* doesn't count. If you said he *didn't* drive a pickup, then I'd be impressed."

"Well, let's see, he's bald."

Oliver leaned forward. "And Jojo, for the two-thousand-dollar question, is the man bald?"

"No." Jojo laughed. "You're human, Doc. Michael has a full head of red hair."

"Oh." Brandon frowned. "I hate when that happens."

"And now," Marco stood, "I believe it's time for dessert and some *Vin Santo. Sì?*"

We responded with a unanimous, "*Sì!*"

Chapter Thirty-One

After much deliberation, I decided I wasn't going to avoid Tyler and Bini the next morning. I still rose early*ish*, anxious to get to the café, but had something I needed to do first. I was glad it was Friday. We would have a break from class for two days and I could focus on the investigation.

I trotted down the steps to the kitchen and noticed dirty coffee mugs in the sink. Good, I thought. They're here. I sat at the table and fired up my computer. First on my agenda: google Bini's lawyer, Jack Morris, to see if he was the guy to get the job done. I learned he specialized in wills and estate planning and had an average of two and a half stars on find a lawyer dot com.

I closed my computer and took notes on the investigation. So far our suspects were Sonja, Bartlett, Phoebe and her husband, and Jojo. I still couldn't rule out Brandon because of his access to the salt. His behavior last night was curious. For someone who says he often feels invisible, he was quite the life of the party.

And then there's Phoebe. Oxymoron, someone said. I was beginning to think Phoebe's husband, Michael, could be the force behind her pleas to Jojo. Phoebe was in the kitchen after the will reading. She looked wretched that night. Could Michael have put her up to poisoning the salt and the liquor?

The next step was to find out about the contract for sale of the farm. After generations of his family owning Windswept Farm, why would Kline suddenly be so willing to sell?

Next I typed up a list of questions, printed it out, fluffed my hair, gave my lips a touch of color, and went to find Bini and Tyler.

The air was warmer and the sun was just poking through a bank of gray clouds that hung low over the river. I tossed some breakfast scraps, sans the bread, into the chicken coop and kept walking. Tyler and Bini were at the goat barn. It was a smallish building painted a clean, bright white. Light filtered in between the slats as I entered the barn, the air saturated with the smell of milk and straw.

Bini was perched on a three-legged stool bottle-feeding a kid who sucked eagerly. Tyler sunk his pitch fork into a bale of hay. I held his gaze. He looked tired. His lips turned down and his eyes seemed almost pleading. I crossed my arms but he said nothing. I wondered if he missed me as much as I ached for him. For the first time since Wednesday night, I got a hint that he might be as miserable as me.

"Good morning," I said cautiously. "What an adorable animal." I looked down at the kid. "How old is he?"

"*She* is six weeks," Bini said.

"I've got names for them. Four girls and a boy, right?"

A small smile appeared on Tyler's face. Bini shook her head.

"The first one is Serena. As in Serena Williams. Because she's the GOAT, right? Greatest of all time?"

Bini hitched the kid up higher in her lap.

"The next one I'm stuck on. Meryl Streep or Betty White?"

"Definitely Betty White," Tyler said.

"Both." Bini looked up. "And the male?"

"That one was easy. Cal. As in Cal Ripken."

Tyler's smile grew wider.

"I have something for you," I said to Bini and held the sheet of paper out for her.

"I can't exactly look at that right now. I think it's pretty obvious why."

"Fine, then." I handed it to Tyler.

He pulled a pair of wire-rimmed glasses from his shirt pocket, frowned, and looked up at me. "These are questions."

"For Jack Morris."

Bini huffed out a laugh. "You get an overnight law degree?"

"He specializes in estate planning," I said, accenting my consonants. "If you're not willing to go to Baltimore for a criminal lawyer, you're going to need my help."

Tyler looked down again. "Find out Kline's time of death."

"There's more," I said. "But to sum it up, I've been doing research. It takes just a few minutes for a lethal dose of water hemlock to kill someone after he's ingested it. The sheriff tested the bottle of Maker's Mark in Kline's house. It was loaded. Enough to kill quickly. You need to pinpoint when you left the farm and arrived at Kline's. He was dead when you arrived. If you can present evidence of the exact time you got there, it will clear you of any guilt. The coroner must have determined a time of death. Your lawyer needs to find out from the sheriff when that was. Tyler and I can vouch that you were at the farm most of the morning."

"Were you wearing a Fitbit?" Tyler read the next question. He looked up at Bini. "You wear one all the time."

"Also, did you text anyone? Stop for coffee? See anyone on the road? Or were Tyler and I the last people who saw you before you arrived at Kline's?" They were both looking at me with puzzled expressions, foreheads creased. "Never mind. Just please give those questions to your lawyer, Bini. He needs to be proactive before the trail runs dry."

Tyler gripped the sheet of paper. "How—"

"I have to get to class." I spun around and hurried back to the house. I didn't want to hear their protestations or anymore of Bini's sarcasm. And I wanted to give them time to 'think.' By the time I entered the kitchen, I realized my heart was pounding in my chest and I felt a little light-headed.

I found Oliver at the kitchen table, yesterday's paper open before him. "You look like you saw a ghost," he said. "I was wondering if you had any in this old place. Must be a couple of them hooting around. I hope they're friendly. I wonder—"

"We're leaving. Now."

"Yes, Master Chef." Oliver stood and saluted.

Chapter Thirty-Two

I had a chance to calm down on the way into town and Oliver, who seemed to sense my unsettledness, kept the conversation light.

Once inside, he said he needed to run a quick errand, so I sat at the bar and rested my chin on my hand, waiting for the coffee to finish.

My stomach did a somersault. Why did Tyler have to look so good? That sandy blond hair thick and loose around his head. His work shirt open a few buttons, sleeves rolled up exposing those strong arms. And he was so tall. I loved that he was tall. My favorite place in the world was in his arms, my head on his chest.

My heart plummeted. It was happening again. Another relationship failure. And I felt blindsided. Again. He didn't even let me explain how the sheriff jumped to conclusions. Maybe I was unlovable. What word did Janice use? Difficult?

I traced a circle on the countertop with a finger. But he smiled. I made him smile. So why didn't he come after me? I thought about that some more. I did practically run back to the house. Maybe he did try and come after me.

I knew from the moment I first saw Tyler, we had a connection. It wasn't any one specific thing, just a knowing. We both stopped in our tracks on that first day and took each other in. We had every reason to dislike one another, but instead, I invited him into my home. We took it slow, testing the waters, becoming familiar, gaining trust. And then he kissed me. That kiss. How does the right kiss solidify so much? I laughed to myself. My mother was right. The kiss was everything. It should be lovely, not forced or sloppy. After that kiss, I felt as if I'd found my home.

The aroma of the freshly-ground Costa Rican blend met my nose. I stood as the last of the coffee trickled into the steel carafe. Oliver strode into the café and I noted how ridiculously happy I was that he was here with me through all of this.

"I had to buy a toothbrush. You ushered me out so fast this morning I didn't get to brush my teeth." He headed to the bathroom. A few minutes later he was back. "Ah," he said. "Much more better." He filled two mugs with coffee and looked at me. "Penny for your thoughts? No, wait, five bucks for your thoughts. They're worth at least that."

"I'll be okay."

"I'm here if you need me. You know that?"

"Yes. And thank you." I went into the kitchen and pulled a large wooden board down from a high shelf.

Oliver stood next to me. "Is that Aunt Charlotte's old bread kneading board?"

"The one and only."

"That thing must be at least sixty years old. Do you use it?"

I reached for a canister of bread flour. "It's all I did when I arrived at Barclay Meadow. I made so much bread I couldn't give it away."

"You and Charlotte made bread together all the time." Oliver stared off. "Did I ever help?"

I placed a large bowl on the counter. "You never seemed very interested in food other than eating it."

"Until now. I'm in a freakin' cooking class." He smiled. "Go figure."

"Marco asked me to make some Tuscan bread. Do you know they don't salt their bread?"

Oliver made a face. "Sounds nasty."

"He must have a reason." I slipped my hair into a ponytail and scrubbed my hands. "You know, the kneading is the best part. Want to get out some aggression? Ed took quite a beating those first few months."

"Um, no. I made pasta dough. That's enough for one week."

I sifted a cup of flour into the bowl. "So what did you do while we spent those six weeks every summer with Aunt Charlotte?"

153

"I honestly don't remember. You know, Rosie, I think I'm going to take a walk. Do you mind if I take my mug?"

"The sun is shining for the first time in days. I think that's a grand idea."

He hesitated. "If Tyler can't see your quality, better yet, understand what motivates you, then he doesn't deserve you. Got that?"

"Got it."

Once I finished kneading the bread, I set the bowl near the pilot light and covered it with a cloth. I checked on the beans I had been asked to soak overnight, and added some fresh water. I hadn't eaten anything yet, but I wasn't hungry. I knew the feeling well. My lawyer called it the divorce diet. Haha. Funny guy. But he was right. And here we go again. I stood still and allowed myself to feel the pain that had been burrowing a hole in my gut. It radiated through me and I had to catch my breath. There it is. Duly noted. Okay, now get through this day.

I heard something. A rap on the glass? I went into the kitchen and opened the door for Marco.

"It's a glorious day, Rosalie." He stepped inside, jostling several paper grocery bags. "I've heard your Maryland weather has its merits. It is finally allowing me to experience them."

"*Buongiorno*, Marco. I'm happy to see you." I locked the door behind him

He set the bags on the counter. "Your brother is in the park charming the *Nonne*."

"Is he now." I smiled. "And I am certain they are loving it."

Marco carried the bags into the restaurant. He started his own espresso and began lining up the vegetables, setting aside several large cans of crushed tomatoes. I sat at the bar and watched. I had never seen someone so completely proficient at everything he did in a kitchen. It was like watching a concert pianist, fingers deft, no need for the music in front of you, it was pure instinct, a practiced art he had perfected.

Once the espresso was ready, he picked up the cup and leaned back against the sink. "You are, how you say, blue?"

"I'm sorry. I'm feeling better now."

"Why apologize? Emotions are what they are. And they exist for a reason.

It's what you do with them that matters. Most importantly, don't let them take over. They are just one part of you."

I sat straighter. "That's very true."

He slurped his first sip. "Rosalie, I don't know if I can properly imagine what it must be like to have someone poisoned in your restaurant. I have been thinking about this a great deal. It is a chef's very worst nightmare."

Marco's words sifted through me and I realized I hadn't allowed myself to really process the tragedy of Kevin's poisoning. I was too busy focusing on preventing it from happening again.

"Before you arrived, I was thinking of the reason I opened this café. When my family was still intact, I would cook a three-course dinner for them every single week night. I lit candles and insisted they stowed their phones. When Annie reached high school and Ed was working all the time, we often didn't eat until 9:00. But I cooked a dinner anyway. I was insistent we had that time together. No computers. No distractions. It was my way of nurturing the people I love. Problem is, after the divorce, I had no one to cook for."

"You found the perfect solution. People gather here and I can guarantee they feel nurtured by you. See, you are beautifully resilient." He smiled. "The people you have surrounded yourself with, they are loyal to you, are they not?"

"Yes. I think that's true."

"And your staff, they are happy? No turnover?"

"We have a good team." I studied him. "Marco? Why did you stay? You could have been poisoned, too."

"I thought about it a long time. But we chefs stick together. And the law was handling it. No one would try to commit the same crime twice in the same place. And in Italy, no one questions the *Gendarme*. Not if you want to stay out of prison." Marco came to attention. "I have an idea."

"I'm intrigued."

"My dear, Rosalie, when is the last time someone cooked a meal for *you*?"

"Just me?" I thought for a moment. "Oh, my goodness. Never? I mean, maybe since my mother died?"

He rubbed his hands together. "Go sit at that table in the corner. The one where the sun is filling the space with light. I am about to make you an Italian breakfast. Prepare yourself to be, how you say, nurtured?"

I gave him a wry smile. "I didn't think Italians were too keen on breakfast. Usually just a strong coffee and a biscuit."

He tilted his head. "True enough. But I will make an exception." He spun around and ducked into the kitchen.

Chapter Thirty-Three

I liked sitting at the table in the corner. I could admire the view and be warmed by the sun. I waved as Doris Bird trudged by. Her face lit up when she saw me. Then she stopped and pointed at the steps. She shrugged her shoulders and shook her head. Then she smiled, tapped her watch indicating she was in a hurry, and continued on her way.

I noticed Sonja across the street, her hair streaming down her back, her strides long and deliberate. I hopped up and hurried outside. Once across the street, I called out her name.

She stopped and lowered her sunglasses. "Rosalie."

"How are you?"

"I thought you would call me." Her lips were perfectly lined with a pale pink shade.

"I'm sorry?"

"There is an opening in your cooking school. You were down a student on the second day. And yet you didn't invite me to join you."

"How did you . . . I mean, things were very chaotic. Were you serious about the class?"

"Serious as a heart attack." She smiled slowly. "Oh, well. Things happen, I guess."

"I was hopeful Kevin would be well enough to return." I tried to gather my thoughts. How did this woman always manage to be one step ahead of me? "Sonja, I have a question for you. You spoke of your father in the past tense. Did you come to Cardigan to find him?"

Her lips trembled. "Why did you ask me that?"

"Do you think you'll find him alive?" I hugged myself, her gaze was intense.

"No."

"But you are looking for him?"

Her spine was ramrod straight. "I know where he is. I just haven't figured out how to get to him."

I tried to convey compassion, but the woman was intimidating. "Can I ask why you think he's dead?"

"I don't think, I know. And I know who killed him. You see my father was here for the right reasons. He had a contract with the US government. He watched Russian companies who were up to no good. When they were flagged, he would investigate. He was a very noble man."

"He was here to stop the sale of Kline's farm." My mind raced. "How did you trace him?"

She removed her sunglasses and swiped a finger under her eye. "I was his only daughter. He texted me when he landed in Philly and I put a trace on his phone. I always worried about him. The last signal was from Windswept Farm."

"Why are you telling me this?"

"I want you to help me."

"How?"

"Get Ms. Bennett to let me onto her farm so that I can find my father." She crossed her arms, which was difficult to do with the large red patent leather Chanel bag on her shoulder. "Aren't you curious, Rosalie? Don't you want to know?"

I laughed. "Of course, I do. Do you know if he was able to stop the sale?"

"No. I think Kline killed him before he could do anything."

"I'm curious what the government was concerned about. Were they going to do some sort of surveillance?"

"I don't care about any of that. I just want justice for my father." She flipped her hair off her shoulder. "So you won't help me?"

"When do you want to do this?"

She studied me for a moment. "I'll let you know." She bumped past me and continued down the street. I watched her go, wondering where on earth she was headed. But then I noticed a guy in a pickup hop out of his truck and hold out something for her to autograph.

I spun around and combed my hands through my hair. Marco. I ran across the street, dodging a Subaru. I climbed over the hole in the sidewalk and clamored into the café. I brushed the dust from my skirt just as he backed through the doors with a plate on each forearm. I was in my seat by the time he set breakfast in front of me: a perfectly poached egg, a slice of my signature bread dripping with butter, a side of stewed tomatoes with a basil garnish, and several slices of crisped prosciutto. The aromas filled my head and suddenly I was hungry. Very hungry.

He snapped out a cloth napkin and draped it over my lap. "I will leave you to your thoughts." He smiled. "And your emotions."

"No," I said quickly. "Please stay. I don't want to eat alone."

"Yes, of course." He sat across from me. "I was hoping you would say that."

"It's beautiful, Marco. Thank you."

"It is my deepest pleasure."

I looked at him. "I'm not so sure that's true."

"You would be surprised. Why do any of us love to cook? To eat what we cook? That is never the case. We cook to delight others."

"Food is power," I said.

"In many ways." Marco sat back in his chair. "You took your divorce very hard. No?"

"Of course. It rocked my world."

"That always puzzles me. Why don't we humans realize what an enormous expectation it is to be married to the same person for most of our lives? Humans are driven to find variety."

"I take it you're divorced?"

"My ex-wife and I are the best of friends. I still love her. And we have a wonderful daughter."

"Did she take it hard?"

"Yes. But I was a chef. It's a difficult life to be married to someone who has another love."

"Oh, you had an affair."

"With my restaurants. They can be all consuming. And the hours are unforgiving." He scraped some crumbs into his hand. "She's married to an accountant now."

"And you?"

"I opened another restaurant."

Our eyes met, his gaze so intense I had to look away.

"Rosalie?"

I looked back at him. "Yes?"

"You're not eating your breakfast."

Chapter Thirty-Four

Friday
Day Four of Cooking Class
Cucina Povera/Poor Italy
or
The Bean Eaters

Menu
Antipasti/Appetizers
Cecina pane con rosmarino/Chickpea flour flat bread with rosemary
Rosalie

Prima/First Course
Panzanella/Bread Salad
Joanna and Brandon

Segundo/Main Course
Fagioli Zolfini all' olio novo con salvia fritta/
Zolfini beans in new oil with fried sage
Janice and Oliver

Dolce/Dessert
PannaCotta/Grandma's Cake with Pine Nuts
Rosalie

"Nothing but time is wasted in Italy"
-Thomas Bailey Aldrich

Marco clapped his hands and asked us to gather, but it was like herding chickens. Janice watched her phone while sipping a prosecco. Oliver was next to her doing pretty much the same thing. Brandon struggled to make an espresso and I was worried he might break the Miele. Jojo was at a corner table, her head resting on her folded arms.

"Sorry everyone is so distracted," I said to Marco.

"This is not your responsibility, my dear. But, of course, you would care. A chef has to read his kitchen and his patrons. These people have a lot on their minds. I see that." He hesitated. "As do you?"

"Not so much after that fabulous breakfast."

"Well, then. I believe we both know how to get their attention."

"We start cooking."

"*Sí, Signora.*" Marco rapped a knife on the side of his espresso cup. "My friends? Shall we commence?"

When everyone had gathered, Marco smiled and wiggled his eyebrows. "It is nice to see your faces. I've been looking at nothing but the tops of your heads this morning."

Janice nudged Oliver. "He's talking about me."

"I believe I'm equally guilty as charged."

"I draw your attention to the quote I have shared with you." Marco paused while we all gazed at the chalkboard. "Today we will talk about 'the poor Tuscans.' Or, the bean eaters, as they are often referred to. You see, food was extravagant and readily available to the wealthy families of Florence. But outside the city, the poor farmers, who had to surrender their best grains and vegetables to the wealthy, were forced to eat what remained. But, being Italian, they did not suffer. The food you will be making today are examples of this.

"To begin, we have chickpea flatbread. While the wealthy snatched up the rich semolina flour, the farmers resorted to making chickpea flour. Rosalie

162

will be preparing this savory bread. Joanna and Brandon will make one of my favorite Tuscan dishes, *panzanella*, where day old bread is soaked in olive oil to provide the main component of this delicious salad. Janice and Oliver, who have thankfully stowed their devices, will be cooking with the *zolfini*, the white beans Rosalie so generously soaked overnight.

"So today, my friends, we will eat like peasants. And we won't be hungry or disappointed." He smiled broadly. "Questions?"

"Does that say *fried* sage?" Janice said.

"*Sí, Signora.* It is *delizioso*."

She shrugged. "We'll give it a shot, won't we Oliver?"

"I have a question, Chef," Brandon said. "When do we start?"

While we waited for the beans to finish cooking, I stood next to Janice and looked over her shoulder at her phone. "Is Trevor at Bonnie's today?"

"No sign of him."

"And yet you continue to watch."

"I'm freakin' obsessed. But my guy keeps turning the camera on the house next door. I think maybe Trevor's onto the private detective. I think he's going through the back door or through the neighbor's back yard. That's why he keeps his camera on that house. See," she said and pointed. "This is the house next to Bonnie's. There's a bunch of guys carrying equipment and stuff into it. So who the heck cares about that?" She frowned. "I keep trying to see in the back yard."

"Can I look?"

Janice handed me her phone. I moved my fingers over the screen to enlarge the view. "Looks like someone is moving in." Several large men in dark suits carried boxes into the house. Suits? Who wears a suit to move? Perhaps it was a fancy moving company. Some sort of gimmick. "Maybe he got bored and was trying to figure out who those people are." I narrowed my eyes. A tall man carried an open box with a large antennae jutting out of the top. I noticed lettering on the side. I'd seen those words before.

"Hey," Janice said, "give me my phone." She placed it face down on the bar. "Now who's obsessed?"

"It is a little addictive. But what about smart phones isn't addicting?" I walked around to the other side of the bar. "Was Trevor there yesterday?"

"For a quickie. Twenty minutes tops." Her lips turned down into a small pout. "Crappity crap crap. I don't know what to do. He was so sweet to me last night it made me cry." She plopped down onto a bar chair. "Isn't that what they do? Act all nice because they're getting their needs met somewhere else? Everything is all lovely and new? Why not be nice to your wife?"

"Once you are convinced something is going on, Snow White, it's easy to find evidence to prove your theory. Maybe you could just enjoy cooking school and not think about it. Your private detective is on this."

"It's not that easy, Rose Red. I've been with Trevor since high school. He's my world. I could never do what you did. Get a divorce and start over. I'm not cut out for that." She shook her head. "No way, no how."

I wanted to say, neither was I, but this wasn't about me. This was Janice facing a terror she'd never imagined. "I can see why you're scared. But maybe have a little fun here today? Let the food heal your soul?"

"I know you're right. I should enjoy this while I can. But the mere thought of food makes me nauseated. My birthday is in a week. I love birthdays. And Trevor always rocks mine. But now I'm dreading it. It will all be a big fake."

"I know how you feel. I have been there for sure. But this feels different to me. For some reason I want to give Trevor the benefit of the doubt. At least for now." I met her gaze. "He would be more lost without you, than you without him. You are his world. I see how he lights up when you enter a room. How have you forgotten that?"

"Yeah, well, he can't have it both ways." She picked up her empty champagne glass and trudged into the kitchen.

As I scooped fresh berries onto the panna cotta, I noticed Brandon and Jojo had finished their dish. They sat at the bar together, close enough for me to overhear their conversation.

"How are things with your brother and sister?" Brandon said. "Have they calmed down at all?"

Jojo's lips were pressed together. She had dark circles under her eyes for the first time since I'd known her. "I haven't heard from Barty in a couple of days. When this first happened, he was out at the farm every day all day."

"Well, that must be a relief."

She shook her head. "Not really. When I'm around him at least I know what he's thinking."

"Have you thought about when you'll move in?"

"Actually, yeah. I don't think the house should be empty. Plus I've got to take care of the farm. But I don't have a clue what I'm doing. I don't even know how to fire up a tractor. Let alone cultivate a field."

Glenn appeared next to me. Our eyes met and he gave me a knowing look.

"It's a big place," Brandon said.

"Have you seen it, Doc?"

"I google-earthed it. It's quite a sizable piece of property."

"I guess I need to have Barty start working again. He said something about spraying the fields."

Glenn stepped closer. "Um, Jojo, my dear. This is none of my business, but maybe you might want to start doing things the way *you* want to do them."

Jojo frowned. "What are you saying, Mr. Glenn?"

"Well, for one, did you realize your brother wants to spray chlorpyrifos on the crops?"

"What's that?"

"A very deadly and toxic pesticide. It's illegal in some states. And it will be in Maryland by the end of next year. It's been linked to several cancers."

"My goodness," she said. "That's really awful." She placed a palm over her forehead. "But I have no idea how to do this. I mean, where do I even start?"

"Jojo," Brandon said, "how about you and I have a glass of wine at that new wine house in town after class. They serve warm olives and bruschetta. I'll take my computer and we can do some research."

"Oh, I like that idea a lot. But don't you have somewhere to be, Doc?"

"I believe I mentioned my assistant is handling things."

"I don't mean to butt in," I said. "But I'm sure Tyler would be happy to help you, too. He knows everything there is to know about organic farming."

"Wow," Jojo said. "I'm the luckiest girl on the planet. You guys are awesome."

Chapter Thirty-Five

Steam rose from the last of the plates as Glenn removed them from the dishwasher. "Thanks for the help," he said as he lifted a glass and buffed it with a clean towel.

"We haven't had a chance to talk in forever," I said. "What did you make of Phoebe last night?"

"She seemed desperate to me."

"And she rescued a spider."

"As our Doctor Brandon said, a woman with many facets of her personality."

"I take it you didn't go to her house this morning?"

"I couldn't, Glenn. She looked terrified when I suggested it." I wiped down the stove top. "Her husband must be a tyrant."

"Maybe she is her husband's messenger," Glenn said. "Perhaps he is the suspect and she is doing his bidding. Maybe she's very consistent after all. A placater, peacemaker kind of person."

"She rescued a helpless spider," I said. "Perhaps she feels helpless in her own life."

Glenn untied his apron. "Any thoughts about Brandon?"

"He sure was having fun." I rinsed the sponge. "Although he comes across as very forthcoming. I wonder if there are secrets." I picked up a dish towel. "But who doesn't have secrets by the time you hit your thirties."

Glenn leaned against the sink. "Back to Phoebe. Maybe we could find out more about her husband. Could he be capable of murder? Or better yet, murder by proxy with a wife who, as you said, will do his bidding? Poisoning is a violent crime. But the perp doesn't have to do anything physical. If she also hated her uncle, perhaps it wasn't a stretch for her."

"All good points, Mr. Breckinridge," I said. "According to just about everyone, Kline was a mean man. All three of those children were damaged by him." I combed my hands through my hair. "I have an idea." I sat at the restaurant computer and brought it to life. "Let's google Phoebe's husband."

"Better yet," Glenn stood behind me, "log onto the website where you can check court records. MDreigstry dot com."

"Yes. Better idea." I typed the website into the search box.

Glenn placed his hand on the back of my chair. "Do you know their last name?"

"Jojo introduced Phoebe to us that first night. Remember? Phoebe Parker."

"That's it," Glenn said. "Let's do a search."

I opened the website and typed in Michael Parker, Devon County, Maryland. We waited while the three-colored circle spun slowly around. And then the list appeared.

"Driving while under the influence," Glenn said.

"Look at this," I said as I scrolled down. "Assault."

"There's another assault and battery," he said. "How is this man not in jail?"

"Glenn, here's another DUI." I looked up. "Remember Brandon guessed he had a fall from grace of some sort? Maybe he had dreams of playing college football before he got kicked off the team. That would be a tough break to handle."

"Yes, that would do some damage." Glenn adjusted his glasses. "Keep scrolling. I'm looking for a domestic violence charge."

We both studied the screen as the list continued. "I don't see any. I wonder if Phoebe would press charges even if that were the case."

"I think we're on to something." Glenn placed his hands on his hips.

"Agreed." I shut down the computer.

"Um, Rosalie, my dear?"

"Yes?"

"Are you still up for meeting at the Tavern or do you have a date tonight?"

"I'm going to make a little stop and then I have every intention of meeting you at the Tavern."

"Good. I'll see you there, in, what, an hour?"

"Yes. Most definitely." I checked my watch. "I need to get going."

"I think we are in good shape. I'll lock up after you leave." He reached up and aligned a coffee mug with the others. "And is it safe to assume you'll tell me about this little stop you're making when we meet?"

Bonnie's house was in a modest neighborhood not far from the small hospital in town and just a block from the college campus. I recognized it immediately from the video feed. I pulled behind a midsized white Ford sedan in need of some touchup paint and shut down the engine. I managed to get out of the café in time to catch Janice's private investigator still on duty.

I rapped on the passenger side window. The man behind the wheel was so startled he threw his Big Mac into the air. After composing himself, he buzzed down the window halfway and said, "I have every right to park here. It's a free country."

"Yes," I said. "Let's keep it that way."

He frowned. "What do you want?"

"I'll start over. Hi. I'm Rosalie Hart, a friend of Janice Tilghman's. I just wanted to chat with you. I promise I'm here on friendly terms." I hesitated. "Honestly? I'm really worried about my friend." I looped my fingers under the door handle. "Do you mind?"

He gathered up his sandwich and unlocked the door.

I climbed into the passenger seat and kept my feet close together. The floor was littered with empty water bottles, soda cans, cardboard coffee cups, and Nacho cheese Dorito bags which appeared to be his food of choice based on the number of them. The air was stale and filled with all kinds of scents ranging from old food and bad coffee to stagnant body odor. I was relieved when he didn't close the window.

He shifted in his seat. "Do you know how many people have asked me what I'm doing? I've had to move my car seven times."

I noticed a small digital camera mounted on the dashboard. "Janice is obsessed with your live feed."

"Happens all the time." He slipped an errant pickle into his sandwich and took a bite. "They all want to watch. It's like they want to see it, but they don't."

I glanced at him. A small paunch hung over his belt. His hair was shaved close to his head. Thick dark glasses framed his eyes. "Do you think Trevor is having an affair with the woman who lives in this house?"

"I don't know that, Ma'am. I just take the video."

"Can you see in the windows?"

"She keeps her blinds drawn. That's as far as I go. If Mrs. Tilghman wants me to tap his phone, that's gonna cost a little more. But these days, all she has to do is figure out his pass code and she can find out herself. Call history. Text messages. Instagram. Probably a voicemail or two. I tell 'em what to look for. Does he always have his phone by his side? Grab it if there's a text before she can see it? But I guess she wants the visual proof. Phone flirting ain't as bad as the physical stuff. Or maybe it is." He turned the sandwich looking for his next bite. "My industry is changing by the minute. I mostly do the tech stuff. But this here client wants to catch her husband in the act."

"This is not a tech industry I'm excited about. But, I guess I understand the necessity."

"You one of those romantic types?"

I looked over at him. "Used to be. You?"

"Dabbled in it." He checked the camera and adjusted the angle.

"Janice showed me the video of Trevor's truck right here in front of the house yesterday. And you saw him walking in?"

"Yeah. That happened. First and second day." He took another bite of the Big Mac.

"Has he been back?"

"Why do you think I would tell you that before Mrs. Tilghman?"

I tugged on my skirt. "I have no idea. That's not really why I'm here anyway."

He finished chewing. "I'm sorry?"

"I was watching the feed today. Janice was at my restaurant. She's attending my cooking school. You switched your camera angle to the house next door."

"Got bored. No sign of Mr. Tilghman."

"I saw the suits. Was there any audio?"

"They aren't speaking English. They all drive these giant black SUV's, tinted windows, the whole bit."

"There's a logo on the boxes. Do you know what language that is?"

He studied me as if he was grateful for an interesting conversation. "I googled it. Russian."

"You're a professional. What do you think they're doing here in Cardigan?"

"That's a very good question. I live in Wilmington. Cardigan seems like a nice, quiet little town. But if you ask me? And I kind of think you are. They are setting up some sort of operation."

I stared at the house. It needed some love. No hardy mums like Bonnie's house. The paint was chipping and the porch sagged. It looked like something the college would swallow up eventually and convert into an alumni relations office. Maybe admissions? "Again. Cardigan?"

"I am as intrigued as you are, Ma'am. Want me to keep a second camera on this house?"

"Charge it to Janice?" I laughed. "Just kidding. But, if you want to. Okay. How much?"

"Honestly? I don't like one bit of what I think is going on here. Sleepy little American town? Set up some kind of headquarters? I won't charge you a cent if you figure out what this is. I'm sitting here anyway."

I studied him. "Why do you do it?"

"You mean why am I a private detective?"

"Yeah."

"It's my job and I make good money."

"Mm, no." I shook my head. "There's always a reason. What compelled you to take your first case?"

"Why are you here?"

I smiled. "Excellent question. I think uncovering the truth helps me to deal with the mysteries in my own life. Does that make any sense?"

"My wife left me. And I still don't understand why. It haunts me every day."

I thought for a moment. "I totally get that." We took each other in. "It was really nice to meet you,—"

"Clifford."

"Thank you, Clifford." I grabbed the door handle. "You work weekends?"

"If someone is going to pay me, yes, of course."

I pulled a piece of paper from my purse and jotted down my phone number. "Let's keep tabs on these guys. Okay?"

"Somebody has to." He bunched his empty wrapper into a tight ball. "This is a crazy world we're living in."

"Agreed." Once I was out of the car, I gave him a friendly wave and shut the door.

Chapter Thirty-Six

An amber twilight sky glowed just above the horizon as I tucked my car next to Glenn's Volvo station wagon in the Cardigan Tavern parking lot. I shut my door and noticed Sonja's Porsche Carrera shining like a red ruby nestled among a pebble bed of pickups.

My eyes adjusted to the dimly-lit room. Pool balls smacked nearby and Merle Haggard crooned at a low volume. I spotted Glenn seated at the bar and sat next to him.

"How was your side trip?" Glenn sipped from a frosty martini.

"Fruitful." I hooked my purse under the bar.

"I started without you. I hope you don't mind."

"I certainly didn't expect you to sit here twiddling your thumbs."

"Oh, I've been doing that too." Glenn smiled. "Did you notice the car?"

"How could I miss it?" I smoothed my hair and smiled at Chuck as he made his way over to us, a dish towel draped over his shoulder.

"It's been a while." Chuck's bald head shone as if polished, and a trimmed soul patch was on the center of his chin. "Welcome back."

"I forgot how much I like it here."

"Glad you remembered." Chuck dipped his head closer. "You two on another case?"

I smiled. "You might say that."

He slapped his hand on the bar. "I knew it. When I heard about Kevin, I was real curious what you were doing about it."

"Everything we possibly can," I said. "And we have no idea who did it. Which means it could happen to someone else."

Chuck picked up a pint glass drying on a rubber mat and flipped it upright. "I'll let you settle in. Blue Point?"

I placed my palms on the glossy wood. "Yes, please."

Chuck set my beer on a cocktail napkin and took a few more orders at the other end of the bar.

I glanced around room. "Have you spotted Sonja yet?"

"Booth in the far corner. She's with a man. Their heads have been ducked together for some time now."

Chuck returned. "Who's caught your eye?"

"The woman in the booth over there. Has she ever been in here before?"

Chuck followed my gaze. "Oh, yeah. She's a crowd favorite."

Glenn removed the toothpick stacked with green olives from his glass. "We love our celebrities. Let's just hope she doesn't start up a reality show in Cardigan."

"Right?" Chuck laughed. "I got to tell you, having her around has perked up my business. When that Porsche is in the lot, place fills up real fast. You know she plays a queen on that HBO show?"

I sat a little straighter. "When did she start coming in?"

Showed up a couple of weeks ago." Chuck eyed me. "You think she has something to do with Kevin. How so?"

"She was in the café the morning Kevin was poisoned. Came in through the kitchen. Had plenty of time to taint the salt Kevin tasted."

"I don't suppose she mentioned why she was in Cardigan?" Glenn said.

"Oh, wait," I said. "I already know this. No need to divulge, Chuck."

"Do tell, my dear," Glenn said.

"Her father disappeared not long ago and for some reason she's looking for him here."

Chuck noticed a man signaling for his check. "Be back in a few."

Glenn leaned in. "Why on earth does she think he's in Cardigan?" Glenn set the toothpick on the cocktail napkin.

"She traced him here through his phone."

"I feel as if I'm a paragraph behind. How on earth does one do that?" Glenn folded his arms and leaned back in his chair. "And your stop this afternoon?"

I filled Glenn in on my visit with Cliff. "Remember Ronnie's contract to sell the farm?"

"I made the connection as soon as you started talking. So this Russian company," Glenn made quotations marks in the air, "is trying to buy a very large farm on a very remote part of the Eastern Shore of Maryland." He thought for a moment. "And you are his closest neighbor. Do you ever hear or see anything?"

"Never."

"What's on the other side?"

"A wildlife preserve. People go there to bird watch."

"So this property is very isolated and yet, as the crow flies, not far from Baltimore or DC." Glenn frowned.

"Good lord, you're giving me chills."

"Hey," Oliver said from behind us. "Sorry I'm late."

"I'm so happy you came."

"As am I," Glenn said.

"Nice to see you out of the kitchen, Glenn." He eyed my beer. "Can I taste?"

"Of course."

Oliver took a sip and caught Chuck's eye. He pointed to my beer and Chuck gave him a thumbs up."

When Chuck arrived with a pint glass, beer sloshing over the side, he said, "You two twins?"

"I'm much older and wiser," Oliver said.

Chuck laughed and moved on.

Oliver had a long sip of beer. "Where did you go after class?"

"I had to make a quick stop."

He looked over at me and winked. "Something sleuthy?"

"Um, yes." I took a sip of beer. Bonnie Raitt purred a romantic song in the background. I felt a tug of longing for Tyler. After a deep breath, I glanced at Oliver and followed his gaze. He had spotted Sonja.

"Who's that guy?" he said. "He looks military."

"Glenn said they've been talking for almost an hour."

Glenn pushed his glasses up his nose. "There's some sort of lettering on the man's jacket. Looks like a picture of a dog. Can either of you make it out?"

"You three look like you need to sit closer to the blackboard," Chuck said. "What are you squinting at?"

"The man with Sonja," I said. "Do you know him?"

"Name's Gunner."

"Wait," Oliver said. "Did you say *Gunner?*"

"It's a pretty common name around here. And I can guarantee there are more Gunners on the Shore than Olivers."

Oliver took another sip. "Duly noted."

"His jacket says something about a tracking dog," I said.

"That's right. Started working with dogs in the army. He did several tours. He takes that dog all over the world. Natural disasters, bombings, you name it."

"Fascinating," Glenn said. "How do you think he knows Sonja?"

"Oh, I know this one too," I said. "If Gunner does searches, Sonja wants him to find her father."

"That's his business," Chuck said. "He can even help people find lost pets."

"That's pretty cool," Oliver said.

"She's trying to hire him," I said. "I wonder if he'll do it."

"How's your martini?" Chuck said to Glenn.

"*Perfetta.*"

"Ok, I'll be back." Chuck walked away and cleared some more glasses.

Bonnie was just finishing up her song. "Did you go home after class?" I asked Oliver.

"You're wondering if I saw Tyler?"

"Am I that transparent?"

"I did in fact have an encounter with Mr. Wells."

"How did it go?" I took a long slug of beer.

"I think he wanted to tell you himself that Bini is cleared. Kline died several hours before she got to his house. I guess her lawyer started asking questions about the time of death and got Wilgus to drop the charges."

"Well, what do you know." I smiled. "That's the best news I've heard all week."

"He seemed disappointed he didn't get to see you."

"Really?"

"We had a beer together. Sat in the front room and he watched for your car the entire time."

"Last I checked, I still have a phone."

"This isn't any of my business, but sometimes a text is far less personal. Maybe he wanted to reconnect in person. That seems classier to me."

I pondered Oliver's words. Tyler wasn't a risk taker. He would have wanted to see my eyes before he made an attempt to apologize. Oliver was right.

Glenn nudged my arm. "Barty's at the end of the bar."

"Well, what do you know. You said we might learn something tonight, and we're in the thick of it. Coming here was a fabulous idea."

"Looks like an intense conversation with the man next to him," Glenn said. "Do you know who the other guy is?"

"No. But Chuck will."

I watched as Sonja stood and shook the dog tracker's hand. They said good-bye and she walked up to the bar and stood next to an attractive woman with a Cosmo in front of her. Their heads ducked together, and the woman barked out a hearty laugh.

Glenn, Oliver, and I had stopped our conversation to watch. Chuck appeared and leaned back on the bar, arms crossed. "Notice how packed it is in here?"

"Now that you mention it," I said.

"Get ready for our Friday night entertainment. And there's no cover charge."

"Who's the woman with Sonja?" Oliver said.

"That's Trixie." A small smile appeared on Chuck's face. "She used to be Patricia. Or Trisha as most folks called her. Went to church every Sunday, ran the food bank, you name it. Then her husband married the babysitter."

"Oh, my," Glenn said.

"Wait," Oliver said, his delight evident in his voice. "So she changed her name to *Trixie?*"

"Bingo." Chuck nodded.

"I can't say that I'm judging her," I said. "Not even close."

"Say, Rosie," Oliver said. "After everything with Ed, maybe you should start calling yourself Roxie?"

"That's actually not a terrible idea," I said. "Buy me another beer and I'll take it out for a test drive."

Sonja motioned Chuck over to them. He filled two shot glasses with vodka and they each knocked one back. Sonja dropped two twenties on the bar and wiped her mouth with the back of her hand.

Chuck returned. "One more of those shots and the karaoke starts."

"No way," Oliver said.

I smelled her perfume before I realized Sonja was standing behind us. She placed a hand on Oliver's back. He spun his chair around and faced her. "No texts," he said. "Give up on me?"

"I have something I need to care of." Her lipstick was a deep red, almost burgundy, her eye liner swooped up at the ends. "How are you, Oliver?" Her hand was still on his back. "Are you taking care of what you came here to do, too?"

My mouth fell open. This was the first time I witnessed her actually acknowledge another person when it didn't have anything to do with her.

"Working on it." Oliver smiled.

"No karaoke tonight, Miss Sonja?" Chuck said.

"No, I'll leave that to Trixie. Charles, will you watch out for her? It doesn't take many shots for her to lose her judgement, unlike my Russian blood that is probably ten percent vodka."

She leaned down and gave Oliver a healthy kiss on the cheek. "You really are delicious." After wiping the lipstick from his face with her thumb, she said, "Maybe we will see each other again one day."

Once the door closed behind her, Oliver said, "That sounded so final."

"Yes," Glenn said. "Agreed."

"Maybe Gunner couldn't help her," I said. "Maybe she's leaving town."

"Or maybe she's going to kill me." Oliver started to laugh but stopped.

"Not on my watch." I stood and straightened my skirt. "I'll be back."

I hurried out into the parking lot. Sonja was leaning against her car, arms crossed. When I reached her, I said, "Is Gunner going to do the track?"

"If Ms. Bennett will let us. Yes, he's in. He can do it tomorrow."

"I'll call Jojo on my way home. Can Glenn and I join you?"

"I'm sure Ms. Bennett will insist on it." She rolled her eyes. "As long as you stay out of the way, yes."

"Deal."

"Here's my cell. I keep it very private but if you could let me know what she says and when we can get there, I would greatly appreciate it."

I accepted the card and gripped it in my hand.

"How is your brother?" Sonja said.

"Better every day."

"That's good." Her face softened. "I'm happy for him. He seemed so sad the first day we met."

"Hopefully I will see you tomorrow, Sonja. Have a good night. And I hope the track gives you something to go on."

"It has to." She climbed into her car and the Porsche rumbled to life. Once the convertible top had tucked into the back, she lit a cigarette, and backed onto the road.

I watched her go, realizing I really didn't know her at all. Was she an actress playing multiple roles? Or was she a devoted daughter trying to make sense of her father's disappearance? When her taillights disappeared around a bend, I headed back in the Tavern and stood behind my chair. "Where did you go?" Oliver said.

"Glenn, if I can get Jojo to agree, want to help Sonja find her father?"

Glenn almost spit out his martini. "Um, that's a definite yes."

I looked down the bar at Barty. "Save my seat." I walked toward the ladies' room but took a slight detour. Barty and the other man were seated at the corner of the bar. I stood in front of a nearby pinball machine where the original Star Wars cast surrounded a looming Darth Vader, and pretended to search through my wallet for quarters.

"Contract ain't no good if he didn't sign it," the man said to Barty.

"The Russians' lawyer said we can make this work. Something about intent to sell."

"What if we forge his signature? We could get one of those handwriting experts."

Barty rubbed his chin. "That's not a terrible idea. Do you know one?"

"You just gonna stand there?" An older man said in a loud voice. "This is my machine. I hold the record. You either play or you move on."

I stepped back, almost dropping my purse. His booming voice was drawing attention.

"You," Barty grunted.

"Who's that?" the other man said.

"Someone who doesn't know what's her business and what isn't."

I tried to smile. "Oh, hi Bartlett. I didn't see you there."

He stood, towering over me. "What did you hear?"

A small dot of saliva landed on my arm. "I was just looking at the pinball machine. It's vintage, I think. I love—"

"That's a load of crap."

I snapped my wallet shut. "I'll just be going back to my seat. It was nice running into you, Barty." I hurried over and slid in between Oliver and Glenn.

Glenn leaned in. "What just happened?"

"I was listening to their conversation a little."

"Um, sis?" Oliver said. "Based on the way those two men are glaring at you, I don't think that was such a good idea."

"Perhaps we should settle up," I said.

"I've got this," Oliver said. "You two can go if you want. Actually, I think you should go right now."

I hopped up. Glenn ushered me out to my car.

"Be safe, my dear," he said as he shut the door after me. "Oh, Rosalie—" He gestured for me to roll down the window.

"What is it?" I gunned the engine.

"The man with Barty?"

I nodded quickly, willing him to talk faster.

"He's Michael. Phoebe's infamous husband."

Despite my growing terror that I was being followed, I called Jojo on the way home and, after a little persuasion, she agreed to let Sonja and Gunner onto her property the next morning. Sonja ended our call with a breathy thank you, and clicked off the phone.

I checked my rear view mirror. No cars. I pulled over and, for the first time in as long as I could remember, buzzed down my convertible top. The air smelled of dried leaves and a charcoal grill somewhere off in the distance. I eased my car back onto the road and drove the rest of the way home with the wind in my hair and the stars crowding the sky overhead and an odd longing for a cigarette.

Once Oliver arrived home, we secured the house, flipping the dead bolts and turning on every outside light. Oliver said Barty and Michael seemed pretty agitated after I left. We agreed that precautionary measures were in order. He decided on a fireplace poker. Gripping the handle in his fist, he said, "I'm not sure if this a good idea or a very bad one."

I chose a heavy flashlight Annie had given me when I moved to Cardigan. "According to Annie, first you blind the intruder with the light, then you bonk them over the head."

"And run like hell?"

"I think that's the idea." As I followed him up the stairs, I said, "Perhaps I should have been more discreet this evening."

He flashed me a crooked smile. "Ya think?"

I skipped a few of my normal nighttime routines, something my mother always warned me not to do, and climbed into bed. I patted the comforter, encouraging Sweeney Todd to join me, relieved when he at last pounced onto my feet. My phone was nearby and I realized I hadn't sent Annie my nightly, *Sweet Dreams!* After typing the text and adding a small pink heart, I hit send. I noticed I had an unopened text. It was the second one Bini had ever sent me.

Thank you

Chapter Thirty-Seven

"Did you get any sleep?" Glenn asked as he struggled out of my car. The air was crisp and cool but the sun had already begun to dissolve the frost that had tipped the grass earlier that morning.

"I think I hit my REM requirement."

"No visits from Bartlett?"

"Thankfully, no. But Oliver and I were ready for him." I gave Glenn a small smile. "A poker and a flashlight were involved."

"Sounds like a game of Clue."

I shut the door and zipped up my jacket. "Looks like they're ready for us."

Sonja and Gunner were in a deep discussion in the driveway of Windswept Farm. We passed a Jeep with Gunner's logo on the side. I flinched when a large dog jumped up and began pacing in the back seat. The entire vehicle rocked from the intensity of the animal's movement. He reminded me of a German Shepherd, only taller and thinner.

Glenn stopped and gazed in the window. "What a beautiful animal." The dog's deep dark eyes stared back. "It's a Belgian malanois," Glenn said. "I love this breed. And if I'm not mistaken, I think a malanois helped uncover Osama bin Laden." The dog's tail wagged. "Look at that focus. It's as if he can see into my soul."

I looked over at the house just as Jojo trotted down the front steps.

"Hey, you two." She was dressed in capris leggings and a loose sweatshirt. Her sneakers were a bright fuchsia with turquoise markings. A matching pink ball cap on her head. "You ready?"

"More than ready. This is going to be fascinating." Glenn rubbed his hands together as he headed over to Sonja and the tracker, his sport shoes glowing white beneath his khakis.

"I'm confused, Rosalie," Jojo said. "If Sonja is trying to find her father on my property, she can't possibly think he's alive."

"Yes, that's the theory." I looped my arm through hers. "Let's join the others."

Sonja shoved her hands in the pockets of her jacket as we approached. She was also in a pair of leggings, but hers hugged every inch of her hips and legs, topped by an equally snug nylon hoodie. Her thick hair was pulled back with a few, I would guess intentional, strands framing her face. "Looks like we're all here." She eyed us, lids heavy. "We've amassed quite a crowd." She faced the man standing next to her. "Gunner, I hope these people won't distract your dog."

Gunner stood trim and fit with an official neon green vest that read, "Dog Tracking in Session." His hair was closely cropped and he was freshly shaven with pale gray eyes. "Not a whole lot can distract my boy."

Glenn shook Gunner's hand. "You have a beautiful dog."

"Best damn dog I ever worked with."

"What's his name?" Glenn said.

, "Randor." He looked at Sonja dreamily. He suddenly didn't seem so tough. "You didn't know that, did you? That I named my dog after a character in your show."

"No, I didn't." Sonja gave him a tight smile. "I'm glad he's your best dog."

I eyed Sonja. Not one inch of her flawless face or perfect posture revealed that she had been cut from the show.

"I watched most of season four last night," Jojo said.

"Okay." Sonja, visibly bored by her admirers said, "Shall we get started?" She picked up a black backpack and removed a large ziplock bag.

"That must be the scent article," Glenn said to me.

Gunner took the bag from Sonja. "Is it clean? No other scents on here? It can't be contaminated in any way."

"It was in my father's hall closet. I wore gloves when I slipped it out from under the collar of his overcoat."

184

Gunner removed the plaid woolen scarf from the bag. It looked to be cashmere. He held it under Randor's nose. With a complete lack of hesitation, the dog started to move. He headed to the front steps and sniffed, nose to the ground.

"My father must have knocked on the door," Sonja said. "He must have stood on that stoop."

Randor lifted his head and froze, his eyes darting back and forth. And then he was on the move.

"He smells something," Glenn said and hurried to catch up to Sonja and Gunner, who jogged easily behind the dog.

Jojo and I walked together, our sneakers squeaking in the wet grass. "Jojo? Do you think it's true? That your uncle could have done something to Sonja's father?"

"My uncle was a very secretive man. And he changed after my mom died. It was like he didn't care about anything anymore. Not us. Not the farm. Not even living."

"So no one knew about Sonja's father being here?" We braced ourselves as we straddled a fallen tree and climbed to the other side.

"No one. Not even Barty."

Dried leaves crackled under our feet as we continued through the sparse woods.

"Jojo, do you know why your mom was so loyal to her brother?"

"Well, for one. She was a nice person and I think she worried about him, even though he wasn't so nice." Jojo pulled a tissue from her pocket and blew her nose. "But then I learned why."

"Can I ask?"

"He had a funny way of showing love. But when she couldn't make the rent for a few months, Uncle Ronnie bought the house we were living in and gave it to my mom outright." Jojo stared ahead. The others had gained quite a lead. "I don't like conflict, Rosalie. It makes me upset. My mom used to say it's because I'm the youngest. That I always wanted to make things better. Are you a youngest?"

"How'd you guess?" I smiled. "And a Libra."

"Holy crap, me too!" Her face relaxed into a smile.

We followed the others down a lane that was really only two worn tracks in a recently cut corn field. Randor had picked up his pace.

"Rosalie? What if they find him? I mean, what if he really is dead? Will they dig him up? Will you want to witness that?"

"Actually, no. I saw a decaying body once in my life and will never forget it."

We passed a small cemetery surrounded by a low wrought iron fence. Grave stones covered in mildew dotted the ground. Most of them jutting up at odd angles from the tree roots underground.

"Is this your family's cemetery?" I said.

"Yeah. They go back as far as the 1700's. If you look over by that lilac bush, you'll see my mother's. And over there," she said as she pointed, "Is Uncle Ronnie."

I followed her gaze. The earth was still in a small mound at Ronnie Kline's grave site. No grass had taken root. Somehow seeing his grave made this whole crazy situation seem more real, more urgent, more sinister.

I took a long sip from my water bottle. "We better catch up."

We brushed through marsh grasses and passed an old well covered with moss. I caught Jojo's arm as she stumbled down a small incline and we continued through the winter wheat until we at last came to a small clearing near the river. A light breeze carried the scent of fish and river mud. The water must be low.

Randor crouched on the ground, tail extended.

"What does this mean?" Sonja said.

"Your father is here," Gunner said.

"Are you certain?" She searched his face.

"My dog doesn't make mistakes, Ma'am." Gunner placed a red plastic marker in the ground where Randor ended his search and removed a hefty pull toy from a pocket in his vest. The dog latched on. After a fierce tugging battle, he patted Randor's back and the dog sat calmly by his side. "Good boy." Gunner scratched behind his ears.

"Are you saying he's really here?" Jojo looked at Sonja. "I didn't believe

186

you. I thought this was some wild goose chase." Her mouth fell open. "No." She shook her head. "No. This can't be true. He couldn't have done this." She dropped to her knees and sobbed into her hands. "No, no, no."

Sonja gazed over at her, eyes cold and emotionless. "Why are you surprised? Surely you knew your uncle was a monster."

Jojo's back heaved. I knelt down next to her. When her cries seemed to be subsiding I looked up at Gunner. "Is it time to bring in the sheriff?"

Chapter Thirty-Eight

Glenn stayed behind while the rest of us returned to the house to meet the sheriff. He was there when we arrived, standing in the driveway, hat low on his head.

Our sheriff took his time, basking in the limelight. After a few moments of frowning and staring at the ground, he adjusted his belt and rested his hand on his gun. "You broke the law, Gunner."

"No, sir, I didn't." Gunner lifted his chin.

"You searched for a cadaver without notifying the law."

"I was searching for a person. We had a scent article. My dog was not on a cadaver search."

"You need to recover his body," Sonja said, her accent thicker than usual. She crossed her arms, one hip jutted out, and met the sheriff's eyes with an intense gaze. If I'm not mistaken, I'm pretty sure he took a step back.

"All right. You can dig him up. But I'm not doing the heavy lifting. Let me call in a deputy so we have another witness." The sheriff looked over at Glenn. Then he peered around him and noticed me. "When did you get here?"

"I wanted her here," Jojo said. "Rosalie has been kind to me." Her mascara had smeared giving her a hollowed-out look.

His face relaxed. "You know, even if this woman's father is in the ground, doesn't mean it was your uncle who put him there. That's a whole 'nother matter."

"What are you saying?" Sonja snapped. "It certainly does."

Gunner stood closer to Sonja. "I got this. Okay? We're going to find him.

I'm certain he's here."

She nodded.

I waited while the sheriff made the call to his deputy. Once he stowed his phone, I inched up to him. "Hey," I said. "Do you have a minute?"

"Was all of this your idea?" he said while continuing to stare straight ahead.

"None of it. I ran into Sonja at the Tavern last night and she asked for my help."

He finally looked at me. I could see my reflection in his mirrored sunglasses. My hair was a mess.

"You hangin' out there again?"

I bit my lip. This was getting to be a thing, me sharing information with the sheriff. I was beginning to think he realized I could be useful. At least that was the theory I was operating under. "Did you recover the documents about the sale of the house in the hidden room?"

"It's not illegal to sell property to a Russian company." He hitched his thumbs in his belt. "But the documents are gone. You said you took a picture?"

"They're on my phone. Also, I overheard Barty and Michael Parker discussing ways to make the sale go through, even though Kline is dead. They said something about forging the signature."

"Oh, boy." He laughed. "You've outdone yourself this time, Hart."

The others were looking our way. Sonja scowled. "What could possibly be funny at a time like this?"

"Are you finished?" I said in a low voice.

The sheriff stood stock still. "How do I know you aren't making all this up? Huh?"

"I've gotten you this far, haven't I?"

This time we decided to skip the walk. Jojo and I drove back in her ATV, something I will never do again. Gunner took Sonja in his Jeep, and the sheriff and his deputy followed in the sheriff's SUV.

After a bumpy, butt-bouncing ride, we finally arrived. Glenn stood from his perch on a log and waved away the billows of dust the caravan had kicked up. Gunner and the deputy each grabbed a shovel and immediately began taking turns plunging them into the ground with the force of their shoes. Sonja stood next to a tree, clutching her father's scarf, her eyes zeroed in on their progress. Glenn, who's eagerness was getting the best of him, leaned in a little too close, causing Gunner to ask him repeatedly to please stand back.

"What's that?" Glenn said when a spot of color shown through the overturned dirt. "I think it's a blanket of some sort."

Sonja crossed herself.

"Sheriff?" Gunner said. "I need you to see our every move."

He nodded.

The deputy nudged the blanket away with the end of his shovel. He knelt down and whisked away some loose dirt with a small broom. A man's hand came into view, the wedding ring on his finger reflecting the sunlight.

"That can't be your father, Sonja. Right?" I said. "Your mother died when you were four."

"He swore he would never remove that ring for the rest of his life." Her voice filled with emotion. "That's him. I would know that ring anywhere."

Chapter Thirty-Nine

Later that afternoon, I stood on the stoop of Kevin and Jake's historic home along the Cardigan River on one of the most beautiful streets in town. They had completely restored the narrow house and turned it into a showpiece.

I had gone home to shower after witnessing the discovery of Sonja's father, unable to get the image of his lifeless hand out of my head. I decided to dress up a little for my visit, wearing a short wrap dress, tights, and my favorite booties. I tucked my hair behind an ear and knocked on the door.

Jake's broad smile gave me hope he was genuinely happy to see me. I prayed it to be so. I had never been able to shake the thought they both somehow blamed me for Kevin's brush with death.

"How's our guy?" I said.

"He's the worst patient on the planet." Jake gave me a friendly hug.

"I've always thought that was a sign of good character."

"Please don't tell him that."

I followed Jake through the house to a wide-windowed room facing the water. Kevin was sprawled on a sofa, sound asleep, head askew, breathing from his mouth. A hand-crocheted quilt of navy's, grays, and cream draped over him.

"He looks so peaceful," I said. "Maybe I should come back later."

"He wants to see you."

"He does?" I peered up at Jake. "Are you sure?"

Jake's shoulders dropped. "As awful as this has been, neither of us blame you." He studied my face. "I promise."

I took in his words. "I would understand if you did."

"You already know this, Rosalie. But Kevin and I credit you for saving our relationship. If it wasn't for your support and encouragement, I would have left him." He gave my hand a small squeeze. "And that would have been the biggest mistake of my life."

Relief washed through me. I looked back at Kevin. "What a beautiful throw."

"My mother made it for us."

"Us?" I said, eyes questioning.

"My family has come around. They adore Kevin now." Jake shook his head. "Sometimes I think my mother likes him better than me."

"That's wonderful news. I know how long they pretended you weren't gay, ignoring Kevin even existed. And now they embrace it? Mazel tov."

"Life is a lot easier when you're not trying to fool the world." Jake smiled. "Let's wake him up. He's been miserable about missing the cooking classes."

I sat on a nearby chair while Jake tapped Kevin's shoulder. He tenderly brushed the hair back from his damp forehead.

Kevin's eyelids fluttered and then opened. "Hi, handsome."

"We have company."

He lifted his head. "Rosalie. Aren't you a sight for sore eyes."

"How are you?" I said gently.

"Hungry."

"Good," I said. "I brought cookies. They're in the kitchen. And just so you know, I made them at home. Although Glenn has been guarding the café like Buckingham Palace."

"That man is a force when he sets his mind on something." Kevin pushed himself up and adjusted the throw.

"So tell me," I said, "what hurts?"

"Mainly my throat and lungs. They kept me on the respirator for a while. And getting your stomach pumped is no picnic. I don't recommend it."

Jake settled in at the end of the sofa and rested his arm on the back cushions. "So who did this, Rosalie? Is the sheriff trying to figure it out?"

"He's actually letting me help him this time."

Kevin grinned. "Oh, god, I love this woman."

Jake chuckled. "You do not disappoint, Rosalie Hart."

"You remember Jojo's uncle, the farmer who recently died? Turns out he was poisoned with hemlock, too."

"Get out of town," Kevin said. "So this is really something."

A lump formed in my throat. "I'm so sorry, Kevin. I can't believe this happened to you in my restaurant." I was surprised at the amount of tears welling in my eyes. I covered my mouth to hide the tremble in my lips.

"If you must know," Jake said. "Not only am I enraged this happened to Kevin, I am boiling mad someone used you as a vehicle to do such a heinous thing." He shook his head. "Steaming."

Kevin picked up the water glass next to the sofa and took a long sip. "And you're trying to figure this out, girlfriend? Any luck?"

"We might be getting close."

Jake propped Kevin's feet on his lap and began to massage them through the blanket. "Are you still having class?"

"Yes. Thank goodness. Oh, Kevin, Marco has a surprise for our last day on Monday." I paused for a little dramatic effect. "I have a hunch he's going to share a secret family recipe."

Kevin frowned. "How secret?"

"He said something about it being passed down through the Giovanelli family for generations. It's not even written down. I think it might be a classic red sauce. He said it would take most of the day to prepare."

"Get out." Kevin gazed over at Jake. "It is worth my life to get that recipe."

Jake took me in. "I love this man." His voice caught in his throat.

"I understand. You decide if you're both ready for Kevin to return. The recipe is yours either way. He's not going to write it down. But I'll do my best to get it straight. We can have our own private class right here when you're better."

"So how does Brandon like the class?" Jake said.

I frowned for a moment. "You know Brandon?"

"Not very well. But I'm on the hiring committee at the college so I was in on the interviews. I see him around now and then."

"Is he liked by his students?"

"Not sure. You know he's from around here? At least his family lived here a while ago."

"Cardigan?" I said. "No kidding. He said he was from DC."

"His family owned a farm a few miles out of town. He tries to hide his roots, pretends he's worldly, you know, sophisticated. But that's one of the reasons we hired him, having some history on the Shore. Helps with PR."

"I had no idea." I let this new information sink in. "Anyway, I should go. I just needed a visual, if you know what I mean."

Jake stood. "Thanks for stopping in, Rosalie. Next time we'll be making some pasta."

Chapter Forty

Once I was back in my car, I noticed three missed calls from an unknown number. I listened to the voice mail. Cliff. He was outside Bonnie's house and wanted me to come over asap.

He was parked on the opposite side of the street from Bonnie's house. I rapped on the window and he popped open the door. "Get in." He tossed a newspaper into the back seat.

"Was Trevor here today?"

"No," he said emphatically. "I wouldn't have called you about him. It's the Russians."

I looked out the window at the house next door to Bonnie's. "What are they doing?"

"They had a visitor."

"I'm intrigued."

Cliffremoved his camera from the tripod on the dash. "This guy's the first one not in a suit to go in there. And he was acting suspicious. Kept looking around to check if anyone was watching him. I think he's a local. I thought you might ID him."

"Okay. Let me at least give it a shot."

Cliff held the camera in both hands. "I know exactly what time he got here." He slid and tapped and slid his finger again. "There," he said. "Check this out."

I hit the play arrow and held the screen closer. A man climbed out of a pickup, shoulders hunched, and checked around just as Cliff had said. He was tall, barrel-chested. I paused the screen just before he turned away.

"Can you enlarge this?"

He took the camera and moved his thumbs over the screen. "It's a little blurry but you might be able to make out his face."

I accepted the camera and stared down at it. I gasped a little as I narrowed my eyes in recognition. "Oh my goodness." I looked at Cliff. "I do know this man." I returned his phone. "Thanks, I'll get back to you as soon as I have something solid."

My mind was reeling as I drove away. I paused for a brief moment appreciating the fresh scent of my car's interior. Although I did have a slight hankering for a Dorito. I pushed the hands free button on my steering wheel and started to search for Glenn's number. I stopped at a red light and canceled the search. This was Glenn's afternoon with Gretchen. He'd been spending all his time either washing dishes or working on the investigation or both. He deserved some time with her.

The light switched to green and I decided to spend the evening doing research. I could tell Glenn about Barty's visit to the Russians tomorrow.

Chapter Forty-One

I found Oliver at the stove stirring something in a wide sauté pan.

"It smells divine in here." I dropped my things in a chair. "I hope you're making enough for two."

"I thought I'd try some risotto."

I peered down at the concoction. "Mushrooms?"

"You bet." He looked up at me. "You know I have a personal chef, don't you?"

"Of course, I didn't know that. My goodness, Oliver. What a luxury."

"She does my shopping, too. Cooks up a bunch of meals in my kitchen every Monday. She makes me protein shakes, kale smoothies, you name it. Crazy, right?"

"Honestly? I think I would hate that." I leaned back against the counter. "So how's it feel to be cooking for yourself?"

"I love it." He grinned. "Why have I had my head up my butt for so long? I've lost touch with everything. Send a text and it's all there. I feel like George Jetson only he was married."

"And he had a dog and a robot."

"I have a salad in the fridge and a nice Sicilian chardonnay I got from The Grande." He peered over at me. "You have plans?"

I brushed my hair from my face. The fatigue from the day was setting in. "I'm very happy to be home and to have you here with me."

Oliver picked up a wooden spoon in one hand, a measuring cup filled with broth in the other, and added some liquid to the risotto, stirring gently.

"Oliver? I'm sorry."

197

He looked up. "For what?"

"This is the first time you've visited me in years, and I am totally distracted. By the cooking school. The investigation. And now Tyler."

"Would you please go open that bottle of wine? I am inviting you to dinner."

"I'm suddenly famished. I haven't eaten all day. What's your time on that risotto?"

"I have 1/2 cup left to add and then in goes the parmesan, so, five minutes?"

"How about some candles?"

Chapter Forty-Two

I fought the covers all night trying to figure out what I was missing. When I finally surrendered, I sat up and noticed a text on my phone. Tyler: *I miss you.* I tossed it back on the night stand and immediately regretted it as my phone slid to the floor with a thud, causing Sweeney to leap up into the air from an almost comatose sleep. I leaned over the edge of the bed and scooped it up. I reread the text. That's it? I miss you? How about, I miss you terribly. Or, I miss you and I'm sorry. I dropped it on the bed and exhaled so hard my hair lifted from my forehead. Tyler was a man of few words. I'd known this since the day we met in my driveway. I glanced back at the device, started to reach for it, but stopped. I'd been fretting and wondering for days what had happened to us. I needed to think before responding. And I had more pressing matters. It felt like I was getting closer to finding out who poisoned Kevin, but I could be a million miles away from finding out the truth.

I threw back the covers and hesitated. I picked up my phone and read Tyler's message for a third time. My heart fluttered with a trace of hope. I really did love that man. But I wasn't going to spend the rest of my life wondering when he would cut me off again. I'd had enough doubt in my life. What I needed now was certainty and trust. So did Tyler. He just didn't know how to recognize it when it was sitting in his lap.

I tapped the text icon and thought for a moment. Then I typed with my thumbs and invited Jojo to meet me at the café for a coffee.

After crawling out of bed, I looked around the room. Clothes were strewn everywhere. I'd been so busy I hadn't had a chance to do any semblance of house work. It was Sunday. My first day in a while without obligations.

I stripped my bed and gathered my clothes, tossing it all into the laundry. I took a long hot shower and got on the scale. How could I lose weight during an Italian cooking class? Stress. I knew that diet and I didn't like it one bit. No one is going to take care of you but you, Rosalie Hart, I said to the mirror. So I moisturized, added a tonic to my hair, spent some time on my makeup, and gave my hair a good styling. Lastly I spritzed on my favorite perfume. I cinched my robe and found a comfortable short cotton skirt and a stylish loose sweater, a surprisingly clean pair of tights, and my favorite booties. And of course, my mother's pearls. I felt instantly better.

Once I organized the café, I removed a batch of muffins from the oven. The aroma of melted butter and cinnamon filled the kitchen. I heard a rap and turned to see Jojo rolling up on her tiptoes and back down again. I opened the deadbolt and let her in. I was surprised at her appearance. She had styled her hair so it framed her face nicely. She had added a little extra makeup defining her wide eyes and wore a short black cotton dress topped with a denim jacket.

"You look adorable," I said.

"Something smells good."

"Muffins. They taste like a good piece of cinnamon toast."

"A personal fave. My mom used to make us that on Sunday mornings."

I followed her into the restaurant and waited while she helped herself to a coffee. She sat at the bar and said, "The sheriff called this morning. He's opening up an investigation into who killed Sonja's father."

I stood across from her and lined up the sugar packets. "He doesn't think it was your uncle?"

"He said it wouldn't be right to assume anything. He wants to get to the bottom of it. But, I can tell you one thing, that blanket he was wrapped in? It was Uncle's Ronnie's for sure."

"Oh, my." I walked over to the Mieles and poured my own cup of coffee. I had hit my caffeine limit but I wanted to keep Jojo talking. "Be right back," I said. When I returned, Jojo was staring out the window, chin in hand. I set a small plate in front of her.

"Phoebe was at my apartment last night."

"And?"

Jojo peeled the paper away from the muffin. "She wants money."

"Are you going to give her some?"

"I think so. She needs it and I just can't sit back and watch her suffer." She took her first bite. "Oh, wow. This is delish."

"Jojo," I said. "Is there a chance Phoebe could have done this?"

"Why would you ask me that?" She dusted crumbs from her fingers. "She wouldn't hurt a fly. Literally. You saw that for yourself when she rescued a spider."

I wrapped my hands around my coffee mug. "She seems so desperate. Do you think her husband is putting her up to all the texts and questions?"

"Phoebs keeps her home life very private."

"So why don't they have any money?"

She shrugged. "Michael gambles. Remember? We talked about this when Brandon was profiling him. Anyway, he gambles. Sometimes he wins. Most times he doesn't."

"That's often the case." I thought about seeing Michael and Barty together at the Tavern. And then Barty at the Russian's house. "Are Michael and Barty friendly?"

"Barty doesn't really get along with anyone. He's been married twice. Neither lasted a year. But those women didn't understand him." She stirred some cream into her coffee. "Barty got the worst of it, Rosalie. From my uncle. I know I've told you a few stories but my uncle was a very mean man. Do you know I went to a psychic once and she said there was a dark cloud in my life? I knew immediately she was referring to Uncle Ronnie. He was bad. Real bad."

"Like how bad, exactly?"

She stopped stirring and set the spoon on the napkin. The coffee spread onto it like an ink blot. "What did you find at his house?"

"He was going to sell his farm to a Russian cartel. Barty's name was on the contract to sell along with your uncle."

She nodded but remained silent. I studied her. Her face was relaxed, not one tic of surprise. "You knew?"

"Sort of. The Sunday before he died? I stopped over to bring him his dinner. There was a dark Suburban in the driveway. It was odd. My uncle never entertained. And when I went inside he stopped me in the kitchen and told me to leave. Usually we'd have a glass of bourbon together. He was always nice to me on Sundays when it was just the two of us."

"Maker's Mark?"

She frowned. "How did you know that?"

"Just curious. Anyway, continue. Did you see who was there?"

"I set the casserole on the table and left. He seemed agitated and I learned long ago not to argue. When I got back outside I looked around a little. Barty's truck was parked behind the barn. It was weird. He never parked back there."

"He didn't want you to know he was there."

"They were up to something. And it made me mad. Barty hated my uncle more than anyone. Why he would be in some sort of deal with him, I will never know." Jojo dropped her hands in her lap. "Why would a Russian cartel want to buy a farm in Devon County?"

"I was wondering that myself. Jojo, did Phoebe know about this deal?"

She looked at me, eyes narrowed. "Yeah. I called her that night. We talk every day. Why?"

"I'm not really sure." I thought hard. Jojo's siblings could possibly sell that farm. Why would she protect them? "You want me to stop looking into this, don't you."

"I think we know what happened. Sonja killed my uncle to get revenge. She knew her father was there. She even brought a scent article. You and I both know she'd been planning that track for a while. She was prepared. Who keeps a plastic bag with a dead guy's scarf in it? One that was, what did he call it, uncontaminated?"

"Your uncle was poisoned. How could she pull that off?"

"You've seen her. My uncle is human. If she showed up at his door with some lame story, he would have let her in. And she recognized me. That first day of cooking school. Remember? She wanted to know my last name. She came in through the kitchen like everyone else. Then she tainted the salt to kill me for revenge." Jojo slurped back the rest of her coffee. "How have you not figured this out yet? I thought that was your thing."

"Does the sheriff agree with you?"

"How could he not? It's totally and completely obvious." She set her mug down and pulled a tube of lip gloss from her pocket. "Why are you so dead set on it being one of my family members? My brother and sister and I have been through hell and back our whole lives. Our dad left us when I was five. But we had a good mom. She kept us sane. And we stuck together. The night Barty had to sleep in the basement with the beast? Phoebs and I took our pillows down there and kept him company."

I studied her, taking in her words. Why was Barty so angry with her if they were all so close? Something didn't measure up. "Jojo, someone else could get hurt."

"I already told you. If it was one of my family members, then I want them to get away with it. But it wasn't. Once the sheriff locks up Sonja, then we will all be safe and sound and back to living in a sleepy little town without movie stars making trouble."

"But you own the farm. Whoever wanted it, didn't get the prize yet."

"You just said it. The farm belongs to me. No one can change that now." She hopped off the tall chair. "I'm meeting Brandon at the Tavern tonight. He's buying me a drink."

"Brandon?"

"Yup."

"Jojo, if the Russians are still interested, will you sell the farm to them?"

"Wait, what? Why did you ask me that?"

"Because they are still in town. I don't think they've given up. They still want your farm." I crossed my arms. "Question is, will you sell it to them?"

"Where did you find that real estate contract?"

"Your uncle has a secret room. Did you know that?"

She did a double take. "What the . . ."

The door is in the back of the closet in the mud room. The key is in the

Stetson on the shelf." Our eyes met. "But the sheriff checked. The document is gone."

"Did you look at it?"

"Yes."

"How much?"

"Five."

"Five *million*?"

I nodded and crossed my arms.

She combed both hands through her hair, eyes wide. "I had no idea."

I walked over to her and gave her a solid hug. "I never stopped being your friend." I stepped back. "This is me wanting to find the truth in all of this horrible mess. I hope you can see that." I handed her a tissue "You're going to smear your mascara. Why don't you go have a nice time with Doctor Brandon. Let him spoil you."

She hesitated. "Five million *dollars*?"

I placed my hands on her shoulders and turned her around. "Go have fun." She started to walk. "And, Jojo? Maybe don't tell anyone about that offer. Okay?"

She looked over her shoulder. "I'm twenty-five years old." She gave me a small smile. "And last I checked, I wasn't stupid."

Chapter Forty-Three

Oliver texted he had just finished having lunch with Sonja at a diner outside of town and was going home for a nap. I had no idea what to make of that. And I was feeling pretty tired, myself. And lonely. I gazed out the front windows. It was a quiet Sunday afternoon. I was past ready to have the café open again.

I noticed Joe Wilgus slumped in the seat of his vehicle in front of the frame shop. My body tensed in a Pavlovian reaction to this man as he stood and slammed the door. He ambled across the street, causing an older woman in a Lincoln to slam on the brakes.

"Everything okay?" I said as he sauntered into the kitchen.

He faced me, hands on his hips. "How did you know about the poison in the bourbon?"

"It was a guess. Tyler said there were rumors about Kline starting every day with a Maker's Mark. It's logic."

"You know, Hart, this is all too fishy for me. You know too much and you ain't even a cop." He stuck his lips out a little. "How did you know Kline's bourbon was full of that poison? You grow it yourself? Do I need to search your damn farm? Maybe I'll get Gunner to sniff around with that dog of his."

I took a step back. "Hemlock is highly poisonous to animals as well."

"You see? Now how do you know *that*? Huh?"

"I have that kind of mind. Okay? And I really appreciate you letting me help out this time. And you actually listened to me. I think we are making progress."

MYSTERY AT WINDSWEPT FARM

One side of his mouth turned up a little. "Nice deflection, Hart."

Relief washed through me. "It's all true."

"We all know Kline killed that woman's father. I was just giving Jojo a little breathing room."

"You care about her, don't you."

"She's a good kid. And I hate the way that family has had to suck up to him their whole lives. And now he finally kicks the bucket and he's still making them miserable."

I tried to get him back on track. "Do you think Sonja could have killed Kline in revenge? You know, she was in the café the first day. She came in through the kitchen."

"I need to talk to that woman."

"I wonder if she has an alibi for the day Kline was killed. She was already in town. Remember? You asked if I knew who was driving a red Porsche."

He frowned. "Good idea."

"What about Barty? No one is keeping him in check. I think he will do anything to get this deal through. And Phoebe's husband is in on this, too."

He tilted his head and studied me. "This Sonja is staying at The Grande. Maybe I'll go pay her a visit." He adjusted his hat. "Got any coffee?"

I walked behind the bar and poured his usual into a cup, noticing a slight tremor in my hand. I was glad to have some distance between us. I snapped on the lid and dropped two muffins into a bag.

He accepted them and glared at me. "So the Maker's Mark? It was all just a guess."

"Yes. And to quote Doctor Brandon, it was an *educated* guess."

"Humph." He adjusted his stance. "So it started with the liquor."

"It often does." I risked a smile and opened the door.

After finally escorting the sheriff out of my café, I collapsed into a chair at the bar and dropped my head onto my crossed arms. My brain hurt. My phone vibrated on the counter. I lifted my head. Was it Tyler? I knew better. Pandora's box was empty. I picked it up. Marco: *I am sitting at The Grande with a marvelous seafood charcuterie in front of me and a glass of California chardonnay. Care to join me?*

"Just what the doctor ordered," I said aloud before I typed the same response. I fished a lipstick out of my purse and topped it with a nice gloss. Before dropping my phone into my purse, I pushed hard on the side buttons and powered down. Enough.

Sonja stood on the porch of the Grande a few steps above me. Her short, flowy black dress swirled around her in the late afternoon breeze.

"Hey," I said. "How was your lunch with Oliver?"

She crossed her arms. "That's none of your business."

"Just a friendly question. Have you made arrangements for your father yet?"

"Again, none of your business."

"Well," I said, "You probably won't answer this either, but will you leave Cardigan once you've interned your father?"

"You," she said, her eyes wide, "are relentlessly annoying." She glanced down the street. "You think this is all resolved?" She looked down at me. "A neat and tidy ending?"

"For you, maybe," I said, "but not for the rest of us."

"I have found my father. I am thankful for that. But there is much that lies underneath this horrific crime." She steeled her eyes into mine. "And I won't stop until the right people have suffered as I have."

"Sonja? Why do the Russians want that house?"

"You don't know? To build a fortress, of course. It is so easy in this country for enemies to infiltrate, steal the secrets, learn the weaknesses, spy, undermine. And what better place than a quiet little town on a farm in the middle of nowhere?"

"We're not far from three major cities. Is that part of the reason?"

"You mean do the Russians want a private compound just outside of DC? What do you think, Miss Rosalie?" She lifted her chin. "I've grown impatient with your naïveté. It is boring. So, if you would excuse me?" She gripped her beaded clutch with both hands and paraded down the steps. Her hair bounced along her back as she continued down the sidewalk. Nice exit, I thought, and made my way into the hotel.

Marco was at the bar talking with Paula, the head chef at The Grande. Marco wore his usual get up, expensive jeans, white button shirt with the sleeves rolled up, and very nice shoes. I caught a whiff of his cologne when I sat on the chair next to him.

He gazed over at me. "And here is the lovely Miss Rosalie."

"Hey," I said, and flashed him a smile. I looked at Paula. "You've met my secret."

Paula was short with a ruddy complexion and coal black hair. Tattoos adorned the sides of her neck and wrists. We were friendly with one another and attended the same chamber of commerce meetings. Our businesses were unique enough that we weren't really competitors. Although I was considering hiring away her bartender. But that was Cardigan. Restaurant workers moved from venue to venue. All the chefs and restaurant owners understood how it worked.

"That looks amazing," I said as I gazed down at the charcuterie artfully displayed on a wood block. "What's under the glass with the smoke swirling around?"

Marco leaned forward. "It's an oyster. Paula has a smoking machine." He winked. "I was saving it for you."

Paula was clearly tickled by Marco's praise, her face a little pinker, dimples forming in her cheeks. "No need to fight over it. I'll bring one for you, Rosalie. And it's all on the house."

"Thank you." I eyed her. "That doesn't mean I'm giving you the secret red sauce."

Her head reared back. "Marco is sharing a secret red sauce?"

"I'll be blacking out the windows and I'm not telling you what day." I smiled at Marco. "We are all sworn to secrecy. But you may want to stop by once I reopen. Fridays will be *Notte Italiano*."

"Speaking of your café, where are your steps?"

"They were stolen."

Marco cleared his throat. "How about a glass for my friend?"

She shrugged. "It's a legitimate question. The place has no steps."

"Don't forget that oyster," Marco called after her. He faced me. "How are you, Rosalie? We only have one more day of class. And I've missed you this weekend." He sized me up. "You look very nice."

"I'm okay. Thank you for asking."

He rested his arm on the back of my chair. "You have a lot on your mind. I wish I could snap my fingers and allow you to relax. Just for this evening."

I shrugged. "It's worth a shot. Give it a snap." I caught a whiff of his cologne again. I was used to Sandalwood soap. But this was nice. I smiled at him. "Thank you for everything you've done. This class has been so much better than I ever could have anticipated."

"I share your sentiment."

"You're having fun? I know we're an odd bunch."

"I've enjoyed being with you."

Paula returned with a glass and the Chardonnay. "Make sure you have some of the smoked trout." She set the glass down in front of me. "Marco selected this. Have you ever had Chateau Montelena? There's a whole story behind this wine."

"Yes, we know the story," Marco said. "Signora?"

I picked up the glass and sipped. "Yummy," I said and smiled at Marco.

Paula was becoming very comfortable being part of our conversation. When she said, "This wine was the first . . ."

Marco interrupted. "How's that oyster coming along, Chef?"

Paula looked bewildered for a moment. Then she said, "Be right back."

Marco turned so that he was facing me. "Rosalie?" His tone more serious. "I have a proposal for you."

I flattened my back against the spindles in the chair. "I'm sorry?"

"I want you to come to Italy. I want you to study with me."

"You do?" I allowed his words to sink in.

He leaned in closer. "You are a talent but there's more. You have the gift. The instinct to know what people want. What they will like." He tapped the back of my hand with his index finger. "It's a rare thing."

"For how long? I mean, I need to reopen. I've been closed for two months."

"There is no hurry. But listen for a moment. Here is what I'm proposing. Study with me and then I want you to open one of my restaurants here in the states. I've never met anyone I could trust to do that. Keep the quality. The authenticity. You pick the city. DC, Baltimore, Philadelphia. We both know it would be a huge success."

I could feel the warmth of his hand behind on my back. The ambitious, dream-big part of me had been nudged awake. "I'm speechless."

He reached for his wine glass, his posture a little straighter. "I knew it was too much. You like your little town."

I took a long, deep breath, exhaling slowly. "That wasn't a no."

One of Marco's eyebrows lifted a little higher than the other. "It wasn't?"

"Can you give me some time?"

He leaned in and gave me a soft kiss on the lips. It was a modest kiss. But a kiss just the same. "Ah, look, here comes the oyster at last."

I gunned the engine of my car and powered up the heat. Part of me was already imagining running one of Marco's restaurants. And to study with a master? In *Italy*? I was shivering although it wasn't that cold. Annie would love it if I went back to DC. Or maybe Philly where I would be closer to the farm. I could do this. I could train Glenn and Crystal to manage the Day Lily. I put a brake on my thoughts and remembered that kiss. Marco's kiss was tender and, as my mother would say, lovely. What was happening to me?

Cardigan was as still and lifeless as a painting. I reached for my phone and powered it up. There were at least seven texts from Annie. The last, asking if I was alive. She had even called Tyler. I wondered what she thought when he didn't have a clue. I typed that I would call her in a half hour and apologized profusely. I just needed to get home first.

Glancing in my rear view mirror, I noticed a large SUV behind me. The grille was practically over my trunk. The windows were tinted so I couldn't make out a face, but there was a faint outline of a driver at the wheel. I started to ease off the clutch when the SUV bumped my entire car, jolting it forward. My foot slipped off the clutch and the car jerked to a stop.

Panicking, I reached for the key but it bumped me again. I needed to move. I quickly restarted the engine and gunned out of there. The vehicle did the same. A chill ran down my spine. Who was that? I thought for a moment. My car had a turbo booster I never used. I flipped the switch and inched up to the green light ahead of me. Okay, dude, whoever you are. Here we go.

Home was left at the light. I glanced over at the crosswalk warning on the adjacent street. Six seconds. Five seconds. I continued to inch along. The flashing orange hand began to pulse. Two seconds. One . . . I hit the gas hard and flew around the corner. I rounded the next and the river came into view. I was up to sixty in no time. I checked my mirror. Nothing. After a mile, I pulled off the road and tucked my car behind a thick clump of trees. A set of headlights appeared. I tensed as they neared, hunching my shoulders as if that would help. It was the SUV. Just like the one the Russians were unloading. They crept down the road, brights blazing. At last they turned around in a driveway and headed back into town. I waited a few minutes before I started the engine. I gripped the steering wheel, trying to slow my heart rate. If that was an attempt to scare the bejesus out of me, it was successful.

After easing back onto the road, I hit the gas. When I hit 60 mph, I rolled down the window and let the wind swirl through the car. I wondered how I could have ever not liked this car. Granted, it was Ed's consolation prize for shopping around for someone younger and blonder than me. But it wasn't the car's fault. And the way it was hugging the road, allowing me to accelerate into every bend, I was growing rather fond of my aging red sports car. I inched up to 70. Not a single screech of the tires. This was actually a whole lot of fun. I checked again. The road was still dark.

Gravel sprayed like confetti as I barreled down the lane. The lights glowed inside Barclay Meadow and I was overwhelmed with how happy I was to be home. I hopped out of the car and ran up the steps. I stumbled into the door, breathless from the exhilaration of my getaway. I locked the door and tried to slow my breathing. I could hear the tinny sound of the television in the next room.

I combed my hands through my hair and fell back against the door, taking in the day. Annie. I needed to call Annie. I pulled out my phone and there it was. Tyler: *I'm sorry. I love you so much. I'm terrified I've ruined the best thing that's ever happened to me.*

I allowed his words to sink in. Okay, Tyler. Thank you for that. But I had just had one heck of a day. If anyone thought I was overreacting to the Russians' attempt to buy the farm, I think they might change their minds. Particularly Joe Wilgus. I rolled my shoulders back and headed for the living room.

"Hey, Oliver," I called. "Want to face time with Anna Banana?"

Chapter Forty-Four

Tyler was at the kitchen table the next morning. I was showered and ready for class. More than ready. After my evening with Marco, I was filled with adrenaline about what my future might hold.

He stood when he saw me, the chair legs scraping the wood floor. "Hey," he said as if nothing had happened. He dipped his head a little and peered up at me.

"Hey," I said.

"You look really nice."

My cheeks warmed. I had put some effort into my appearance, still in my black skirt and white blouse, but added a few extra touches. "Thank you."

"Rosalie—"

"I don't have much time. Class starts—"

"Can you at least give me five minutes?"

Oliver trotted down the steps, did a one-eighty, and headed back upstairs.

"Okay." I crossed my arms and squeezed my biceps. "I wish you would have given me the same five minutes the other night, but there's nothing we can do about that now. What do you have to say?"

"I'm sorry."

My emotions were like a witch's brew coming to a boil. "For what, exactly? I know you pride yourself on mincing your words, but you have to put something out there or I'm going to work." I squeezed a little tighter.

"I don't really know." Tyler shrugged. "What do you want me to say?"

"Oh, well there you go." I bumped a chair as I breezed past the table. I stopped at Mr. Miele. Nope, I could make coffee at the café. I spun around

213

and called up the stairs as I headed for the door. "Meet you in the car." I grabbed my purse and knew I was most likely forgetting something, but burst through the door and marched down the steps. *What do you want me to say? Are you kidding me??* I had decided on a pair of kitten heels in my efforts to dress up a little, and almost twisted my ankle in the gravel. My mind raced. He was blowing this. Were we really going to fall apart? End this relationship? Maybe I would go to Italy. Oh, that would be amazing. I could . . ."

Tyler grabbed the door just as I slid into my car. "Please don't go."

"I have class. A job. A responsibility. What? Do you want me to stay here instead? Tell *you* what to say?"

"Whew." He combed his hands through his hair. "I figured you were upset, but, well, this is intense."

I slammed the door.

"Rosalie." His voice was muffled through the window. "Roll down the window. Come on."

I cracked it open. "I can hear you."

He put his hands on his hips. "Really? I get an inch?"

I nodded and rolled my lips in.

"I'm sorry."

"For what exactly?" I looked up at him. His eyes had filled but he said nothing. No, I thought. No. I buzzed the window down another inch. "I believed I was unlovable. I went there again. It was awful. I doubted my ability to love someone or be loved." My voice cracked. Oh, boy, get it out and get out of there. "I was letting myself love you with abandon. And then . . ." I buzzed the window back up and gripped the steering wheel. Where was Oliver? This was the perfect time to leave. Tyler was likely to slink away any minute.

He rapped on the window. I gave him half an inch this time.

"Will you come to my place this evening after class?"

My jaw dropped. I never went to his house. "Why?"

"So we can talk." His lips curled into an incredibly adorable grin. "Without the window."

Oliver was at the door. I unlocked it so he would know to get in.

I looked back at Tyler. "Maybe." I closed the window despite the warmth in the car. "Fasten your seatbelt, brother of mine, I am about to make an iconic exit."

He clicked it closed. "This is awesome."

I hit the gas and rounded the boxwoods, not a single skid or fishtail as I turned down the lane, shifting gears as the trees breezed by.

Oliver's grin was wide. "You go, girl!"

Chapter Forty-Five

Monday
Day Five of Cooking Class

Menu
i Famiglia Giovanelli Sugo Rossa di Domenica/
Giovanelli Family's Secret Sunday Red Sauce

*Braciole/*Thinly sliced beef, stuffed, wrapped and tied
Rosalie

*Linguine Fresche/*Fresh Linguine
Janice and Oliver

*Polpette/*Meatballs
Joanna and Brandon

"Dolce Far Niente"
Pleasantly Doing Nothing

Oliver and I clambered in the door as Glenn held it open for us. We were both out of breath, wide grins on our faces.

"What have I missed?" he said.

"Oh, Glenn, I have so much to tell you." I dropped my belongings on the counter.

"I only have one thing to tell you." He closed the door and turned the dead bolt.

"What is it?" I said. "Is everything all right?"

"We have steps."

"Oh, that's wonderful news." I hurried into the restaurant and looked out the front door. "They're beautiful."

"So why is the yellow tape still there," Oliver said as he looked over my shoulder.

"They're curing," Glenn said. "Now it's your turn, my dear."

We gathered around the bar later that morning. Jojo and Brandon, side by side, looked relaxed and happy. Janice was quiet. No phone but she seemed sad which made me feel an empathic pang of sorrow for her. Oliver was animated after our ride into town. I echoed the feeling. I noticed he had filled out a little since he arrived.

Kevin had opted out. Jake said my promise of coming to their place and spending a day cooking the red sauce with them sealed the deal. Jake had already selected a high end *Barola* wine. I missed Kevin, though. He had a way of perking up the place by just being there. I had already given him a refund, but so far he hadn't cashed the check.

Marco cleared his throat. He stood at the end of the bar and said, *"Felice lunedi."* His thick brows dipped as he considered each of our faces. "I'm about to share with you a treasured family secret. You can take notes and prepare it as many times as you wish, but you must never share the written version of this recipe with anyone else." He began to pass out sheets of paper. "This is an agreement you must sign before we begin."

Brandon snatched up his paper. "This is fantastic."

I stood next to Oliver and whispered, "Have you noticed how Brandon is dressed today?"

Oliver looked up. Brandon was in a pair of stylish jeans and a white shirt, the top two buttons undone, sleeves neatly rolled up. His glasses were history and he had trimmed his mustache. "He's starting to dress like Marco," Oliver said under his breath. "Looks like you're not the only one who's been Italicized."

Once Marco had received all the signed forms, he dropped them in his leather briefcase and said, "Ready?"

"Oh yeah." Brandon rubbed his hands together. "Let's make some *pomodoro* sauce."

Marco chuckled. "So eager, *Signore*."

Jojo gazed up at Brandon. "Eager and caffeinated."

I studied them. How did Jojo know he was caffeinated? Were they together this morning? Were they together all night?

Oliver leaned in. "You see a ghost?"

"I'm not sure what I'm seeing,"

Marco continued, "If you will all please direct your attention to the chalkboard again this morning. Below your assignments you will see a famous Italian saying. *Dolce Far Niente* which translates to, the sweetness of doing nothing. This is the essence of my culture. And so, while our red sauce is simmering, which will take most of the day before we sit down to eat, I want you to, how you say, meditate on this saying. See if you can master *dolce far niente*."

"I love that," Oliver said. "Whoever heard of such a thing? What have I been doing all my life?"

"Making a bunch of dough," Janice said.

"Let's do this, Jani. Maybe go for a walk today and do nothing."

"All right, my friends," Marco said. "The Giovanelli Family Sunday Red Sauce is a meat-based sauce which is the staple of every Italian household's Sunday dinner. It takes most of the day to cook, but once it is ready, the family gathers around the table and celebrates life and love." He aligned several large cans of pureed Italian tomatoes. "This sauce is different from a quick sauce, such as a marinara that cooks in less time and is meatless. The other difference is the spices. The only spice used in this sauce is basil and it must be fresh and added at the very end of the cooking process."

"No spices?" Brandon said.

"That is correct, *Signore*. Remember, every family's recipe is unique. This is mine. I learned this recipe at *mia Nonna's* side. And I share it with you as a gift to our Rosalie." He glanced over at me. "Shall we get started?"

"*Si, si!*" Brandon said and lifted his espresso cup.

"Rosalie, you will prepare the *braciole*. Oliver and Janice, the fresh pasta. And Brandon and Joanne, the meatballs. You will also begin with the first step of cooking the onions. They should be sliced and salted and then sautéed in olive oil until they begin to brown. Then we remove the onions and the remaining oil will be used for sautéing the meat."

Brandon held an onion tight in his palm. "I think this class may be the best thing that's happened to me in a very long time." He bent down and whispered something in Jojo's ear.

She giggled and picked up the knife sharpener. "Chop, chop, Doc."

"Marco?" I said. "How about if I make some crusty Italian bread to go with our meal."

"*Perfetta.*"

"No salt?"

He shook his head. "No salt."

"Can I ask why?"

"Ah, yes, of course." He clapped his hands. "My friends, your hostess has asked why there is no salt in Tuscan bread. The common belief is that Italian food is so delicious, the bread will soak up all the flavors of the food, so why add salt?" He checked our reactions. "But, if you ask a Tuscan, they will tell you it's because before Italy was unified as one country, the only place to obtain salt in the Tuscan region, was from Pisa. And Tuscans hated Pisa. So instead of giving them money for salt, they did without. And if you ever wondered if Italians were stubborn, here, you see, is an example. We still do not put salt in our bread."

I grinned. "I love this, Marco."

Jojo and Brandon were focused on the onions, and Oliver had begun to form his mound of flour. I flinched when I realized Marco was standing next to me. "Hey." I smiled. "Do you need anything? Are all the ingredients here?"

"Everything is here." He dipped his head a little lower. "You look concerned. Did you sleep well?"

"Of course," I said quickly. "Thank you for last night. For everything."

"I want you to take liberties with the *braciole*. Maybe add your own touch." He straightened. "This is not a test. I'm just curious. Maybe you will find a way to make it even better than it already is."

I gave him a half smile. "Okay. You're on. Oh, and Marco?"

"Yes?"

"Is it all right if I share this recipe with Kevin once he's up to it?"

"Yes, yes of course. That is an excellent idea. How is he, by the way?"

"He's recovering nicely. I'll tell him you asked after him." I started to go back into the kitchen but stopped when Marco said my name.

He held my gaze. "I hope you are still considering my proposal."

"Yes." I warmed at the intensity in his eyes. "Of course, I am."

He winked and headed over to Brandon and Jojo.

Once Marco was out of earshot, Oliver was by my side. "You weren't exaggerating when you said he made you an offer. He wants you to do this, Rosie."

I stood a little straighter. "My brain is spinning."

While Oliver was rolling the dough through the pasta maker, Janice sidled up next to me. "What's with Jojo and Brandon?"

"They had a drink together last night."

"Shouldn't that be against the rules? No fraternizing in cooking school?"

"Well, we are immersed in Italian culture. How was your weekend?" I said while continuing to watch Brandon and Jojo.

"Meh," Janice said. "I missed being here with you and Oliver drinking prosecco."

"Was Trevor home?"

"Every second." She frowned and shook her head. "Guilty little bugger."

"Girlfriend, what are you going to do?"

"I'm paralyzed. Numb. Novacained up. Do you have any by the way?"

"Novocain?" I coughed out laugh. "No, I think I ran out."

"Anything else? Vicodin? Percocet?"

"Janice!" I faced her. "You're scaring me."

"I'm scaring myself. I'm exhausted and nervous at the same time. Do you know my Carson asked me if I was on Adderall? He's twelve. How many kids are taking that stuff? How does he even know what it is?"

"They must sense something's up. Are you going to talk to Trevor?"

"I'm numb. Remember?"

"Hey, Tilghman," Oliver called. "Get your butt over here. We need to dry this linguini."

A small smile appeared on Janice's face. "Your brother is awesome." She looked at me. "How is he such a good guy?"

"Crazy thing about it, he doesn't even realize it."

Chapter Forty-Six

I headed back to the kitchen to start the *bracioli,* pondering what special ingredient I would include.

"Hello, my dear." Glenn loaded the morning coffee cups into the dishwasher. "Any news from the sheriff? Was that man Sonja's father?"

"Yes. He was shot at close range in the chest. Went straight through him. Sheriff said it was a pistol of some sort. And he has also concluded Kline is the one who shot him."

"That was quite a thing to witness, digging up that body. I don't think I'll ever forget it."

I removed a pack of pancetta from the refrigerator and selected a sauté pan from the rack overhead. "Marco's recipe includes pancetta. Is it as bad for you as bacon?"

"Italians are supposedly some of the healthiest people." He started up the dishwasher.

"Everything is better with bacon," I said.

"Very true. But I don't think I've ever had it in a red sauce." Glenn wiped his hands on a towel and took me in. "I believe I need a thumb drive to download everything that's going on in your brain."

I laughed. "Where to begin? Okay, here's what's first and foremost. Brandon and Jojo have a thing."

"You mean romantically?"

"I would say yes. Or bordering on just about to be. Does that make sense?"

"What concerns you, my dear?"

"I don't know. I really like Brandon. He has risen to the occasion with class every time he has needed to." I laid several strips of pancetta in the pan and switched on the burner. "But we have to be open about this. Just like Jojo. Everyone is a suspect. And she is very vulnerable right now."

"What have you learned?"

"Nothing groundbreaking. But Jake said on Saturday that Brandon's family used to own a farm in Devon County. He said that's also one of the reasons they hired him. He was almost a local. So that led me to think, what if he has a connection to Kline?" I separated the strips with a fork. "Or does that sound too far-fetched?"

"Not so far-fetched." Glenn sat down. "Who else owns a farm in Devon County?"

"Kline." I thought for a moment. "And now Jojo. Glenn, is there any way to figure out if there's a history between the two families?"

"Honestly? We are on the Eastern Shore, my dear. That could be one of those things that is family lore. Never made the papers. Maybe never made it into a land transfer." Glenn frowned.

"I'm curious about Kline's farm. It's almost three hundred years old. There's got to be a rich history there."

"Any chance you could so some research?"

"I'm already on google. But just not near a computer." Glenn rubbed his hands together. "I'm looking forward to this."

"Ok. Brandon's full name is Brandon Preston Hitch." I reduced the flame under the burner.

"Hitch is a common name around here. But if there's anything to this, I hope to find out."

I grinned. "Thank you for being my friend. From that first day in memoir class when I felt as lost as Alice in Wonderland. I don't think this café would exist if it wasn't for you."

"You give me way too much credit. But you are most certainly welcome." Glenn nudged his glasses up his nose. "I think it's time for you to flip the bacon."

I picked up the tongs. "I almost forgot to tell you. I was chased through town by an enormous black SUV last night."

"No," Glenn said with concern. "How awful." He frowned. "Black SUV? Like the one the P.I. was filming?"

"It had to be the Russians."

"Barty and Michael. They know you overheard their conversation. They are trying to intimidate you." Glenn eyed me. "Were they successful?"

"I outran them. It was awesome."

"Just be cautious, Rosalie. This is getting more serious by the minute."

The sauce was simmering, the meatballs and *braciole* submerged in the tomatoey goodness, and the bread dough rising in a warm corner of the kitchen. Marco had offered us a little break for our *dolce far niente*, so I stepped out for a bit. As I slipped my purse on my shoulder, Marco said, "You added slices of hard-boiled egg to your *braciola*. Can I ask why?"

I hesitated, worried he didn't like the idea. I took a deep breath and said, "I wanted to add some texture and a little depth to the flavor."

"I love it."

The sun was directly overhead making my car warm and toasty as I headed to the Cardigan Tavern. There were very few hours in a day when it wasn't open. And I'd heard they served a decent lunch with fried rockfish sandwiches, but the bar was empty when I got there. Chuck came out of the kitchen when he heard the door.

"Rosalie. What a nice surprise. Blue Point?"

"It's nice to see you, too. No thanks on the beer but I do have a question for you." I set a white paper bag on the counter, the top edge neatly folded. "Cinnamon toast muffins. For you."

He wiped his hand on a dish towel. "A bribe?"

"Of sorts. Just one quick question. I don't think it will betray anyone's privacy."

Chuck braced his hands on the bar. "I heard something about that actress's father being buried on Ronnie Kline's property. Was it Gunner who found him?"

"You bet. And that's why I'm here. She arrived in town a few days before

Kline was murdered."

"Okay."

I folded my hands together. "Can you remember her ever being in here the same night as Kline before he died?"

Chuck smiled. "I don't know, Rosalie. That's a big ask."

"Could you try? This famous actress shows up at your bar. That would be a night to remember. It would have been about three weeks ago."

"Wait a minute. I do remember her coming in here. It's easy because it was a Ravens game. Everybody was excited about the new quarterback. That game filled the bar."

"And?"

"New guy played hard. After the game, everyone was pumped up. You know, maybe we'd have a winning record again. Nobody wanted to go home right away. So Ronnie kept drinking. Then he got to talking."

"What did he say, exactly?"

"He was just being Kline. But he did start talking about the government being a bunch of criminals. You know, all kinds of crap. He said they should let a farmer do what a farmer wants to do. Not try to tell an American citizen how to conduct his business. And then he went off on a tangent. He said something like the only good Russian is a dead one."

"How did people react?"

Chuck leaned back against the bar and crossed his arms. "Lucas Jennings said he agreed but for the most part everyone was hoping Kline would shut up and go home. But it was a Ravens win. People were drinking. And Ronnie Kline was always shooting his mouth off, nothing new there."

I played with a stray cocktail napkin. "Alright, here's the question. Is there any chance Sonja Volkov was here that night?"

Chuck looked out at the U-shaped bar, nodding his head at each bar stool. I leaned forward, amazed at his ability to remember who sits where, when, what they drink. He smacked his hand on a thigh. "She was right there. Last stool on the left."

"No way. Did she come in before or after Kline?"

"That I don't remember. She was keeping a low profile. You know, ball cap, sunglasses. No one had recognized her yet. I only noticed her because she had that exotic accent." He faced me. "But I'm positive it was her because right after Kline stopped bragging about putting Russians in their place, she ordered shots for the whole damn bar. Not just any shots. Lemon drop shots. Can you believe it? That's how I knew she was Hollywood or something. Took me almost an hour to get one out to everyone. Cleared me out of Citron vodka. You don't forget a thing like that."

"She knew Ronnie killed her father. And Kline was still alive. She could have killed him. She practically had the confession right there."

"This is intense, Rosalie. What are you going to do?"

"Not sure yet."

"So you think she's the one? You think she killed Kline?"

I hopped off the bar stool. "It's certainly a possibility." I reached under the counter and removed my purse from the hook. "I've got to go eat some pasta." I smiled. "Thank you, Chuck. Your memory is formidable."

"As are you."

Chapter Forty-Seven

As I drove down Main Street on the way back to the café, I noticed Glenn opening the door of the Historical Society building on the corner. I whipped into the first empty parking spot. I really did love this car.

A display of Devon County in the Civil War filled the store window. A black and white photo of an African American regiment was adjacent to one of slaves working in a tobacco field. Both Union and Confederate uniforms were arranged on headless mannequins, the brass buttons dingy, the fabric frayed.

A bell rang as I pushed open the door. Glenn stood in front of a high glass display case brimming with relics and old books. An elderly gentleman sat on a stool behind it. He eyed me over the top of his spectacles. "All of a sudden this is a busy place."

"Hello." I closed the door.

"Rosalie," Glenn said, "I'd like you to meet Daniel. I thought perhaps he could help us."

I gripped my purse and approached the glass case. "I've never been in here before. I hope we're not disturbing you."

Daniel glanced around the empty room and back at me. "I suppose you could get in line. But that would be silly because you two are the only ones here. Only customers all day, as a matter of fact."

I smiled. "I guess I'm not exactly sure what you do here."

"Well, we do just about everything we can to preserve the history of Devon County. Actually, the entire Eastern Shore. Its buildings, artifacts, history, you name it."

"I can't believe I've never been here before, either," Glenn said. "This place is a real treasure."

Daniel stood and crossed his arms. He was taller than I expected. His posture straight, shoulders level, his stature one of confidence and, well, wisdom. He slipped his wrinkled hands into the pockets of a wool cardigan.

"I'm Rosalie. It's a pleasure to meet you."

He looked at Glenn and then me. "You are in search of something."

"Oh, my." Glenn and I exchanged a quick glance. "How did you know?"

"Most people come in to look at old photographs, pick up a brochure for the walking tour, or maybe just chat about interesting spots to visit. But you, I believe, are seeking information."

Glenn tugged on his sweater vest. "I'm getting a sense we came to the right place."

"I don't suppose you would like some tea?"

"If it isn't too much trouble," Glenn said.

While Daniel busied himself in the back, we browsed around the room. I discovered a framed photograph of Main Street from 1916. "Look, Glenn, this is the café," I said. "Right here." I pointed. "It used to be a bakery."

Glenn stood next to me. "Oh, my. Will you look at that. Are those bicycles parked out front?"

"A bakery. They must have had wood-fired ovens. I would kill for one of those. Can you imagine? The bread and flatbread pizzas?"

"You're making me hungry," Glenn said.

"Me too." Daniel had returned. "You're the proprietor of the Day Lily Café?"

We turned to look at him. "Yes. I am. And Glenn is my right-hand man."

"Well, bravo to you, Rosalie and Glenn, for keeping it a thriving business. Now, come and sit. Let's see if I can answer your questions."

We followed Daniel over to a grouping of musty, overstuffed chairs in the corner. "I noticed your display in the window." I took a delicate sip of tea.

He formed a tent with his fingers. "So you are interested in Devon County's role in the Civil War?"

"We're not sure," Glenn said. "What we are curious about is a historic property named Windswept Farm. Do you know the place?"

"Ah," Daniel said. A warm smile graced his face. "Now we're talking the essence of Devon County history."

Glenn sat forward, gripping his tea cup. "So you do know about it."

"One of the oldest farms in the county." Daniel took a sip of tea. "If those walls could talk."

"If only they could," I said. "You probably heard that Ronald Kline died not long ago. His niece has inherited the entire estate."

"Yes, I did hear that. Who hasn't? It's the talk of the town."

Glenn set his tea cup on a small coffee table. "We're curious about the history of the property. Do you happen to know if the Kline family has always owned it?"

"The original owners were sympathizers to the crown. When the Revolutionary War heated up, they packed their things and took the first ship back to England. A local Colonial Naval officer was awarded the farm and took up residency there with his family. I believe the farm belonged to them until the late 1700's. That's when Mr. Kline's ancestors took over the property."

"I'm curious how you know all this," I said.

"Homes like Windswept Farm are in the historical registry," Daniel said. "All this information is public if you know where to look."

"This is fascinating," Glenn said. "Is there any other significant history? Was land ever exchanged or fought over? For instance, Rosalie owns Barclay Meadow, right next to Kline's farm."

Daniel crossed his legs and cupped his knee. "That display window of ours tells it all."

"The Civil War?" Glenn looked over at me. "I knew it. Remember I asked Jojo if her ancestors owned slaves?"

"The answer is yes," Daniel said. "They grew nothing but tobacco. Did you know that in Maryland there were troops from the Eastern Shore for both the Union and the Confederacy? We were divided. Sympathizers of the South saw it as economic issue. They had thousands of dollars invested in their slaves. Those siding with the North had their own reasons, mostly moral, especially those involved in the Underground Railroad, but the Eastern Shore was changing."

"Yes," Glenn said, "I've heard some of this. Wasn't there one particular battle involving Devon County men on both sides?"

"Yes. Brothers fighting brothers. Cousins fighting cousins. Men like Kline's ancestors hung on until the very end. Thing about it is, most Eastern Shore farmers had stopped growing tobacco. They switched to other crops that didn't require slave labor to be profitable. And they diversified, I would imagine much like you are doing now, Rosalie."

"And Kline's farm?" I asked.

"Even before the war, that soil was practically worthless from growing only tobacco. They had to sell off part of his land to keep it going. When was your home built, Miss Rosalie?"

"Right before the Civil War." I nudged Glenn. "This is incredible. I had no idea our farms were so connected."

"Some say Windswept Farm is cursed. Others say the Klines are just mean." He took a sip of tea and set the cup down on a small side table covered with a crocheted doily. "I've lived here my whole life. I've seen the Klines damage more than one family."

Glenn cleared his throat. "This is a long shot, but did they ever do harm to a family with the name Hitch?"

"Absolutely." Daniel studied Glenn. "How did you know? I thought you were new to the area?"

I pressed my toes into the soles of my shoes. "What happened, Daniel?"

"Theodore Hitch owned a small farm next to Kline. It would be on the opposite side from yours. He had some dairy cattle, raised spinach, family-run for generations. But Theodore got irritated with how many illegal immigrants Kline used. Thought he treated them badly. And also that he was taking jobs away from hard-working Eastern Shore men. So he turned him in."

"And?" Glenn leaned closer.

"Ronnie Kline ruined him. I don't know the details, I just know they had to sell. Mr. Hitch shot himself not long after. Family moved away. Not sure what happened to them."

"And how long ago was this?" Glenn said.

"Oh, I'd say about twenty-five years ago."

"Were there any children?" I said.

"Oh, yes. Quite a few of them. Do you think you know someone from this family?"

"It's a long shot," I said.

"The number of Hitches in this area is quite astounding." Daniel studied me. "Be sure you get it right."

"Thank you for everything, Daniel." I checked my watch. "Glenn, we should get back to the café."

"Thank you, Sir." Glenn stood and shook Daniel's hand. "It's been an absolute pleasure."

"One more thing," I said. "Is there any way I could get a copy of that photo of Main Street?"

"I think that can be arranged." Daniel eased himself out of the chair and escorted us to the door. I stopped when I noticed a photography book of Devon County. The cover was a gorgeous photo of an old schooner sailing into the Cardigan River. While I paid for the book, Glenn said to Daniel, "I don't suppose you are in need of volunteers?"

Chapter Forty-Eight

Glenn unlocked the back door of the café and we were met with the aroma of simmering red sauce loaded with Italian sausage, meatballs, and *braciole*. I checked the bread. It had doubled in size. I switched on the oven and followed Glenn into the dining room.

Oliver, Janice, and Marco had all returned from the break. A bottle of red wine was open on the bar. Glenn reached for two glasses from the rack over the condiments tray.

"Ah, Rosalie, you have returned," Marco said. "As soon as Brandon and Joanna arrive, I will show you the most important secret of the sauce."

"I am so ready for that." I accepted the wine from Glenn. "What did you guys do during the break?" I asked Oliver.

"We took a walk. Sat on a bench by the dock and watched the ducks."

Janice shrugged. "I only do that when I have out of town guests. It was nice."

"We savored the sweetness of doing nothing." Oliver flashed a wide grin.

"And Marco?" I said.

"Someone had to mind the sauce. And then I began researching the restaurant market in Philadelphia."

"You don't say." Oliver eyed me.

"Would you like me to put the bread in the oven?" Glenn offered.

"Can you glaze it with an egg wash first?"

Glenn frowned. "I can't do something wrong with that, right?"

"You got this," Oliver said. "Why don't I help?"

"The dough smells like pizza," Glenn said. "I would tell you a joke about pizza, but it would be too cheesy."

Oliver erupted into laughter. "Did you just tell us a joke, Glenn?"

"Yes," Janice said. "A very cheesy one."

"These jokes are beginning to remind me of parsley," Marco said.

Oliver's eyes danced. "And why is that, Chef?"

"It shows up everywhere."

Our laughter resounded in the room.

Oliver slapped Glenn's back as they walked into the kitchen. "That was a good one, Mr. Glenn."

"I'm really quite surprised I said that."

I took a sip of wine. "Where are Brandon and Jojo?"

"Honestly?" Janice said. "I don't want to know. Those two need to step back."

"Too much chocolate." Marco smiled. "I'll check the sauce." He picked up his wine glass and went into the kitchen.

"You just got a text, Rose Red."

"I know," I said without looking at my phone. "It's not the first one."

"Who doesn't answer a text?" Janice noticed Brandon and Jojo on the stoop outside. "'Bout time. I'll go let them in."

Brandon closed the door behind him and placed his hand on Jojo's back. "I hope we didn't delay anything."

"Mm." Jojo walked up to the bar. "That sauce is smelling good."

Brandon went into the men's room and flipped the lock.

"Where have you two been?" Janice took a long slug of wine.

"I took Brandon out to my uncle's farm. I mean, *my* farm. He wanted to see it." She filled a wine glass. "I got a letter from my lawyer. Barty is contesting the will. He found some clause he thinks will work. But it has to happen in thirty days."

"Did you tell Brandon about that?" I said.

"Tell him what?" Janice came to attention.

"How much the farm is worth."

Jojo tucked her hair behind an ear. "I guess I did. I told him about Barty and Michael and how they're trying to get it back. So, yeah, I guess I told him about the price they would sell it for."

"I know about these things," Janice said. "How much do they think they can get?"

Jojo took a sip of wine. "Five mil."

Janice scowled. "They can't get that much."

"Yes, they can, right, Rosalie?"

"It's not theirs to sell," I said. "At least not yet. So what did Brandon think of the farm?" I studied Jojo's face, looking for some sign of what she was feeling, why she was spending so much time with Brandon. Was she really smitten? Or just using him as a distraction? Jojo liked her distractions.

"He loved it. He knew all about the house and its historic features. Like, he showed me the newel post? You know, the bottom part of the banister with a marble cap? He said once a house was built, they put the plans in the newel post. I wonder if there's any way to check and see."

"Sounds to me like you're getting more comfortable with owning the farm." I narrowed my eyes.

"You think so?" Jojo had another sip of wine. "I'm not so sure about that."

"None of this is making any sense." Janice refilled her glass. "Jojo, you're going to have to start dealing with this inheritance. If you aren't going to move in and start farming, why don't you just sell it to Barty yourself?"

Brandon emerged from the bathroom and clapped his hands. "Isn't it about time to eat?"

"Is everyone ready?" Marco called through the door. "Come into the kitchen."

We gathered around the large commercial stove. The scent of baking bread had filled the room. Marco lifted the lid of an industrial-sized Dutch oven and reached for a box of baking soda.

"What the heck are you doing with that?" Janice said.

"Most Italian red sauce recipes involve adding carrots or sugar to counteract the acidity. *Mia famiglia*? We add baking soda." Marco scooped out a teaspoon and sifted it into the pot. The sauce fizzed and popped like a fireworks display.

The applause was deafening.

Once we finished eating our classic Italian meal, we all agreed to chip in with the clean up. Glenn tried to shoo us out of his domain, but Brandon turned on some *Bocelli* and we waltzed around performing our tasks. Once the place was spotless, Marco stood at the head of the bar and clapped his hands. "My friends. I am very sad this is our last day." His eyes sparkled. "But I am very glad we are all still alive. *Si?*"

Oliver stood next to me. "Now he's a comic?"

"Kind of not funny yet."

"Before we say our goodbyes, I have an announcement." He paused until everyone had given him their full attention. "Due to the unfortunate events last Tuesday, I feel you have not received your full Tuscan cooking experience. I am not leaving Caridgan until late Wednesday. Which means tomorrow I will be free. So I have put together a little surprise for Rosalie. I will present it to her tomorrow promptly at 9 AM. Then she will prepare a meal with what I have given her. You are all invited to watch or help or both."

Chapter Forty-Nine

I 'm pretty sure Tyler texted me a dozen times throughout the day reminding me I was invited out to his place that evening. And by the end of the afternoon, I agreed. I had no idea how it would go for a lot of reasons. I had only been to his house a few times before, but only for brief, purposeful visits, never to be entertained by him.

Tyler's property was in a remote part of Devon County. As I neared his place, the endless farmland had segued into nothing but trees and meadows. After almost five minutes of more of the same, I turned down the lane to his house where a signpost read: *East of Eden*. That was Tyler in a nutshell.

His house was small with cedar shake siding and a roof covered in solar panels. My heart fluttered around in my chest like a bird in a bath. I had no idea what would happen. And as scary as that was, I was actually enjoying the feeling. I passed a maple tree whose leaves had turned a brilliant shade of eggplant and knocked on the door.

"Welcome to my humble abode," Tyler said as he opened the door.

"Thank you." I stepped over a sleeping Dickens and entered the kitchen.

The room was spotless, with tiled countertops, a small range, and a stainless side-by-side refrigerator

"I'm not sure if you know," Tyler said as walked up next to me. "I'm off the grid."

I leaned against a counter where a row of copper canisters were lined up like nesting dolls. "Completely?"

"I have back up. But for the most part I am powered by solar, geothermal, a wood stove, and a very nice down comforter when it's cold."

"I had no idea. Why do we spend all of our time at my house?"

"We have a lot to figure out. That's why I thought you coming here might change it up a bit."

I hugged myself. "I should have brought something for us to eat. You must be hungry."

"No way, you're at my place this time." He opened the refrigerator. "I didn't know if you would come, but I put this in to chill anyway." He stood next to me. I could feel the heat from his body, the scent of his soap. "Didn't know I was an optimist, did you?" He smiled an adorable sheepish grin and I felt myself begin to relax, ever so slightly.

"Veuve Clicquot." He peeled away the foil and eyed me. "Guy at the liquor store said it was the best."

"Wow."

"Want to sit outside?"

I followed Tyler out the back door. His house bordered a small creek, a tributary of the Cardigan River. The sidewalk ended at a narrow dock with an upside-down kayak moored to a piling. A blue heron stood stock still beside it. Instead of a lawn, Tyler had wild flowers. A pileated woodpecker made waste of a suet block while the last of the hummingbirds tucked its beak into a flowering day lily.

We sat on two white Adirondack chairs. I smoothed my skirt and crossed my ankles, drumming my fingers on the wide arm of the chair while Tyler eased out the cork. After a muted pop, he filled two elegant champagne glasses.

He raised his glass. "Thank you for agreeing to come here."

We clinked our glasses together. "I wanted to. I mean, well, anyway. I'm here."

We sipped our champagne and I gazed out at the water. The heron had hunched down, annoyed at our presence, yet refusing to leave. When a large fish popped out of the water and landed on its side with a significant splash, I understood why.

"How many acres?" I said.

"Fifty. None of it is farmed."

"But why?"

"Trying to do my small part to counteract greenhouse gasses. And give the critters a safe haven during hunting season." Tyler took another hefty sip of the champagne. "Don't get me wrong, I don't judge hunters. I've done plenty of it in my day. But this place is my Charlotte's Web, so to speak."

"It's amazing, Tyler. You rarely talk about your home."

I felt his hand warm on my arm. I looked over, his gaze so intense I fought the urge to look away.

"I see you, Rosalie."

I laughed a little. "Well, that's good."

He didn't return my laugh. "I guess I don't want you to think I'm trying to change you. I love who you are. How you care so much about other people. But I realize now I was disapproving of your curiosity." He cleared his throat. "I will never ask you to be anyone other than yourself again. I got it so wrong."

Tears welled in my eyes. "But—"

"Shh." He held an index finger up to his lips. "There's more. I know you are a woman who loves hard and I can't believe I was in your cone of light." He slipped his fingers through mine. "I thought I'd lost you forever. That once I screwed up, that was it. And I did screw up. I didn't even let you explain."

"Why, Tyler? It seemed way too easy for you to jump to conclusions. That you could believe so readily that I would deliberately hurt Bini."

He took a deep breath and exhaled. "I've been thinking about it a lot. I believe some part of me anticipated you leaving me. Eventually. Just because that's my history. So it was sort of like ripping off a scab. Get it over with." He frowned. "And then you showed up with that list of things to ask Bini's lawyer. And I realized you hadn't given up. On me, on Bini, on anything."

I eased my hand out of his and looked down at my lap. "I wanted you to come after me that morning."

"I've been kicking myself ever since that I didn't."

"How am I supposed to trust you won't do it again?"

Caressing my fingers with his thumb, he said, "I want to be with you for the rest of my life."

My eyes widened. "Tyler, we've only been at this for a short time."

"Long enough for me to know I never want it any other way."

"I . . . I'm speechless." I brushed my hair back with my free hand. "I mean, I love you, I do. I—"

"I'm not asking for a response. I'm just telling you how I feel. So, it's out there. You know I'm all in. That's all I need."

The grip of tension that had surrounded my heart for the past five days loosened. I inhaled, held it for a moment, and let go. I studied his rugged face, the slight smile on his lips, allowing myself to take in his words, accepting this man actually loved me. "Thank you," I said, my voice barely audible.

He squeezed my hand. "How am I so lucky you showed up in my life? Nothing has been the same since I first saw you toss your phone in the gravel."

A tear escaped. I shook my head. "Why did that have to be your first impression of me? Why couldn't I have been on my way out to a party in a hot little black dress and heels?"

"Well, I certainly would have noticed. But I don't think I would have been as intrigued. You showed vulnerability that day. And yet you stood up for yourself at the same time. And then you invited me in for the best coffee I've ever had."

"My coffee." I laughed. "It's always about the coffee with me."

"And you are the most beautiful woman I have ever known." Tyler's lips were on mine and I wrapped my arms around his neck. He pulled me closer and more tears filled my eyes. When we separated, he brushed back my hair and took me in. "God, I love you."

I swallowed, hard, trying to catch breath. I hadn't been romanced in, well, maybe never? Ed was a practical guy. His proposal was more about how logical it would be for us to get married, that we had similar interests, would make attractive children.

I pulled away and took a long sip of champagne, trying to quell the emotions overwhelming me. And the tears. I didn't want to cry.

Tyler refilled my glass and we sat quietly, drinking more champagne, me faster than him. There was some sort of energy field vibrating between us. For a brief moment, I thought about Marco. The world he could show me. And when I looked into Tyler's eyes I knew. He was my home.

I startled when he set his glass down. He reached out for my hands and pulled me toward him, close, chest to chest, his gaze so direct I shuddered. He laced his fingers through mine. "This okay? I know we decided to take it slow. Ease into this. But I've never been more ready to make love to anyone in my entire life."

"Yes," I whispered. Then he scooped me up in his arms and carried me inside.

Later that night, I found my phone amongst the tangled sheets and texted Oliver. "I'll see you in the morning." Then I snuggled under Tyler's arm and had the best sleep I'd had in as many years as I could remember.

Chapter Fifty

Tuesday
Day Six of Cooking Class

Menu

?

T he sun showed up in all its glory for the last day of cooking school with Marco Giovanelli. Time had sailed by with countless unexpected and unwanted interruptions. I wanted to savor every minute of the final hours. After I dashed into the house for a quick shower, Oliver and I headed into town. When I parked in my slot behind the café, he finally spoke, "I hope you are happy."

"So far so good." I looked over at him. "Do you think I'm being an idiot?"

"On the contrary. I think you're following your heart no holds barred. I've never done that in my life."

"It's terrifying."

"And I would imagine a little exhilarating."

"You think Tyler's a butthead."

"He was *being* a butthead. And, if you recall, I believe I said I liked him a whole lot better than Ed. Now, Ed, he *was* a butthead, all the time. Tyler . . . I'll give him another chance." Oliver finished his coffee and set the mug on the floor mat. "You went to his place?"

"I did."

"Did he grovel?"

"A little. But it was better than that. He was positive. The thing that got me is he said, I *see* you. No one has ever said that to me before. But I liked it." I gazed over at Oliver. "When you think about it, feeling that attention, being listened to, taken in, it's the most amazing gift one human can give to another."

Oliver stared out the windshield. "You make a good point." He cleared his throat. "I'm happy for you, Rosie. Good for you." He got out of the car and walked down the sidewalk.

"Where is Oliver going?" Janice said as she watched him pass by the window.

"I have no idea. He just started to walk."

"Is he coming back to see what Marco has for you?" She crossed her arms, a small pout on her lips.

"Absolutely." Oliver turned the corner and was out of sight. "He's leaving on Friday. I think he has mixed feelings about it."

"I have mixed feelings about it, too. He's been a really good friend to me." She huffed out a sigh. "Any idea what we're doing today?"

I looked around the room and stopped at the chalkboard. "I sort of feel like this is a test. But he's already asked me to study with him. I hope I don't screw it up."

"Wait, what?" Janice scowled. "He asked you that? Are you going to go? What about Tyler? What about the farm? What about our friendship? You can't just—"

I stood next to her. She reared back. "I'm not going to touch you, relax. Look, he asked me and I said I have to think. But you're right, Cardigan is my home. If I go, it won't be permanently."

"I'm sorry I overreacted. I'm kind of having a break down, Rose Red." Janice's fingers trembled as she sat down at the bar. She gripped the edge to stop the tremor.

"You're going to get through this, girlfriend."

"My birthday is tomorrow. It's not a milestone, so I was thinking I would just hop on a train to New York and do some shopping. Maybe take in a show." She eyed me. "Want to come with?"

"Maybe." I crossed my arms staring at the door. Jojo and Brandon were together again. Glenn was on his way to let them in. "If I have figured out who has been poisoning people by then, I would love to hop on a train with you. I'll bet you could get us tickets to Hamilton."

"I bet I could."

Marco pushed through the kitchen. "*Signoras!* How are my two favorite ladies this morning?"

"We are very sad it's the last day," I said. "You?"

"Terribly depressed."

I studied him. He had a wide grin on his face. His words clearly didn't match his affect. "Where will you go first?"

"Austin. I've heard amazing things about the food scene there. Maybe I will add some Tex-Mex to my menu in Florence." He accentuated the x's, making tex-mex sound sexy.

"Where's the menu for today?" Janice said.

"It's a little complicated. I will explain when the others are here." Marco headed for the espresso machines.

Once everyone had arrived, we gathered around the bar for the last time.

"You have all chosen to come back today. That is a good sign. I think we have accomplished something very important here this last week. And made lifelong friendships. So, shall we have some fun?"

Glenn had joined us. "Do you have any idea?"

"No." I shook my head, not taking my eyes from Marco.

He jaunted back into the kitchen and returned with a large picnic basket. "I believe there is a television show that does something like this. But here is your basket, Rosalie. Inside are ingredients you must use. You may add whatever else you like, but you will be preparing a meal for us."

"Get out," Jojo said. "*Chopped*. Right? Rosalie, this is so cool."

"I'm not convinced."

"Open the damn thing," Janice said.

Glenn dried his hands on his apron. "We are all intrigued."

"As am I." I approached the mysterious basket and unbuckled the leather fasteners. "Is something going to jump out of here?"

"No." Marco laughed. "But that would have been a good trick, right Glenn?"

I rubbed the tips of my fingers together. "Okay, here we go." I opened the basket and stared down at a random assortment of ingredients.

"What 'cha got, sis?" Oliver said.

"I have to see." Jojo hurried to my other side. "Check it out, there's porcini mushrooms. Oh, I know those. You have to soak them, right?" Her elbow bumped my arm as she removed them from the basket. "And, what's this? An artichoke?"

"A petite one, yes." Marco's eyes danced with delight at what he had done.

"Oh, no you don't." Janice took a sip of prosecco. "I buy the jars. Those things are a royal pain in my buttinsky."

"What else?" Brandon said, craning his neck.

"We got some ricotta cheese . . ." Jojo hesitated. "Am I taking over, Rosalie? Do you want to look first?"

"No, no, I'm good. Please, you keep it up while my brain kicks into overdrive."

"Carry on, Jojo," Oliver said.

"Okay, we got clams." She looked up at me. "Clams? Holy crap."

"You can thank my cousin for that ingredient," Marco said.

"And Cas . . . casavel . .. I can't pronounce this, Marco. What kind of olives?"

"Castelvetrano. They are not pitted, by the way. I don't want anyone to lose a crown."

"They are delicious," Brandon said. "My favorite."

Janice wedged herself between Jojo and me. "Keep going, Jo."

"Okay, raisins. Raisins?" Jojo set the bag on the bar. "With clams?" She shrugged. "Last but not least, Phyllo dough sheets." She looked at Marco. "They're starting to thaw, Chef. Want me to stick them in the freezer?"

He shook his head, hands behind his back.

"Holy cow, Rosalie," Jojo said. "I would not want to be you right now."

I put my hands on my hips and surveyed the merchandise. "Main dish?

Appetizer?"

"Yes," Marco said. "Everything but the salad. We can sip Vin Santo for dessert and Brandon and Joanna will be preparing the salad."

"Oh, thank goodness," Janice said. "Okay, girlfriend," she said in a louder voice. "You have thirty minutes. Starting . . . now!"

"Haha," Marco said. "You have as long as you want. Your sous chefs are Janice and Oliver. And I am very curious to see what you will make for us."

Oliver smiled. "Maybe there is a test after all, Rosie."

"Would anyone mind if I put on some music?" Brandon said.

"Depends on what," Oliver said.

"*Verdi?*" Brandon pulled a CD from his jacket pocket. "I've been listening to Italian opera lately."

"*Perfetto,*" Oliver said. "You got your apron on, Jani? We are your humble servants, sister of mine."

My mind was reeling, but the dishes were coming together in my head. I assigned the initial tasks and grabbed the phyllo dough.

In no time *La Traviata* echoed through the dining room. It seemed the perfect background for our last day together. I glanced at Marco as he stood next to Janice, showing her how to peel the bottom leaves from the artichoke before steaming it. What a gift he had given us. I couldn't believe my good fortune. My world was beginning to right itself now that Tyler and I had found one another again.

Oliver attempted to chop the first Castelvetrano olive but had a difficult time working around the pit with a small paring knife. Marco approached. "It's like the garlic. Flatten the blade of a knife over it, push down, and pop it open." He pulled a large knife from the butcher block and placed it on the olive. After a quick push, It fell into several pieces, the pit easy to remove.

"That's awesome. Hey, Rosie, I mean, master chef, how big do you want the pieces to be?"

Marco waited for my answer.

"Chopped, not minced."

"Do you know what that means?" Oliver said to Marco.

"I do indeed." He picked up a piece of olive. "This one is just right."

245

Brandon stood in the middle of the room, "Okay, everyone, let's get some life into this place. This song is a *Brindisi*, a drinking tune!"

Jojo laughed. "Oh, my lord, doc. What are you doing?"

"I'm inspired. Do you know *la traviata* means the fallen woman?"

"I'm sorry?" Oliver caught my eye and mouthed, *what the . . .*

I studied Brandon. He was already getting a little tipsy. And he was wearing the same shirt and jeans from yesterday, only now the shirt was wrinkled, the shirttail untucked.

"Come, Joanna," Brandon started for the kitchen. "We need to select our salad ingredients and open some more wine."

Not long after, Glenn slumped into a chair at the bar. "Mind if I sit for a moment?"

"Never," I said. "Joanna and Brandon? Getting a little heated back there?" I pushed out the edges out of the phyllo dough with a rolling pin.

Glenn's face flushed. "Brandon is quite animated today, bordering on boisterous." He shook his head and I could see his he was trying to make sense of Brandon's change in behavior. He took a deep breath and exhaled. "This is the last day of class. What are you doing tomorrow morning?"

"Having coffee with you," I said. "Any insights to share?"

"I'll have a nice hot toddy when I get home and organize what we know. I like to put it all on my whiteboard. Each suspect. Can we meet at my place?"

"Oh my gosh, yes." I straightened, rolling pin tight in my grip. "I just remembered, the sheriff said he was going to interview Sonja. I wonder if he learned anything." I pushed my hair back from my face, my forehead dotted with perspiration. "I think I'll stop in to see him on way home. Oh, wait. It's going to be too late."

Glenn cleared his throat. "If you don't mind my saying, you are going to need a respite after this class. You haven't stopped running for three weeks."

"I can't stop until we know who's done this. Can you?" I heaved out a sigh, realizing he was right. I was running on nothing but adrenaline. "Tomorrow morning is a good idea. But not tonight?"

Glenn smiled my favorite Glenn smile. "Not tonight, my dear. Not tonight."

Chapter Fifty-One

Oliver and Janice teamed up and we went to work on the mystery basket. *Verdi* arias inspired us and the dinner began to come together. I decided the phyllo dough would be the base for a savory appetizer. Marco had helped Janice snip the top of the artichoke, peel away the outer leaves, and set it to steam. Meanwhile I rehydrated the porcini mushrooms with boiling water and asked Oliver to chop them once they cooled.

Next they removed the remaining leaves from the cooked artichoke and chopped up the heart. We tossed it in some melted butter with the mushrooms and garlic, and I added the raisins. I brushed the phyllo dough with melted butter and spread the ricotta cheese over it. I topped it off with the artichoke mix. Oliver, using his dough mastery, covered it with another piece of phyllo and brushed it with more butter.

Janice slid it into the oven and we got started on the main dish. Linguini with clam sauce. Oliver steamed the clams while I played with the sauce. I melted butter and added olive oil. Next I added some smashed garlic cloves, capers, the Castelvetrano olives, a tablespoon of tomato paste, and chopped tomatoes. Janice cooked the linguini al dente and our meal was ready.

Much like the night we had the feast, Glenn and Marco readied the café so we could be together for our final meal. The candles had been relit and the room glowed. We sat around the table, each with a small plate of phyllo squares, and a glass of chilled white wine.

I felt Marco's eyes on me and looked up. His face was flushed, his eyelids at half-mast.

"You don't like them?" I asked.

He shook his head slowly. *"Au contraire.* These will be on my menu."

"Really?" I flattened my palm over my heart.

"These are crazy good." Jojo licked a finger. "Can you write down the recipe?"

"I'll tell you what," Marco said. "I'll compile all of the recipes we've made and send them to you in a nice tidy folder."

"Even the red sauce?" Brandon said, eyebrows arched.

Marco shook his finger back and forth. "Never the red sauce."

"I'd order these things in a restaurant." Janice picked up her third square. "And you know, artichokes aren't so bad. I've always thought they were a little scary. But it wasn't so bad cooking them." She looked around the table, stopping at each face. Tears welled in her eyes. "I've learned a lot about myself in this class. I didn't expect to, you know? I just wanted to get out of the house." She wiped an eye with a knuckle. "This cooking thing is kind of magical. Look what we did. Together. I feel like I can do this. Cook. For me. For my family. And the candle thing is so cool." She wiped her hands on a napkin. "I'm going to start an Italian night for my family. And I'm going to cook." She gave her head a sharp nod. "I'm going to need to find a red checkered tablecloth."

"You know, Jani?" Oliver said. "I feel the same. I made risotto the other night and it touched something in me. Something deep. Like I had been avoiding a basic part of living."

"I've been known to quote Bourdain before," Marco said. "But one of my favorites I think you will relate to. Bourdain said, and I know this one verbatim, "Food is everything we are. It's an extension of nationalist feeling, ethnic feeling, your personal history, your province, your region, your tribe, your grandma. It's inseparable from those things from the get-go."

"That's wonderful," I said.

Brandon cleared his throat. "And if those things weren't passed down to you, or at least you weren't interested in what they were selling . . ." he took a long sip of wine. "Then you can go to cooking school and start your own traditions." He had begun to slur his words.

"Um, kind of the same thing," Janice frowned at Brandon. "That sounds a little bit more like sticking it to the man."

Brandon popped another square into his mouth and brushed his hands together. "No, I'm talking about taking your life into your own hands and learning skills you were never taught." He lifted his glass. "You don't always have to keep playing the hand you were dealt. Knowledge enables that. And I learned a lot here thanks to Marco. So? A toast?"

"To Marco," Oliver said, and we chimed in with a clink of glasses.

After we finished the clams and a *panzanella all'* Brandon and Jojo, I walked Marco to the door. "Thank you," I said. "I actually enjoyed creating under pressure. That adrenaline thing can be fun."

"Then you are, as I already know, a true chef."

"The clams came out pretty well. Did you like them?"

"They will be on our American restaurant's menu."

My heart warmed from the food, the wine, and Marco's praise. "I guess this is good-bye?"

"I will stop by in the morning. *Sí?*"

"Yes, please."

"It is good what we have done here, you and me. Everyone is a little different than when they started." He nodded his head. *"Better* than when they started. We have healed some souls, have we not? You have given me this gift, Rosalie. My heart is happier too for this opportunity to help others." His eyes were moist. "I wasn't expecting that."

"Food is power," I said, for the first time truly understanding the depth of meaning to that quote.

"Ciao, my dear." Marco kissed both my cheeks and left.

Oliver carried the last of the dish bins into the kitchen where Glenn and I were cleaning up. "I'm going to head over to The Grande. Do you mind? Or do you need me to help out some more around here?"

"Do you want some company?" I said.

"I got a text from Sonja. She asked me to meet her there."

Glenn and I exchanged a concerned look. "She hasn't had her revenge, Oliver."

"I didn't get that vibe. I think she's getting ready to leave. She said she's been talking with her agent about making some changes. And she wants to fly her father's ashes back to the west coast. We're just going to have a glass of champagne. It will be fine. Oh, she has an alibi for the day Kline died. The sheriff checked it out. She was at the Grande the whole time."

I chewed on the inside of my cheek. Oliver had come so far. And I still didn't understand Sonja. One minute she was kind and thoughtful, the next, angry at the world. "If she is indeed leaving, please tell her I wish her luck." I felt a tug of worry for Oliver. The sheriff asked her for an alibi on that day. But who's to say when she poisoned the liquor? She was in town days before Kline was murdered. She could have done it the night before and waited at the Grande for the news Kline was dead.

"Please tell Sonja we'll be watching the next season," Glenn said.

Not really, I thought, but kept quiet.

"Are you sure I can't help around here?" Oliver said.

"You've done enough. Call me when you're ready to come home and I'll pick you up."

"No Ubers in Cardigan?" Oliver smiled.

"Just Rosalies." Glenn returned a sauté pan to the over-head rack. "Has everyone gone?"

"Place is empty." Oliver grabbed his jacket and walked outside. "I'll see you two later."

I loaded the dishwasher with the last of the dishes. "I got a text from Cliff, the private detective."

"Anything new with the Russians?"

"He sent a video of both Michael and Barty going into the house."

"So they are still trying to do this deal?"

"Yes, they are." I frowned. "Glenn, if they are going through with this, and they have hired a lawyer to contest the will, why would they want to kill Jojo? If she's dead, the will would go into probate and they may never get the farm."

"So you're saying you don't think they're the murderers? Either one of them?"

"I think they're trying to do a very bad thing, and they are most likely incredibly greedy, but if they were going to kill Jojo, they would have done it by now. They wouldn't be going through other channels. And why would they have murdered Ronnie Kline if he was on board with the deal?"

Glenn sat on a nearby stool and rubbed his knee caps. "So is it Jojo?"

"She has the motive and access."

"And that beautiful farm."

"I just don't get it, Glenn. She's been bewildered by all that's happened. She's more the type to react to things, not make them happen."

"That only leaves one person."

"I haven't ruled Sonja out completely, but I agree. Is there any way for us to find out if Brandon is the Hitch who lived next to Kline?"

I stopped talking when I noticed dark circles under Glenn's eyes. A lock of hair had fallen onto his forehead. "You've worked hard, my friend. Why don't you head home and I'll finish up. Get some rest and I'll see you in the morning."

"Are you sure you don't need me here? There's still so much to do."

"It's Tuesday. We don't reopen until Monday. I have plenty of time to get things back in shape." I crossed my arms and smiled. "Besides, I want to take all this in. I'm going to miss these classes. And Marco, too."

Glenn pushed himself up to a stand. "Maybe I'll stop by and have some tea with Gretchen. I'll see you at my place in the morning? And don't do too much. It's like you said, everything can wait. We have plenty of time."

I said good-bye to Glenn and flipped the dead bolt to the kitchen door. I hadn't been alone in the café for quite a while. I filled the soap dispenser and started the dishwasher. After texting Tyler that I loved him and couldn't wait to see him tomorrow morning, I dropped my phone in my apron pocket, and went into the dining room.

I pulled the tables apart and moved them back to their original location while planning the new menu in my head. I wondered where I could find zucchini blossoms in October. I heard a noise behind me and spun around. Brandon was walking out of the bathroom.

"You startled me." I fanned myself. "I didn't know you were still here."

"I thought we could share one last glass of wine together. Reminisce about the class?"

His fists were clenched. As he brushed past me I noted a faint stench on him, as if he had just finished exercising, or was stressed by something.

"I wasn't planning on staying long, Brandon. Tyler is expecting me."

"And who might Tyler be?"

"My significant other." I took a step toward the kitchen."

"How lucky for him to feel significant." He walked to the bar and draped his jacket over a chair. "Looks like there's one last bottle of this delicious chianti. Did you know it is a Sangiovese? I knew it from the first sip. I really do know a lot of things." He pulled two glasses from the shelf overhead. "But then, you do too. That's unfortunate, don't you think? If you were a little stupid, we wouldn't be in this predicament."

"And what predicament is that?"

"You're not going home, Rosalie." He wiped the beads of perspiration from his forehead. "One more glass is all you need."

Fear gripped my heart. I looked out the front door measuring the distance. Could I run? But where? Main Street was quiet. It was a Tuesday. Everything closed by five. Darkness had fallen over my beloved Cardigan.

The cork unleashed with a loud pop. I glanced at Brandon just as he finished filling two glasses.

"Shall we?" He gestured toward the nearest table.

I sat gingerly in the chair opposite Brandon as he set a glass in front of me.

"Do you remember when you said this wine tasted peppery?"

"Yes, of course."

"So much has happened since that afternoon. Why don't you take a sip?"

My stomach knotted up. Could he have poisoned the wine? But I watched him open the bottle. Wait, no I didn't. I was staring out the front door. "You first."

"But of course." He lifted the glass and took a long, hefty draw. After setting it back on the table, he said, "So, Miss Rosalie. Have you solved your mystery?"

I studied him. "Yes, Brandon. I believe I have at last."

"Do tell."

"Jojo already told you about the deal to sell the farm to the Russians. Barty hasn't given up and I don't believe he will. Five million dollars is a lot of money." I pinched the stem of my glass.

He leaned forward, elbows on the table. "So it was Barty. Did you tell the sheriff?"

"We're meeting tomorrow morning."

"And the evidence?"

"Barty's been spending time with the Russians. They rented a house on Cedar Avenue. I have video of him going inside."

"But why poison Kevin?"

"He already had the method because he poisoned his uncle. He was in the café right after the will reading. He was upset. He wanted either to kill Jojo and/or throw the sheriff off track." I shrugged. "Who else could it be?"

Brandon drained his glass and filled it again. "Sonja Volkov. Jojo is certain it was her."

"I suppose it could be her, too. See?" I shrugged. "The case is not closed."

"You're not drinking," Brandon said in a low voice, almost a growl. "And you're a terrible liar."

I straightened my spine. "Sometimes you have to trust your gut. I think I know who did this. It might have been Sonja, but my money is on Barty. You can't escape your genes and everyone says the Klines are mean. Whether Michael was an accomplice in some way remains to be seen. But I'm pretty sure he got involved later. After the poisonings."

"Take a sip."

"Why?"

"So you know it doesn't contain any hemlock."

"Hemlock. Your MO."

"Ah, see, you should have been a little more stupid. But you can't help yourself. Now that you've said that, it's clear you know it was me. *Brava*, Rosalie Hart." He tapped his fingertips together. "You solved your mystery. Now take a sip. Then you can go home to your significant man."

I lifted the glass, my hand trembling. All the research I'd done on hemlock poisoning flashed through my mind, the speed of its devastation, how only a very small amount was enough to kill. I set the glass back on the table. "Brandon, if no one has any proof, why are you doing this?"

"I want you out of my way. You are a bit player who is too curious for her own good. But I'm not the first to tell you that. Now, the sheriff? He will never figure out it was me. I am invisible to him. But you? It was just a matter of time. I know you went to the historical society. I know you wondered about my name. So I need you to step out of the way and let me finish this. So? Have a peppery sip."

I looked around the room, wondering if someone had forgotten something. Or maybe the sheriff was idling out front in his vehicle. I clutched my phone with my free hand. It vibrated. "I have a text."

"What are you doing?"

"It's from Oliver. He wants me to join him at The Grande." I leveled my eyes with Brandon's. "If I don't respond, he'll think something's happened to me."

"Show me."

I held the phone out to him.

"Type your response and I want to see it before you hit send."

I clicked rapidly. *Having a glass of wine with Brandon. Still at the café* "There? That okay?"

"Take me out of it."

"Fine." I deleted the having a glass of wine sentence, knowing Oliver would wonder why I was still here. At least I hoped he would. As I hit the backspace I managed to type h-e-l-p. I hit send as fast as I could and dropped the phone back into my apron.

"Keep your phone where I can see it."

I placed it face down on the table.

"It's been the perfect crime so far, Miss Rosalie. I have left no evidence."

"Except if you kill me."

"When did you realize it was me?"

"Only recently. You are really quite good at this."

"Thank you." He leaned back and smiled.

"So why Kevin? Why did you poison the salt?"

He rolled his eyes. "You said it yourself. To throw the sheriff off track. And it did just that, I believe."

"Why are you spending so much time with Jojo? Is she in danger?"

"It's the perfect twist. I seduce the niece. Move onto the farm. Who knows what could befall the lovely Joanna. Once she's written her will, that is."

"How did you know she was taking the class?"

"I've been watching her ever since I took this job. Stalked her on Facebook. She posted in Cardigan Life about the class, that she had signed up. I even knew she did yoga sometimes on Mondays and wasn't always with her uncle in the morning. I had everything in place and this was just what I needed. A way to endear myself to Joanna."

"I know about your family, your father."

His face paled. "No one knows about that."

"The Klines ruined him because he turned them in for abusing migrant workers."

"He paid them nothing, let them work fourteen hours days. It was as if that farm had slaves again." Brandon's face darkened. "My father shot himself. My mother found him. She was never the same." He stomped over to the bar, grabbed the wine bottle, and filled his glass to the brim. "It will be better for everyone when the Kline family is obliterated."

"How'd you get Kline to drink the bourbon?"

"I tell you that and you drink the wine."

My mouth had dried. No one knew Brandon was here. He could easily get away with this and it would be one more unsolved poisoning. His prints were all over the café. But he could wipe the glass clean, have plenty of time to erase any evidence. He might even play some opera, although by the looks of him, Brandon's giddiness at having pulled off the perfect crime was eating away at his soul. My guess is he hadn't slept for a few days based on the redness of his eyes, the intensity of his face.

"How?" I pressed.

"I offered him a better deal."

"What do you mean?"

"To buy the farm. That's why he never closed with the Russians."

"How did you know about the Russians?"

"As I said, I watched that family closely. Several people were abuzz about the Russians, what they were here to do."

"You bettered the deal?"

"I offered six million. He could retire in Florida. He thought about it for a bit. He mumbled a lot. Said he was feeling regret about selling. That he had gotten tired of Barty's greed and had rewritten his will in a drunken haze to give everything to Jojo and gotten it notarized by his lawyer the day before. But then he thought for a bit and said going to Florida was a good idea and Jojo would have to find another way to get rich. Plus, selling to me meant he didn't have to do a dirty deal with the filthy Russians. It was the perfect solution."

"And you celebrated with a Maker's Mark toast?"

"Once I learned Jojo was to inherit the farm, my plan was complete. So, yes, I poured us each a glass, just as I have done here with you." His smile sent an icy chill up my spine. "You can find out anything you want to know about anybody in a tiny pathetic little town."

I stared at the door. Where was Oliver? I noticed the dead bolt was locked. There was no way for him to get in. I was trembling. There had to be a way.

Brandon stood. "And now the popular Rosalie Hart will die in her own café drinking the wine of her dear friend, Alessa. It will be the tragedy of the century."

"I suppose you're going to watch."

"You die?"

I nodded.

He removed a cigar from his shirt pocket. "Yes. And now I'm going to dim the lights and wait behind the bar in case we have any passersby." He stood and walked over to his jacket. My eyes widened as he removed a rope from the pocket.

"What is that for?"

"I'm bored with your questions." He looped the rope through the slats in the chair. I flinched when he touched my hand.

"Brandon, I have a case against Barty."

"I know how self-righteous you are. You could never let me walk away." He tightened the rope around my wrist, grabbed the other hand, and tied them together. I stiffened with terror as he returned to his jacket.

"Well," I said, slightly out of breath, "guess I can't drink the wine now. Maybe you don't know everything after all."

"Shut up," he snapped. He closed his eyes and held them shut. "Of course you can." His nostrils flared. "You can drink it with this." He removed a straw from his jacket and dropped it into the glass.

"I won't do it, Brandon. This is wrong and you know it. Your father was a compassionate man. What would he say about this?"

"Shut up!" He slapped my cheek. My head jerked to the side.

"I won't do it," I said in a softer voice.

"I was hoping it wouldn't come to this." He dimmed the lights to their lowest setting and lowered himself to the floor. "Will you drink to save a friend? Glenn, perhaps?"

"Glenn doesn't know anything. I swear."

"Thank you for that information. Apparently I'm not finished after I leave here." Brandon peeled the cellophane from the cigar. "What else . . ." He frowned. "Oh, I know. Don't you have a daughter? I believe her name is Annie. She's a junior at Duke. Studying—"

"No!" I screamed, my eyes wide. I swung my head toward the glass as hard as I could. The wine bled all over my beautiful café as the glass shattered on the floor.

"You . . ."

I tried to wiggle my hands free as Brandon struggled to get up. I screamed and ducked my head as a bullet burst through the front door. A hand covered in a pink sweater pushed away what glass remained and flipped the deadbolt. Oliver and Sonja rushed in. Brandon started to run but slipped on the wine.

He steadied himself and headed for the kitchen.

"My gun is pointed at the back of your head," Sonja said in a thick accent. "And I've been itching to shoot someone for weeks."

Chapter Fifty-Two

The lights blazed in the café, Sonja at the bar smoking a cigarette, Oliver next to me, his arm tight around my shoulders.

Sheriff Wilgus brought me a dish towel filled with ice and placed it on my cheek while his deputy walked a handcuffed Brandon to the cruiser. "So the wine on the floor has hemlock in it?"

"Yes." I nodded, but I couldn't stop shaking. "He was waiting for me to drink it."

Oliver squeezed my shoulder. "What a sick thing to do. What's wrong with that guy?"

"You're lucky, then," the sheriff said. "Why do you think he didn't force you to drink it?"

"He was about to." I held the towel to my cheek. "He wanted to watch. He was going to smoke a cigar while I died."

"What a disgusting man," Sonja said while exhaling a cloud of smoke. "The death penalty would be too good for him."

"You got a way for me to get a sample?" the sheriff said.

"I got this." Oliver stood and went into the kitchen.

I studied the sheriff's face. His eyes drooped a little, his lips turned down. "I was going to call you on my way home," I said. "Tell you Brandon was the killer."

"I know," he said. "I could tell you were getting close." He sat across from me. "You gonna be okay?"

"Eventually," I said. "Thank you, Sheriff, for your concern. It means a lot."

"You know what, Hart?"

259

"No."

"I think I'm ready for you to call me Joe. How's that?"

"Okay." I smiled. "Thank you, Joe."

Chapter Fifty-Three

O nce Oliver told him what happened, Tyler met us at the farm that night, Dickens by his side. He slept in my bed, holding me close until I finally stopped shaking. Every time I startled awake, he soothed me, telling me over and over again that I was safe. That he was here with me. Dawn was breaking when I at last fell into a deep, REM sleep.

Everything was easier to handle in the daylight. My night terrors had subsided and I relished the sun-drenched morning, knowing we had all survived Brandon's insanity and the investigation was over at last. After lots of coffee and a steaming hot shower, Tyler accompanied me to the café where I would be saying *arrivederci* to Marco Giovanelli.

I hesitated when Tyler and I arrived, swallowing back the fear and muscle memory of the night before. "Tyler," I said as I took in the room. The restaurant was spotless, everything in place, no evidence of Brandon, the rope, the wine, the overturned chair. "Do you know who did this?"

"I sure do. Your loyal staff to the rescue."

"Glenn."

"He's kicking himself for not checking to see if the café was empty before he left."

"Of course, he is. But we all thought everyone had gone home. Oliver did too."

I felt a pang of nostalgia for the classes as I looked around the restaurant. And then I noticed the front door. Plastic had been taped over the opening where the glass had shattered. It breathed in and out like a lung. I felt a wash of relief we all survived. Everyone, including Tyler and me.

I fluffed my hair and smoothed my hands over my skirt. Tyler was at the coffee machines.

I looked up to see Marco walking toward the café. I opened the door and a crisp fall breeze followed him into the room. He stepped inside, the classic Italian male, solidly comfortable in his own skin.

"Rosalie, I heard what happened." He gripped my arms and kissed me slowly, one cheek at a time. "Please tell me you are okay. I can't believe it was Brandon who was behind the poisonings." He startled when he saw Tyler, and let go of my arms.

I stood back. "Marco, this is Tyler Wells."

Tyler extended his hand, although he was frowning. They exchanged a quick shake.

While massaging his hand, Marco said, "I didn't know there was a Tyler Wells. Where have you been these past two weeks?"

Tyler cinched his thumbs in the front pockets of his jeans. Then he smiled a sheepish grin, his dimples framing his mouth. "Missing opportunities."

"Ah," Marco said, seeming to appreciate Tyler's self-deprecation. "That's a tendency for our male species. Have you recovered?"

Tyler caught my eye and winked. "I sure hope so."

"Marco, Tyler is the farmer who leases my land. He farms organic, and if all goes well, we can call ourselves sustainable once we receive our certification."

I watched Marco closely. I had a pretty good idea about his feelings for me. And yet he took Tyler in and nodded. "I cannot say another word until I have had an espresso." He walked around the bar, and his familiarity with my restaurant gave me that sort of homesick feeling—the tug in your belly when you realized something wonderful was going to end.

Once the Mieles spat out a rich dark espresso, Marco finished it off in one quick gesture. He turned to face us. Another man in my life who didn't wait for his coffee to cool. "*Signore,*" he said. "Have you ever heard of the Island of Naxos?"

"No." Tyler settled onto a chair and gripped his coffee mug. "Why?"

"I shall tell you." Marco propped his leg on a low sink under the bar and leaned forward. "Naxos is a beautiful island in an archipelago off the eastern coast of Greece. They call these islands the Cyclades because they form a circle around the sacred island of Delos." He made a circular motion with his hand. "They are all temperate and beautiful."

I watched carefully, allowing these two intriguing men to find a common ground.

"In the Aegean?" Tyler said.

"Exactly." Marco's eyes danced. "You know your geography. This island? If for some reason the apocalypse happens? That is where I want to be. You see, it is entirely self-sustainable. It has the mountain to keep it cool, lush green earth to grow crops year-round, farm animals for dairy, an abundance of fish in the sea. And long ago the natives built a cistern at the top of the city that can hold enough water to sustain the population for an entire year for when the island was under siege."

Tyler's eye narrowed. "Sounds incredible."

"It is a beautiful place. The sea is a deep *azzurro*, teeming with fish. The people are warm and welcoming. And the food . . ." Marco puckered his lips and kissed his fingers . . . "they have the best tomatoes I've ever tasted." He bowed his head. "Better than in Italy." He crossed himself. "Don't tell anyone I said that."

"Not a word," Tyler said. "How have I never heard of this place. It sounds too good to be true."

"Blame the gods," he said. "They are self-indulgent." Marco cocked his head. "But you see, most importantly, it is not unlike your farm. When you are sustainable, you protect your land, you don't pollute your water, you honor the earth, the animals, the things that," he spread open his arms, "sustain you."

Tyler hadn't taken his eyes off Marco. He seemed mesmerized. It occurred to me as I observed their interaction that Tyler rarely encountered someone not of the Eastern Shore. Although he was extremely well read, sometimes a person had to experience it firsthand. I smiled, pleased they had a chance to interact. I didn't want it to end.

"And there you have it, Rosalie," Marco said and gazed over at me.

"I don't want you to stop talking." I smiled. "You live in a wonderful world."

His brown eyes drooped like a puppy. "Walk me to the door?"

"Yes, but I need to get something." I reached under the counter and removed the photography book I had bought at the Historical Society. I held it against my chest and followed Marco outside.

"There's a Tyler," he said.

I nodded. "Yes. There is."

"So you will not come?"

"Oh, I want to come and study with you."

A small smile formed on his lips. "Really?"

"I have a lot to figure out. But your offer is a dream realized. Can I take some time to think about it?"

"But of course."

"Is there an expiration date?"

"I have been searching for you. I told you that. I want to open a restaurant here. And you are the one. I hope you will agree."

"Thank you, Marco. For coming here." I offered him the book. "This is for you. So you don't forget you have grateful friends on the Eastern Shore of Maryland."

"It's perfect. Thank you." He gave me a strong enveloping hug. "*Ciao*, my *Rosalia*. I will see you in Italy." He wiggled his eyebrows. "How do you say? The sooner the better."

Chapter Fifty-Four

Later that day, Tyler and I were in his pickup on our way to Janice's house. Trevor had invited us for dinner to celebrate her birthday. I was dreading it more than a little, not sure what to expect. But I knew I needed to be there for my friend. I had scooted over to the middle of the bench seat, feeling like I was on a date in high school, and loving every minute of it.

Tyler draped an arm around my shoulders. "Marco's a fascinating guy. I see why you're so taken with him." He squeezed my shoulder. "I'm actually very impressed. He's the real deal." He glanced over at me. "Congratulations, Rosalie."

"Thank you." I crossed my legs. "It's pretty amazing. But for now I'm excited about getting the café up and running again. I have so many new dishes I want to serve. Oh, and I need to teach Custer how to make fresh pasta. I hope all my favorite customers haven't found somewhere else to go."

"Not a chance." Tyler sat quietly for a moment. "Rosalie? What do you say we go to Greece in the spring."

"What?" My mouth fell open. "Are you serious? You would travel to Europe?"

"I studied the classics in college. I've always wanted to go to Rome and Athens. And now I want to go to Naxos. You in?"

"Ask me twice, Mr. Wells." I coughed out a laugh. "Would you spend that much time away from the farm?"

"If I'm with you." He wrapped a tress of my hair around a finger. "My life ain't so pretty when you're not in it."

I snuggled next to him. "Oh, I've really missed you."

He turned down the lane to Janice's house, spinning the wheel with the palm of his hand.

After angling his truck under a spindly pine tree, he shut down the engine and pulled me closer. "You okay if I just love you like nobody's business?"

"Yes, please do." I slipped my hand into his.

Tyler looked out at their very large and beautiful home. "So Trevor is having an affair with Bonnie Tucker. And we are about to sit down to dinner with the two of them to celebrate her birthday?"

"That's correct. She has video of Trevor going into Bonnie's house two days in a row. The first time he was there over an hour."

He opened the door and climbed out. I picked up the bottle of wine we had brought, gripped the steering wheel, and shifted across the seat.

Tyler took my hand. "You just bring the one?"

"Welcome," a petite woman said as we stood in the entryway of the Tilghman household.

"Bonnie?" Tyler said.

His face had paled. When I caught his eye, I mouthed, *Bonnie?*

He gave me a quick nod.

"Why, I haven't seen you in years," Bonnie said. "Come on in."

I stepped gingerly into the foyer. "Where's Janice?"

"She's not here yet," Bonnie said as she took the wine from me. "Don't you want to put some sort of tag on it? How will she know it's from you?"

"Because we plan to have it for dinner."

"Oh, that's right," she said, overly enthusiastic. "You're here for dinner."

"Bonnie," Tyler said. "Where's Trevor?"

"He's right inside."

I placed my palm over my stomach, trying to quell the lump of dread. "This is so awful," I whispered to Tyler.

"Do we have to stay?" he whispered back.

"I can't abandon her." My mind raced. I had to warn her somehow. I dug through my purse for my phone.

"Come on, come on," Bonnie said, waving us inside. "Everyone is in the conservatory."

"Everyone?" My head shot up.

"Yes." Glancing at her watch, she said, "Janice will be here any minute. You have to shut the door."

Trevor strolled into the foyer. "Remember, Bonnie, they have to be out here. Janice is expecting to see them. We don't want her to know until the last minute."

"Hey, Rose Red." He walked over and gave me a quick kiss on the cheek. "Know what exactly?"

"She doesn't know about the surprise party. I've been planning it for weeks." He grinned. "Bonnie's helped me. She made the cake, decorations. You name it."

"I started my own business after my divorce," Bonnie said. "I plan parties. It's perfect because I can get it all done while my kids are in school."

I felt a little dizzy. "That is the best news I've heard in a long time."

Bonnie's forehead furrowed. "Why is that?"

"Where is everyone else?" Tyler said. "I want to see who's here." He shut the door and we followed Bonnie and Trevor through the house.

The conservatory was standing room only, filled with animated people clutching champagne glasses under streams of silver and gold crepe paper. I spotted Oliver chatting with the man next to him. "You did all this?" I said to Trevor.

"There's no way she knows," he said. "She's only turning forty-seven. Who throws a surprise party for a forty-seventh birthday?"

"Oh," I said. "She will definitely be surprised." I smiled at him. "Nicely done, Trevor. I always knew you were a good guy."

"Okay," Bonnie said, "you two go out into the living room. And hurry!"

The tears erupted immediately when Janice entered the conservatory to shouts of 'surprise'. And then she took in Bonnie. And that's when I knew I was there for a reason. I rushed to her side and said, "Bonnie is a party planner." I forced her to look at me. "Janice. Do you understand? They've been planning your party together for weeks."

Janice gave me a blank stare. I placed my hand on her cheek and smiled. "Snow White. He was planning your party. Not having an affair. He did all of this for you."

She looked at Trevor. "You're not?"

"I'm not what?" He wrapped his arms around her. "You're really surprised?"

"Oh, hell yes." She looked back at me. I was beyond shocked when she embraced me in a bear hug. "Thank you for being my friend." She sniffled in my hair.

She let go and wiped under her eyes. She scanned the room and finally, a wide grin brightened her face. "Now will someone *please* get me a glass of champagne."

Chapter Fifty-Five

E arly the next morning I drove into town to pay a visit to Joe Wilgus. I found him in his office, pumped up like a peacock in full plumage. "Someone is having a good day," I said. "Did you by chance polish your badge?"

"You noticed."

"What happened with the Russians?"

"Been busy around here." He leaned back in his seat. The springs in his desk chair sounding as if they were at their breaking point. One day, I thought, one day they're going to blow.

"Homeland Security got out here yesterday. They searched the house on Cedar Lane."

"Did you go with them?"

"Heck, yeah. They pride themselves on working alongside the local law. I got the search warrant and off we went."

I sat in the chair opposite him. "Were they up to something?"

"House was loaded with surveillance equipment." He clasped his hands around his belly. "All kinds of stuff. Most importantly, detailed maps of DC and Baltimore. Even the Bay Bridge."

"That's terrifying." I suppressed a shudder.

"Oh, and get this, they had some kind of device that taps into cell phone towers. Never seen anything like it."

"I need to tell Cliff, the private detective. Oh, and he has lots of video if they need any more evidence." I smiled. "Nicely done . . . Joe." I checked his reaction. He seemed to take it in stride that I called him by his first name.

"They took all three of those guys in for questioning. But we're pretty certain they were up to something smelly. Confiscated all their computers, too." He sat forward again. "Little old Cardigan could make CNN."

"And what about Barty and Michael?"

"It all depends on how much they knew about what the Russians were up to—if they were willing to sell knowing they were going to do something illegal, something that would threaten our national security. I think we'll know more once they've sorted through all of the evidence."

"Cliff also has video of both of them going into the house on Cedar Lane. That's got to be worth something." I crossed my legs and sat back. "Maybe we stopped something, you and me. It's like Glenn said, a remote farm in Devon County? Seems miles away from anything important. But as the crow flies?"

"Baltimore, DC, you name it." He checked his phone. "I got the boys watching the house just to be sure."

"And can I ask where Brandon is?"

"In the cell. You know he's here." He narrowed his eyes. "You doin' okay?"

"I think so. The last thing he did before Oliver and Sonja burst in was threaten my Annie. I think that was the worst of it. To think he could have—"

"The man will most likely end up in the psych ward."

"He loves to play games with words, manipulate people to believe he's someone he could never be. I just hope they never let him out." I picked up my purse. "I've called Annie so many times she finally told me she was in the middle of mid-terms. I may drive down there anyway. I think I need a visual."

He frowned. "I thought you were reopening."

I laughed. "Good point. Opening day is Monday. Oh, and my coffee supplier is quite excited about some new organic Honduran Roast. I'll need your opinion, of course, before I start serving it."

"I'll be there first thing Monday morning."

Chapter Fifty-Six

Oliver and I strolled down to the river that evening and sat at the end of the dock, dangling our legs over the edge. The trees on the opposite bank glowed like brass-coated lanterns as the sun dipped behind us, backlighting the view. It was his last night with me. I didn't want him to go.

"You need to get a boat," he said.

"Would that lure you back?"

"Oh, no, I don't need a dangling carrot. I'll be back for certain."

"I apologize for the craziness. I know you needed quiet."

"Quiet isn't what I needed. And there is craziness everywhere. It's random. Not in our control."

"So what did you need?"

"To reconnect with you?" He looked over at me. "Or maybe to connect with you. Maybe we never really did have the bond that I feel with you now."

"Oh, my, I am going to miss you. I feel like it's the first day of school and I have to brave the world on my own again."

"I remember that feeling." Oliver smiled. "Look, Rosie, I don't know how to tell you this, but you've changed my life."

"*You* changed your life." I smiled back.

"Nope. You're very seldom wrong, but you are now. You showed me what I have been missing my whole messed up life."

"What?" I said, my throat tightening.

"You said it yourself. Or Tyler said it. Anyway, you made me feel visible.

You didn't let me disappear into my own narcissism. You kept pulling me back. And then, when you helped me so much, I realized how I've lived my life. Who I was in relationships. Always a step back. No real connection. Slipping away if it got too real." He shook his head. "I never helped you when we were kids, either. And the worst of it? I stayed away when your husband left you. That's unforgivable."

"You're here now."

"That's true. For the first time I showed up."

"You saved my life."

Oliver shook his head adamantly. "I believe that was Sonja. She was the one with the gun."

"You showed up. That's what matters."

"Maybe I did. And now I think it's time I showed up in my own life. You know, Mom was so right. She saw it but didn't know how to tell me."

"This is huge, Oliver."

"I knew I needed to come here. Something was nudging me." He gazed out across the river. "I'm going to buy you a boat. Maybe just a pontoon. And then we can cruise around with Anna Banana, drink some wine—"

"As long as it isn't chianti."

He looked over at me. "How do you feel about champagne?"

"Oliver? What will you do next?"

"I called Sylvie last night. At first she tried to hang up, said she's been dating other guys, that it's going well. Then I asked her to just talk. About herself. About her dreams. Just talk. She said I sounded different. And she started talking. When she stopped, I asked her to meet me in Richmond."

"Virginia? Why?"

"I'm taking her to the farm. Just like Mom asked."

"But it's sold."

"I just want to see it. I also like the idea of meeting her somewhere that's not New York. I want it to feel fresh. And after the farm, we'll stop in and visit Annie. I haven't seen that kiddo in way too long."

"Oh, that's a wonderful idea, Oliver. Thank you for that."

"I can't believe she agreed. I have so many questions for her. Things I never bothered to ask. And I'm going to hang on every word."

"And what about Sonja?"

"She's on her way back to LA."

I smiled at him, my heart full. "You really did find what you were searching for?"

"If you mean, how to connect with another human being? The answer is yes."

"Bravo, Oliver."

"Just so you know, I'll be here for a week at Christmas. I hope that's okay. And I'd like to make Christmas dinner for you guys. I already have some ideas."

Chapter Fifty-Seven

The envelope was propped in the middle of the kitchen table against a ceramic blue and white striped bowl filled with Macintosh apples. Bini, Tyler, and I encircled the table, no one willing to pick it up.

"Jojo is going to start converting her fields to organic," Bini said.

"That's amazing," I said, still staring at the envelope.

"Phoebe is moving in with her. She left her husband. Jojo is buying her chickens so she can sell the eggs at the farmers' market."

"That's lovely," I said, not moving. "Those will be some very happy chickens."

Tyler cleared his throat. "Will one of you please open the damn envelope?" He combed his hands through his hair.

I looked up at him. "It has to be you."

"Why?"

"She's right, Ty," Bini said. "You, more than anyone, has gotten us this far."

I reached out to hold Bini's hand. She let me.

Tyler searched our faces. I nodded. He picked it up and turned the envelope over in his hands several times, smoothing his hand over the front, as if trying to see what was inside. At last he inserted his thumb under the flap and popped it open. It was a hefty tri-folded document. My heart skipped a beat as I remembered my mother watching me open my acceptance letter from the University of Virginia. *You don't need that much paper to say no.*

"Tyler?"

He sorted through the pages and flipped to the last one. He looked up. His emerald green eyes moist. "We did it." Our eyes met. "We're sustainable."

Acknowledgements

To Bob Roth, for making me feel visible and loved.

To my daughters, Elizabeth and Madeline, for just about everything I can think of. I am so lucky to have you in my life.

For Chris, Paul, Stacy, and Terry, for your love and for getting me through the pandemic, and always having my back.

To Lindsay, Kyle Marisa, and Sage, for allowing me into your lives and embracing what I have with your dad.

To Dawn Dawdle, for believing in me when I thought I had hit a dead end.

To Shawn Reilly Simmons for your guidance, enthusiasm, and support. The Dames of Detection rock.

To Joe O'Connor. A fallen soldier in the Covid war. You were a dear friend and fellow writer, a talent, and one of the most intuitive people I've ever known. Thanks for being one of my besties in the few years we had together.

To my critique group friends and writers, you have all brought me to a new level of writing. You enrich my writing and my life: Susan, Mary, Denny, Jon, Terese, Bill, Rick, Ronny, Frances, Linda, Alice, Ken, and Joe.

And to all the support and kindness I've received from readers of the series. Book lovers are the nicest people on the planet.

About the Author

Wendy Sand Eckel is the author of the award-winning Rosalie Hart Mystery Series. Eckel, who studied criminology and earned a Master's Degree in Social Work, lives on Maryland's enchanting Eastern Shore.

SOCIAL MEDIA HANDLES:
   FACEBOOK: www.facebook.com/wsandeckel
   TWITTER: www.twitter.com/wendysandeckel
   PINTEREST: www.pinterest.com/wendyeckel
   GOODREADS: www.goodreads.com/wendysandeckel

AUTHOR WEBSITE:
   www.wendysandeckelauthor.com

Also by Wendy Sand Eckel

Death at the Day Lily Café

Murder at Barclay Meadow

Educating Tigers
   AmErica House, 2000